D1328036

MAGAZINE

Tin House

Volume 15, Number 1

*"The voice is a wild thing. It can't be bred in captivity.
It is a sport, like the silver fox. It happens."*

—WILLA CATHER

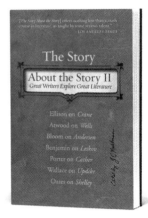

THE REVOLUTION OF EVERY DAY

a novel by Cari Luna

In the midnineties, New York's Lower East Side contained a city within its shadows: a community of squatters who staked their claims on abandoned tenements and lived and worked within their own parameters, accountable to no one but each other. With gritty prose and vivid descriptions, Cari Luna's debut novel, *The Revolution of Every Day*, imagines the lives of five squatters from that time and the rifts within their community, which prove to be almost more threatening than the city lawyers and the private developers trying to evict them.

"Cari Luna shines a light in the dark corners of New York that most people don't see. Her vivid portrayal of the squatters of Thirteenth Street and their fierce struggle to keep their community alive is an elegy for a city that no longer exists."

—ELLIOTT HOLT, author of *You Are One of Them*

Available October 2013

THE STORY ABOUT THE STORY, VOL. II

edited by J. C. Hallman

The Story About the Story, Vol. II documents not only an identifiable trend in writing about books that can and should be emulated, it also offers lessons from a remarkable range of celebrated authors that amount to an invaluable course on both how to write and how to read well.

"There is no better path to the heart of a great writer's expression than keen intuition born of a deep regard, and no one more likely to have both than a fellow writer. This collection of master reader-writers appraising their admirations is not in the least predictable. Turn the pages: surprise, surprise, surprise!"

—SVEN BIRKERTS, author of *Reading Life: Books for the Ages*

Available October 2013

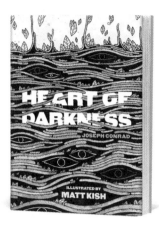

HEART OF DARKNESS

a novel by Joseph Conrad
illustrated by Matt Kish

THIS IS BETWEEN US

a novel by Kevin Sampsell

Following his massive—and massively success-ful—*Moby-Dick in Pictures*, artist Matt Kish has set himself upon an equally impressive, and no less harrowing, task: illustrating each page of Joseph Conrad's masterpiece, *Heart of Darkness*. Kish's rich, imaginative drawings and paintings mirror Conrad's original text and illuminate Marlow's journey into the heart of the Congo, and into the depths of the human soul.

Kish's introduction lends context to his approach, details his relationship and struggle with Conrad's work, and explains his own creative process.

Available November 2013

Chronicling five years of a troubled romance, *This Is Between Us* offers an intimate view of one couple's struggle—from the illicit beginnings of sexual obsession to the fragile architecture of a pieced-together family. Full of sweet moments, emotional time bombs, unexpected humor, and blunt sexuality, the daily life of this man and woman, both recently divorced, with children and baggage in tow, emerges in all of its complexity. In this utterly engrossing debut novel, Kevin Sampsell delivers a confessional tale of love between two resilient people who have staked their hearts on each other.

"Here is the quiet, funny, heartbreak truth of Real Love. Read it and weep."

—AMELIA GRAY, author of *THREATS*

Available November 2013

TEXAS STATE UNIVERSITY

The rising STAR of Texas

MFA

FINE ARTS

with a major in
CREATIVE WRITING
and specializations in
FICTION OR POETRY

*We now offer classes
in creative nonfiction.*

*In the Texas Hill Country
right next door to Austin*

THE ENDOWED CHAIR IN CREATIVE WRITING
2012–2014 Cristina Garcia
Tim O'Brien, Professor of Creative Writing

FACULTY

Cyrus Cassells, Poetry
Doug Dorst, Fiction
Tom Grimes, Fiction

Ogaga Ifowodo, Poetry
Roger Jones, Poetry
Debra Monroe, Fiction

Kathleen Peirce, Poetry
Nelly Rosario, Fiction
Steve Wilson, Poetry

ADJUNCT THESIS FACULTY

Lee K. Abbott
Catherine Barnett
Rick Bass
Ron Carlson
Charles D'Ambrosio
John Dufresne
Carolyn Forché
James Galvin
Amelia Gray
Saskia Hamilton
Shelby Hearon
Bret Anthony Johnston

Hettie Jones
Patricia Spears Jones
Li-Young Lee
Philip Levine
Carole Maso
Elizabeth McCracken
Heather McHugh
Jane Mead
W.S. Merwin
David Mura
Naomi Shihab Nye
Jayne Anne Phillips

Alberto Ríos
Pattiann Rogers
Nicholas Samaras
Elissa Schappell
Richard Siken
Gerald Stern
Rosmarie Waldrop
Sharon Oard Warner
Eleanor Wilner
Mark Wunderlich

RECENT VISITING WRITERS

Kevin Brockmeirer
Olga Broumas
Michael Dickman
Louise Erdrich
Nick Flynn
Richard Ford

S.C. Gwynne
Yiyun Li
Thomas Lux
Mihaela Moscaliuc
Karen Russell
George Saunders

Charles Simic
Robert Stone
Justin Torres
Wells Tower

Visit *Front Porch*, our literary journal:
www.frontporchjournal.com

$60,000 W. Morgan & Lou Claire Rose Fellowship for an incoming writing student

Additional scholarships and teaching assistantships are available.

Tom Grimes, MFA Director   Phone **512.245.7681**
Department of English   Fax 512.245.8546
Texas State University   **www.mfatxstate.com**
601 University Drive   **mfinearts@txstate.edu**
San Marcos, TX 78666-4684

time	space	support
3 years	*Austin*	*$25,000 per year*

MFA IN WRITING

THE MICHENER CENTER FOR WRITERS
The University of Texas at Austin

www.utexas.edu/academic/mcw
512-471-1601

MFA at PSU

Fiction | Nonfiction | Poetry

Diana Abu-Jaber

John Beer

Paul Collins

Charles D'Ambrosio

Michele Glazer

Michael McGregor

A. B. Paulson

Leni Zumas

James B. Norman, *The Portland Bridge Book*

www.pdx.edu/mfa-creativewriting

Application deadline for 2014: January 6, 2014

Portland State
UNIVERSITY

Tin House

MAGAZINE

EDITOR IN CHIEF / PUBLISHER
Win McCormack

EDITOR	Rob Spillman
ART DIRECTOR	Diane Chonette
MANAGING EDITOR	Cheston Knapp
EXECUTIVE EDITOR	Michelle Wildgen
POETRY EDITOR	Matthew Dickman
EDITOR-AT-LARGE	Elissa Schappell
POETRY EDITOR-AT-LARGE	Brenda Shaughnessy
PARIS EDITOR	Heather Hartley
ASSISTANT EDITORS	Desiree Andrews, Lance Cleland, Emma Komlos-Hrobsky

CONTRIBUTING EDITORS: Dorothy Allison, Steve Almond, Aimee Bender, Charles D'Ambrosio, Brian DeLeeuw, Anthony Doerr, CJ Evans, Nick Flynn, Matthea Harvey, Jeanne McCulloch, Christopher Merrill, Rick Moody, Whitney Otto, D. A. Powell, Jon Raymond, Rachel Resnick, Peter Rock, Helen Schulman, Jim Shepard, Karen Shepard, Bill Wadsworth

DESIGNER: Jakob Vala

INTERNS: Erin Gravley, Stephanie Herwig, Allyson Paty, Janet Matthews, Veronica Martin and Jeremy Scheuer

READERS: Stephanie Booth, Susan DeFreitas, Polly Dugan, Megan Freshley, Ann-Derrick Gaillot, Mark Hammond, Christie Hinrichs, Bryan Hurt, Erika Klyce, Aaron Kroska, Alina Labrador, Louise Wareham Leonard, Sarah Marshall, Shannon McDonald, Maya McOmie, Lisa Mecham, Foster Mickley, Aurora Myers, Cynthia-Marie O'Brien, Hannah Pass, Stacy Heiney Perrou, Jeremy Scheuer, Annie Rose Shapero, Neesa Sonoquie, Joel Statz, Lee Steely, Jennifer Taylor, JoNelle Toriseva, Megan Udow, Linda Woolman

DEPUTY PUBLISHER	Holly MacArthur
CIRCULATION DIRECTOR	Laura Howard
DIRECTOR OF PUBLICITY	Nanci McCloskey
COMPTROLLER	Janice Carter

Tin House Books

EDITORIAL ADVISOR	Rob Spillman
EDITORS	Meg Storey, Tony Perez, Nanci McCloskey
ASSOCIATE EDITOR	Masie Cochran
EDITORIAL ASSISTANT	Desiree Andrews

In our mitigated, cultivated world, is it possible to still be wild? With no wilderness, will our natures turn tame? These are two of the challenges we threw out for our Wild issue, and because writers are creative, and therefore untamed, they came back to us with very different answers. Olena Kalytiak Davis pushes into the wilderness of language, pursuing taboo thoughts well past the point where tamer poets would dare tread. Often the word *wild* is associated with otherness and primitiveness. Artist Matt Kish explores this idea in his dark, haunting interpretation of Conrad's classic tale of madness, *Heart of Darkness*; Lauren Groff's single female heroine loses herself to otherness in the story "Salvador"; and journalist Inara Verzemnieks chronicles a transient community that colonized a highway rest stop. In an excerpt from his novel-in-progress, Donald Ray Pollock lets his southern gothic run wild, while in Ben Marcus's fiction, a single sentence is stretched to its limits. The doggedly inquisitive Ginger Strand tackles the elusive sex trade in Vegas and traces the not-so-wild roots of the Wild West. Ursula K. Le Guin, herself no stranger to the great wilds of this and other worlds, makes a case for H. L. Davis's underappreciated western novel *Honey in the Horn*. And while many of us welcome the uncontrolled and unpredictable outdoors, those who live daily with its dangers, like Rilla Askew, whose family's property in Oklahoma is crawling with rattlesnakes, have a more complicated relationship with the untamed. Whatever your inclination, we hope you heed the words of Isadora Duncan: "You were once wild here. Don't let them tame you."

CONTENTS

ISSUE #57 / WILD

Fiction

Poetry

Features

Lost & Found

Readable Feast

FICTION

Salvador

Lauren Groff

The apartment Helena rented in Salvador had high ceilings, marble floors, vast windows. It always looked cool, even when the blaze of the Brazilian summer crept inside in the late afternoon. If she leaned from her balcony, she could see the former convent that curved around her street's cul-de-sac; she could see over the red tile roofs of the buildings across the way to where the harbor opened into ocean. She was so close she could smell faint littoral rot and taste the salt on the wind. For the first few mornings, she sat on the balcony in her cotton nightgown, drinking coffee, and watched as the water swept greenly toward the horizon, ocean and sky faltering into haze where they met.

One morning when she was on the balcony enjoying the nightgown's graze against her ankles and the sharp summer sunlight, she looked down to find the shopkeeper from the grocery across the street staring at her. He had a broom in his hand but he wasn't sweeping. His round, dark face, always glistening as if just brushed with hot butter, was turned up toward her. His lips were open and his tongue was flicking rapidly into the gap between his two front teeth, all pink and wet and lewd.

She went inside and shut the glass door hard and put her coffee cup down very carefully on the dining table. She felt ill. She went into the bedroom to look at herself. The same light that fell across the balcony was slicing through the windows in her room, and she stood in a spill of it to see what he'd seen. In the mirror, all was apparent: she could see her entire body—legs, dark pubis, round brown nipples—as if her nightgown were only a pale shadow of her own skin. Helena thought of the man's view from below, the pink soles of her feet pressing through the keyhole shapes in the balcony's floor, the line of her legs to her bust, her head topped with dyed yellow hair brazenly unbrushed. "Jesus Christ, I look like a whore," she said. Helena laughed at herself, and the laugh broke the spell, and she showered and dressed and went out for the day. As she passed the grocery, she stared straight ahead, unwilling to give the shopkeeper the satisfaction of looking into the dark recesses of his store.

Helena was in that viscous pool of years in her late thirties when she could feel her beauty slowly departing from her. She had been lovely at one time, which had slid into pretty, which had slid into attractive, and if she didn't do something to halt the slide, she'd end up at handsomely middle-aged, which was no place at all to be. She was the youngest daughter of a mother too perennially ill to live alone, and, being the youngest and unmarried at the time of her mother's first bloom of illness, Helena was the one to fall into the caretaking role. For the most part, her life with her mother was calm, even good, with whist and euchre and jigsaw puzzles and television programs, with church on Sundays, in Latin, with veils. Helena herself believed in no god but the one that moved in her mother's face when she genuflected on the velvet and forgot how ill she was.

> She could see her entire body—legs, dark pubis, round brown nipples—as if her nightgown were only a pale shadow of her own skin.

She was, on the whole, all right with the arrangement. It had to be said, however, that love was impossible with a sick and saintly mother patiently bearing her insomnia in the bedroom next door. There was no question of dates, either, because her mother needed help every few hours to go to the bathroom or remember a pill or a shot. On her bad days, she needed a lap to lay her head in and a hand to wipe away the moisture at her temples.

Helena's sisters felt horribly guilty watching their beautiful sister fade in such dutiful servitude, and so they gave her a good chunk of money every year and each came to spend two weeks apiece caring for their mother in Helena's stead. For a month out of the year, Helena had the freedom and funds to spend her time where she would. She mostly chose to visit quiet places bedaubed with romance—Verona, Yalta, Davos, Aracataca—and to stretch her cash reserves, she rented a furnished apartment and ate only dinners out. She'd spend the days in museums and coffee shops and botanical gardens, and at night, more often than not, she'd come giggling back home with her pumps in one hand, exchanging sloppy kisses with a stranger in the elevator.

She had no trouble finding men, even if it was undeniable that her looks were slipping. If, at the restaurant she chose, a man didn't approach her, she went to the bar of a nice hotel. If nothing happened at the bar, she went to a nightclub and picked up a drunk boy half her age. She preferred blond businessmen above all, but there was a different and sometimes more intense pleasure in these young men, natives of the places she visited, something delicious in the way their languages glided past each other, barely touching.

> The boy drew her away by the waist, his voice warm and sibilant and nonsensical in her ear.

Men were not as disciplined or as smart as women, she thought; men almost always took what they were offered, their appetites too crude and raw to put up much resistance. They were like children, gobbling down their candy all at once, with no thought about the consequences of their greed. She and her visitors often kept the neighbors awake, but the neighbors rarely complained; when they met her later in the hallway, they usually became confused by the neat and elegant gray dresses Helena wore, her severe tight bun, her pale and haughty face. It felt wrong, somehow, to make such an embarrassing complaint about a woman whose posture was so very correct.

After her month of slaking her thirsts, Helena found she was almost eager to return to the close, doily-riddled apartment and her mother's half-swallowed cries of pain in the night.

A week after the shopkeeper had seen her in all her glory, two weeks into her stay in Salvador, she came home early one morning with one of her boys. She'd met a group of flight attendants at a bar, and their lone man was clearly uninterested in her, or perhaps in women in general, and so she'd gone along with the giddy bunch to a local nightclub. There they were out of place among the gorgeous young creatures with their barely-there clothing, their feline sleekness. The flight attendants eventually vanished and Helena was left dancing with a tall, very dark-skinned man of eighteen or so. Though his English was limited to the rap lyrics he mouthed to the music, she managed to convey what she wanted to do to him. He grinned beautifully. They rode his scooter to her part of the city, she pressing her pelvis against him as they rode, touching him, and he went so fast he nearly lost control when they hit the cobblestones. They laughed with relief and something richer when he turned the bike off, and they climbed down, and, hushing each other, went through the wrought-iron fence. She pulled the gate closed and glanced out into the street as it clanged. She was startled to see the moonfaced shopkeeper. He was in a crouch, about to pull up the metal gate protecting his storefront, and watching her. She felt the smile fall off her face as he gave an imperceptible shake of his head and turned his back to her. She had a sudden urge to call out to him, something desperate and true, about the long, dry months spent in the wilderness of her mother's illness, but the boy drew her away by the waist, his voice warm and sibilant and nonsensical in her ear, and when she looked back, the shopkeeper was gone.

Helena woke midmorning to find the boy gone. In the kitchen, she discovered a plate he'd left with a smiley face drawn on it in hot sauce, and she set it in the sink and watched as the face dissolved under a stream of water. She spent the morning slowly caring for her person, taking a long bubble bath and exfoliating and depilating, filing and polishing, seeing elaborately to her hair. The gnawing feeling she'd woken to hadn't gone away, and so she put on her primmest outfit, a long black dress and sturdy walking sandals. She hesitated, then threw a shawl around her shoulders to give an even fustier impression. She hadn't, as yet, bought anything from the grocery across the street—the owner of the apartment had warned her in his letter that the prices at the clean chain grocery three blocks northward were half what the local shop's were—but she needed some bananas and papayas and coffee and bread and so she gathered her courage to face the shopkeeper.

The store smelled strongly of fruit on the cusp of rot, and the shelves were packed, the rows tight. Two people with baskets could have hardly passed one another. There was nobody else in the store, she was relieved to see, save the shopkeeper and another man chatting by the register until she came in. She gave them a small nod, and they nodded back, both unsmiling.

She browsed for a while, and the men began to speak again in a low tone. Back by the toilet paper and festive paper napkins, there was a little narrow doorway in the wall that was empty when she first walked past it. When she passed it again, though, she saw a small foot, then a hand, a dark head. When the whole person came into the light, she was either a very short woman or a young girl. Helena assumed she was indigenous, brown skinned and broad cheekboned, then wondered if she was the shopkeeper's daughter, though she had assumed that the shopkeeper was black; he was only slightly lighter than the boy from last night. But Brazil was so confusing this way, Salvador especially so, with its slave-trade blight of long ago: you never could tell exactly where people belonged. She had been surprised to find that this city upset some deep Northern Hemisphere sense of order that she hadn't known she treasured.

The shopkeeper saw the girl or woman and said something in a harsh voice, and by the swift fear Helena saw on her face, the way her shoulders dropped subserviently, and the speed with which she vanished from sight, Helena thought there was something wrong. She didn't know what to do; she had to rest her head against the cool metal of the shelves to pull herself together. When she took her purchases up to the shopkeeper, her hands were trembling and she could barely look at him, getting only an impression of shortness and powerful shoulders. She fixed on a small tin statuette in the window above his head, a woman knee-deep in sharp-looking waves. Yemanjá, she remembered from the marketplace, goddess of the sea. The man pointed at the numbers on the register with a blunt finger. Helena paid the money to Yemanjá, not to him.

By the time he put her purchases in a plastic sack, she was able to look him full in the face, saying silently, *You are a bad man and I am watching.* For the rest of the day, she fretted over the girl, wondering if she needed rescuing, and savored the way the shopkeeper had flinched under her eyes.

For three days, Helena dressed with ostentatious primness and made small purchases at the grocer's, but the shopkeeper never greeted her and she never saw the girl or woman again. Helena's ardor had cooled by the third day, and she began to wonder if the girl weren't simply the man's wife or girlfriend or stock person, someone whom it certainly wasn't right to speak to in the way he had spoken to her, but it was not a crime, either. She began to feel a frisson of guilt that she had jumped to such conclusions—what an arrogant, American thing to do!—and to avoid the whole marshy emotional terrain, she began making her purchases at the chain again.

On a trip back from the other store, her milk and eggs swinging in a bag by her hip, she saw the shopkeeper, and he looked first at her bag, and something folded in his face and he gave her a not-unfriendly wave, and she, confused, pretended not to see him.

Upstairs in her apartment, she fretted. Was she never to walk out of her house without being swamped with bad feelings? Was the shopkeeper going to ruin her entire vacation? She made herself a fruit salad and sat vengefully on her balcony to eat it. A great thick cloud had formed, and the wind had risen, and when she finished, she stood to take a look at the ocean. She watched as a distant wall of water descended from the black cloud and sped toward her, drawing a thick curtain over the cruise ships outside the harbor, then the fishing boats motoring in, then the harbor itself, then the church steeple. When it hit the red rooftop across the street, she stepped inside and shut her glass door a breath before the storm smacked loudly at her, as if raging that she was dry and safe when all the rest of the world was vulnerable.

A great thick cloud had formed, and the wind had risen, and she stood to take a look at the ocean.

The storm against the many windows was terrifically loud. For two days, Helena was stuck in the apartment, unable to go out to her museums or films or restaurants and bars and nightclubs. She read two books and wrote letters to her sisters and mother, telling them of this strange, dreamy town with its pastels and hills and wandering bands of drummer girls who danced under the streetlights and played ferociously, the former slave market filled with textiles and handicrafts. She wrote of the first man she had met there, though she stretched the truth far out of shape, taking what was simply a torrid jet-lagged hour or so and implying a love affair, as she always did in her letters during her months at large. Her mother was a romantic to her bones, and her sisters, stuck in their happy marriages, only pretended to tsk at and censure her entanglements, gorging themselves for a full year on Helena's hints and subtexts. She wrote of visiting the Church of Nosso Senhor do Bonfim, translating it as Our Lord of Happy Endings, knowing her mother would hear only the sonorous Portuguese and imagine a dark-skinned Jesus on a cross, that her sisters would get the joke and laugh behind their hands.

When a navy kind of night fell over the afternoon, she felt desperate, and tied a plastic shopping bag over her head and wore the only trench coat she'd brought, because it was supposed to be summer in the Southern Hemisphere, after all. She ran, holding her shoes, to the convent-cum-fine hotel at the end of the street. At the very last second, the bellhop opened the door for her and she burst into the lobby, laughing and shaking the water from her yellow hair and untying the plastic bag from her head. This was much better, she thought as she surveyed the hotel with its jungle of plants and woodwork, then checked her hair and makeup in a vast gold-framed mirror. She was flushed and very pretty. She slid on her shoes, and the bellhop gave her a little round of applause and gestured to the fire.

But she shook her head and sailed over to the bar, which was normally far too expensive for her. The storm had kept her in for too long; she couldn't give a fig any more for budget; she needed to make up for lost time and her sort of businessman frequented this kind of hotel. She caught her breath and sipped her Scotch and watched the display behind the bar, blue-lit bubbles in some kind of oil rising with preposterous slowness.

> She took off her shoes, marched out, and immediately knew that she had made a mistake.

There was a pair of American men who smiled back at her, but who were joined instantly by their wives in print dresses. She winked at an old fellow who looked alarmed and tottered away; she slowly put on a coat of lipstick in the direction of a Japanese businessman who only had eyes for his computer. There was no one else, and the bartender was a woman. Helena ordered a hamburger with a luxurious heap of fried onions and Gorgonzola on it and ate it slowly, in neat bites, sitting sideways so she could watch the doorway. But nobody entered.

The lights flickered and went out, but there were candles on the table in a soft constellation. She watched the bartender light more, until the room was again twilit.

She felt full of frantic energy by the time she had finished her food, but from the deafening sound of the rain outside, it was going to be a dud night. Nobody in his right mind would go out in such weather. Reluctantly, in the light from the fire and the scattered candles, Helena tied the shopping bag over her head again and put on her unpleasantly soaked trench coat. At the door, however, the bellhop shook his head and said, "No, no, miss!" and waved his arms.

"I know it's storming, but my apartment is literally fifty feet away," she said, touched by his distress. She tried to show him through the glass but the rain was so thick and the night so dark that the world melted away a foot from where they stood. She grinned at him—he was cute, big-eared, in such a pinch he would do—but he only turned toward the reception desk and called out something. A woman rushed over. She was tall, a German Brazilian, Helena thought, with hazel eyes and long, streaked hair, and Helena felt a warm burst of hatred rise in her, for the woman was more beautiful than Helena had ever been, even in her prime.

"Miss," the woman said, "we cannot let you go. It is a tremendous rain. With winds. What is the word?"

"Not a hurricane," Helena said. "There are no hurricanes in the south Atlantic." She knew this because her mother had fretted, and Helena had found the entry on Brazil in the old set of encyclopedias to put her mind at ease.

"Well," the woman said, shrugging. "But even if it is only a storm, you must stay."

Helena explained again about the apartment so few feet away and suggested that she bring the bellhop with her, glancing under her lashes at him, wondering if he'd take the hint. But he took a step backward, and there was such terror on his pale little face that she laughed. "I'll be all right," she said.

"Stay," the woman said. "I will give you a room for half price."

Helena felt herself flushing, but said, "Which is?"

The woman said a price that was the cost of the entire month of her apartment's rent. "Too much," Helena said.

"Quarter price," the woman said in distress. "I am not authorized to go more low."

"Thank you," Helena said. "I'll be all right." She took off her shoes, snatched open the door, marched out, and immediately knew that she had made a mistake.

She took a dozen steps before the wind carried her breath from her mouth, the rain pounded into her eyes, and Helena stepped back until she felt the hotel's stucco under her hand. She couldn't see the doorway or the rug she had just been standing upon, and she was able to breathe only when she made a windbreak out of the crook of her elbow. She was not one to go back, though, not ever. Her place was a few steps away; it had taken her a minute, at most, to run here barefoot a few hours earlier. She dropped her shoes and felt her way painstakingly over the curve of the old convent to the wrought-iron fence around the courtyard. She pulled herself hand over hand, like a sailor along the yardarm, until she reached the next stucco texture, the next building.

By the time she got to this building's doorway, she was weeping. She stopped and pressed her body against the glass and tried the door, but it was either locked or the wind was holding it shut. She breathed for a while in the lee of a mailbox until she stopped crying, wiped her swollen eyes, and started out again. *Stupid woman*, she said to herself. *Stupid, foolish, terrible woman. You deserve what you get.*

She inched forward. There were three more doors, she thought, before her own wrought-iron gate that swung inward, that the wind would whip open as soon as she touched it and pull her inside the courtyard, home. Or maybe four doors; she couldn't quite remember and she couldn't believe she hadn't paid much attention before now.

But as she reached the third door, she tripped over something, went sprawling, and felt the skin of her knee open painfully. She curled into a ball to gather her strength and lay there, crying with anger and exhaustion. She was alone and she conceded to her aloneness; she would always be alone, she would always be in these puddles that grew even as she lay in them. For a very long time she focused on breathing, and it wasn't terrible, despite the wind and rain upon her. It was only blank.

Something rushed out of the storm, something seized her wrist, and she felt herself being dragged over the cobblestones, her limbs cracking against the hard ground. And then there was the absence of first the wind in her face, then the driving rain, and she opened her eyes to darkness. She was so grateful to be breathing that she didn't wonder where she was until her breath calmed and she hushed the whimper she had just heard rising from her chest and she listened to a harsh metal clang that muffled the storm even more, then a pounding that was the wind, angry to be left outside. She pulled herself up painfully and drew her legs in, the cut on her leg smarting terribly, and leaned against whatever was behind her, so soft and covered in plastic. She felt with her hands and knew she was leaning on wrapped paper towels, and only then did her dulled mind grasp that she was in the grocer's, that he of all humans on the planet had saved her. Now the smell of the place rose to her, the sour half-rot and flour. She heard him shoving something heavy before the door.

An ugly flicker began to stir in her, and she pushed herself farther against the paper towels, up onto the shelf, letting the displaced rolls pad down on the floor. She was shivering, and she put the collar of her dress between her teeth to keep them from chattering. The place was darker than dark, the only light from a distant red pulse that illuminated nothing.

Helena hoped for the girl or woman she'd seen on her first visit to be there. She longed for the little body to come close to hers, to hold her hand and warm her, but she listened so acutely that she could hear there was nobody in the store but them, she and this man; their breathing was the only breathing. She forced herself to listen to him, his heavy shoes shuffling closer to where she was sitting. It was maybe an accident that he kicked her calf when he drew near; she couldn't tell what he could see. She held her breath, but he knew every inch of the store, of course, and stepped even closer. She could smell him, a particular sweat of feet and armpits and denim that has been worn to grease.

He said nothing, just stood for a long time over her. He gave another shuffle closer and the fabric of his jeans brushed her face and she was glad for the dress in her mouth or she would have shouted.

Then he said something in his gruff voice, but she didn't understand and didn't bother to respond. She tried to keep her breathing light and unobtrusive, but her stomach, so upset by her struggle and the heavy food, gave a gurgle, and he laughed unpleasantly.

> She could smell him, a particular sweat of feet and armpits and denim that has been worn to grease.

The shopkeeper moved away, and she felt the tension fall out of her shoulders. She could hear him rummaging, then the double kiss of a refrigerator opening and closing, across the room. She thought wildly of running now, but knew she couldn't get the metal door up in this wind and was fairly sure there was no back way out of the store. And as bad as he might be, she had been in the storm outside, and though she wasn't entirely sure, she thought it must be worse.

The man came back. Instead of standing, he sank down across from her, and she felt a sharp and sudden pain on her throat, which made her gasp. But then the pain translated to cold, and she knew that he was holding out a glass bottle to her, and she took it in her hand. On her cheek, then, there was another feel, a slick plastic, and the man said, "Biscoitos," and she took the package of cookies in her other hand and ate one to be polite. "Obrigado," she whispered, but he said nothing back.

The drink was beer. She clung to the heft of the bottle in her hand. Though he far outpowered her, he had at least given her a weapon. She drank sparingly, to make the weight of the bottle last. Across the dark gulf of the aisle, his gulps were thick and loud, and he must have brought more beer for himself, because every so often she heard the clink of an empty bottle on the cement floor and the hiss of a new beer being opened and the chime of a cap falling to the floor. The storm roared outside steadily and her feet on the floor began to be tickled, then lapped by water. The water was coming in.

Worse than being in the storm was not knowing what the storm was doing. The evidence of it was everywhere: in the cold water up to her rear on her little shelf, in the blasts of wind, the rattle of the building and the sounds of distant crashes, boats, most probably, smashing into the shore. She wondered about fires blazing through the rickety old structures of this part of town, and what would be left in the morning. If she survived this night, this hulk of a man across from her in the darkness, she could close her eyes on the taxi ride to the airport, she could get on a plane, she could soar over the wreckage until the plane landed in the ice, her mother in a wheelchair beaming at her from the bottom of the escalator in baggage claim. It would not be her mess to clean up. She was a visitor, only; she could be absolved. But this was cold comfort, barely any at all. The end of the storm was unreal and she was beyond tired. The hours of waiting in the dark here, the years of waiting in the darkness at home, were too much; they overcame her in waves of exhaustion. There was no telling how fast the water would rise. It didn't matter: the man was already here. And Helena waited for his sudden lunge, his powerful body, which her own thin one couldn't resist for long.

> She felt her anger blaze alive in her and she jerked her leg away, but his hand found her ankle again and clamped down.

There was a pop outside, and the man's bulk came closer, and he said something gruff, and she cringed, but he didn't touch her.

She was lulled by the darkness, the man's immobility, save for his drinking. *It must be morning by now*, she thought. Her fear had dulled and her thoughts were thick with sleep. She rested her head against the towels in their packages and shifted so the cramp in her rear was soothed and shut her eyes, as if she could make the dark darker and push the storm and the man farther from her.

The shopkeeper stood three times, there was the kiss of the refrigerator three times, he sloshed back and groaned to the floor opposite her three times. The third time, she was nearly asleep when he leaned over and put his hand on her ankle. He had been holding a beer, and his skin on hers was shockingly cold.

She had feared this for so long, it seemed, that when it was here, it was almost a relief. She felt her anger blaze alive in her and she jerked her leg away, but his hand found her ankle again and clamped down to the point of pain, then beyond. She gave an involuntary cry and he laughed, as if to say that wasn't even close to the limit of his strength, and she bit her lip until it bled, and he loosened his hand again.

She thought of her mother, at home in her warm bed, the snow softly falling in her dark window, the crucifix in the shadows above the bed; she thought of the small tin orixa, the goddess of the sea, calm above the register in the dark. She found herself praying, and it didn't matter to whom the words were addressed because the act without direction was all she could do.

The shopkeeper removed his hand only to fetch more beer or food. He crunched and breathed heavily and smacked his lips, and she remembered how he had tongued the gap between his teeth that day he gazed up at her on her balcony, how pink and pulsing and obscene it was. Whenever he returned, he put his hand on her leg again, each time higher on her calf. The gate rattled with less desperation now; the wind appeared to have died down a little. When he reached her knee, he felt the raw wet mouth of the wound there, and despite herself, she pulled in a hissing breath, and this shook something from him.

He ran his finger over the edges of the wound. Every once in a while, the finger would dart forward and touch inside the cut, and she would gasp, and he would laugh. He began to talk. He was beyond drunk, this was clear, and his tongue was thick and his words were strange, and she was sure she would never have understood his Portuguese, even if she spoke the language.

She felt sick with anticipated pain. She clutched herself, waiting, and found her brain translating surreally, the long strands of language broken into short strands, swept into a semblance of rhythm. She took comfort in the images that rose in the darkness before her. *Bull's blood zucchini flowerstar,* she imagined he said. *Cinema collation of strange mad zebras.*

She listened. His words thickened. His hand fell away from her knee, down her calf. Outside, she heard the wind through leaves—there were still trees, then, and the trees still had leaves—and the occasional plink of rain against metal. It could be the eye of the storm, she told herself; and if it was, she could have to bear the intensification of wind again, this man's heavy presence, and she knew what would happen if she had to wait with him once more through the terrible roar outside. She would not be able to be still enough for him to forget her. But at last, the shopkeeper fell silent and a whistling started up in his nose and she understood that he was asleep.

In tiny increments, she extracted her leg from under his hand. She stood from the puddle on the shelf where she'd been sitting and moved, stiff and old, toward where she remembered the door to be. She had to put down the beer bottle that she had clutched all night to move a shelf out of the way and to lift the lock. In a burst of strength, she ripped the gate up and away from the ground.

The day dazzled with sun. Steam rose from the street, a clean sheet of liquid light covering the cobblestones, a wet skin glittering on the buildings. Gold drops fell from the tree limbs and a cool gentle wind swept the hair from her face. Her leg was caked with blood, the wound livid, her body racked in the joints. She didn't care.

Behind her, the shopkeeper shifted to his feet, bottles ringing on the wet floor as he struggled. She turned, ready to shout, but he was gazing beyond her to the outside. The reflection from the street pushed into the dark of the store, made his round and greasy face shine with moving sunlight. He held on to the shelf before him, and she saw his fear, different and subtler than hers, rise from him and move deeper into the shadows of the room. The shopkeeper tilted his head and closed his eyes and soon he said, "Campainhas," and this was a thing she understood, because she also heard the church bells ringing into the morning. She said, "Yes." He looked at her as if surprised to find her there; he had forgotten her; she was merely the postscript to his tempestuous night. She was a mere visitor. She was nothing. Helena reached over to the tin orixa above the cash register and found it to be sharper and lighter than she had imagined it, a thought turned to matter, an idea that fit in the palm of her hand.

For a long while, she stood in the doorway, listening to the bells, happy for them; but they went on and on, and she began to listen for them to stop.

Each peal, she was sure, would be the last. The bright sound would dissolve back into the sea-touched wind and the ordinary noises of Salvador would rise to take the bells' place, the calling voices, a scooter, a dog barking, a drum; and Helena would be freed to move forward, outward, up. But each note disintegrated and was followed by another and then another and she felt stuck where she stood, a wild feeling rising in her. Her body grew unbearably tense; her heart began to beat so fast it felt as if it were winged.

And then she saw, plain as the street before her, her mother in her dark bedroom at home, pale among her pillows. Helena could not tell if she was alive or dead. She was so peaceful, so very still. A snow sifted gently against the window. Helena was alone.

Helena's hands flew out to stop the vision; her index finger hit the doorway and began to throb. The wet street was again spread before her, the air still full of horrid bells. She sent one last rattled look inside the store and found the shopkeeper kneeling amid his ruin. He held a can washed free of its label, a roll of undamaged toilet tissue in pink paper. His face was strange, as if it had collapsed into itself. He was making a low whistling sound through the gap in his teeth.

She took a step toward him without thinking; then stopped. She hated herself for her first impulse, to comfort. It wasn't who she wanted to be, but it was who she was.

She watched herself as if from above as she moved back into the store, picking over the rubble. The shopkeeper stood as she neared. He smelled of wet denim and sweated-out alcohol and sour private skin. Up close, he looked at her face briefly, with a doggish expression, something hungry and ashamed. And then he closed his eyes, as if she, this morning, were too much for him.

She reached out to touch him, but in the end, she couldn't. She took a step back, and picked things up off the ground. A pen. A dustpan. A bath toy. One perfect orange, its pores even and clean. She piled the items gently in his arms. And when he didn't move, she stooped to collect more, then more, then even more. 🛡

THE POEM SHE DIDN'T WRITE

began
when she stopped

began in winter and, like everything else, at first, just waited for spring
in spring noticed there were lilac branches, but no desire,
no need to talk to any angel, to say: sky, dooryard, _____,
when summer arrived there was more, but not much
nothing really worth noting
and then it was winter again—nothing had changed: sky, dooryard,
_____, white, frozen was the lake and the lagoon, some froze the
ocean
(*now you erase that*) (*you cross that out*)
and so on and so forth
didn't want
didn't want to point, to catalog to inquire,
to acknowledge, to uncover, not even to transcend
wasn't ambitious, wasn't ambiguous, wasn't
_____-reflexive, _____-referential,
the "poet-narrator" did not "want to be liked"
got even stronger: no longer wanted
"to be"
until "wasn't"
was what was missing
was enough

the paper need not (was) not
function(ing) as air *(please stop)* *(please shut the fuck up)*

THE POEM SHE DIDN'T WRITE

had no synecdoches, no metonymy, no pattern, if it rhymed—it was
purely accidental,
no non sequiteur, no primogenitor, wasn't
influenced by homer or blake or yeats   auden   contained
no anxiety, hadn't even heard of
louise glück franz wright billy (budd?) collins

(in the margin: *"then why are you so sad?"*)

spring summer fall
and so on and so forth
it was and it was and it was

done

she did not read it to anyone
she did not send it out "for publication"   when asked
she said she "was not writing" because
"she wasn't"

But somehow   (like a rumor)

THE POEM

SHE DIDN'T WRITE got out   maybe
she talked about it in her sleep   maybe
she was betrayed by a lover

(and in the margin: "*and why are you so sad?*")

In   THE POEM SHE DIDN'T WRITE
there was nothing poetic.
In   THE POEM
there were no hidden references to _____.
In   THE POEMSHEDIDN'TWRITE
arthur rimbaud was not a hero.
In   THEPOEMSHEDIDN'TWRITE
people did not turn to each other in mania or desperation
preservation
In   THEPOEM
away in boredom   disappointment   despair

THE POEM

was equally hailed and dismissed by the critics.
harold bloom said: "otherness to such a degree that loneliness was
created and alleviated at once."

helen vendler wrote: "a posthumous consciousness imputed to the
poet's corpse; a hoped for future represented as though it has already
happened."

_____: "the marriage of marivaux and poussin, i.e.,
poussinesque maurivaudage"
:"an anti-master floribund disaster"
:"fawn meets wolf"
:"exudes sexuality like a dark french perfume"

poets turned in their tombs
hopkins's skull shifted   nothing could be counted   was this finally
S=P=R=U=N=G rhythm?
there was hysteria and histrionic personality disorder   low affect
aphonia apophasis andyet
            THE POEM
(people need(ed) shorthand and so the rest of the title began to be
elided) was   some how   able to act
some said   THE POEM

        "could not exist, because it, um, didn't"
some said "it existed only in that space between "out there" and "in
here"   catullus's mistress's   sandaled foot stepping/suspended
over the threshold
some exegesised that "rilke had already not written it"
some opined that like all the other poems— it only didn't exist in
academia, if it didn't exist at all
        i.e., somewhere in a park near athens   "duh," said

some, "ever heard of derrida? as the poet need not be present then,
why present the poem?"
some said its presence   as with all poetry   written or not was
"contingent

      on a reader (or non-

      reader, as the case may be) and only if that reader bent over it late
at night

      called it 'beloved'"
others agreed because now they could quote some stevens: "yes, yes,"
they said,

                    "late and leaning"
others maintained that it SO didn't matter, they would go on the way
they had been doing and their parents before them and their parents'
parents

          (a cat's flux)

:"tries, but fails, to cross over into different worlds"
:"not worthy of my love"
:"an assassination at an assignation"
:"(nothing is(n't) real, everything is(n't) possible)"

but the lilacs, the lilacs
blooming, blooming   (on) (in) winter

i.e., nothing had changed   and yet   and   none
the   less: a new world order
the point had been made: things that didn't exist   existed more
existed ever   existed over . . . (*watchit!*)
("*because complexity never made anyone feel better")
she had given them permission (not) to   proceed
soon   hopefully   other writers would stop

(writing(:))
        THEPOEM

was somebody's thesis and somebody's else's dumbest joke
it made literary terms like _____ and _____ obsolete
it made literary theories like _____ and _____ sound
stupider than ever

in the 22nd century they would talk about   "she" being hit with a
"fish"
they would confuse "she" with all the great poets who really weren't so
good, were they?
        (all small and flawed men)
five hundred years later a fragment would be found   a fragment
        that also couldn't   didn't
exist
and so forth and so on   on in

lilacs   on in
winters

        THEPOEM

   was repeatedly misattributed   it crossed and recrossed
genres
some said it had once been   a charlie kaufman movie or
                a novel by davidfosterwallace
was it rauschenberg or   was it dekooning?
who erased whom?

          what?

it was the ascension and the ceiling and the sonnets except
better   'cause refused   to be
refused to participate in a world made up of and by   ants and
dogs and   armadillos   peacocks
skunks
(rf. swarthmore chart)

my name is verdant greene.

i am the HUNTER GRACCHUS.

call me.........

BUT by now (then)   every   one   was   dead

but for now,

in the year of
            THEPOEM
20___
finally:

a poetry the masses could rally around—
"so simple" they intoned "and yet so brilliant"
people began crossing poetry off the list of what they, too, disliked
someone began carrying a sign, as if it was a demonstration: "CLEAR
YOUR MIND OF CANT" someone else copied it but added an apostrophe
splinter groups became political (INSERT SOMETHING HERE ON KANT) (*the
starry skies above me and the moral law inside me?*)
"why didn't the poets invent it sooner?" they bemusedly wondered
(smelling their faux lilac boutonnieres)
slightly giddy with relief they became a little careless and self-
aggrandizing
"why didn't WE think of it?"
"my six-year-old could have done it!"
"how did we live (not) not thinking about poetry, when, after all, that was
all there ever wasn't."

COMMENTARY

depends on the day; today:
the first show/snow of march.
we are proceeding
from winter to winterstill the windowsill
thick with icicles/gnarled spindly geraniums ancient
in human years. the soft
cat in her soft bed. the hard
hip at the hard (kitchen) counter, as always, all
stay and delay and nothing, and sometimes, just
nothingyet, and timesother:
nothingfuckingever.
nothingfuckingmore

(fuckingnoonenewnow)
(fuckingnoonenew!)

sat this
morning that
poem came
walking by. said: "pup,
get back to breathing." said: "shut up
and write this down":

it must be more spectacular in its absence!

(*you* must be more spectacular in your absence . . .)

mind strayed. "i" stayed
'til the alarm went off. there is a hole
in the tree outside the (bedroom) window —into
which i sometimes
looks. aftertimes "i" finds: it is not

a hole
at all.

ESSAY

THE LAST DAYS OF THE BALDOCK

Inara Verzemnieks

Say your life broke down.

Given the chance, the more sentimental among them would probably return in summer. Summer was when it seemed as if all the residents of the Baldock threw open the doors of their homes to the bronchial, hawking churnings of the passing semis and wheeled coolers out to the picnic tables that had not yet surrendered to rot. There they would sit, cans clutched in cracked hands, as their dogs whipped smaller and smaller circles around the trunks of the Douglas firs to which they were chained. In those moments, it was possible for them to imagine that they had merely stopped there briefly on a long road trip, that they were no different from the men and women with sunglasses perched on the tops of their heads who trooped in and out of the nearby restrooms, mussed and squinting.

Sometimes they walked over to the information kiosk and collected travel brochures, and they would rustle the pages and pretend to plan journeys to state attractions they knew they would never reach. *Crater Lake is the deepest lake in the United States . . . Shop Woodburn Company Stores!* When it grew dark, they crumpled the sun-warmed paper in their fists and used it to start fires in the barbecue pits. After the flames died, they would toss whatever leftovers they had to the dogs, leaving them to thrash beneath the trees. Then they climbed inside their cars, stuffed blankets in the window jambs, reclined their seats, and let the freeway's dull squall, constant and never ending, gradually numb them to sleep.

Without any kind of written record or historical archive to consult, the question of who first settled the rest stop must be answered by one of its oldest former residents, a vast, coverall-clad man named Everett, who claims to have arrived in 1991, after years of wandering the bosky wilds along the interstate with his pet cat. Together, they set up house in the secluded farthest corner of a rest stop named for Robert "Sam" Baldock, "father of Oregon's modern highway system" and "honor roll member of the Asphalt Institute," first in the bushes in a rough hut assembled from scrap, and then in a ragged van that remained more or less parked in the same place as one decade turned into the next. In that time, dozens more joined Everett and his cat, drawn by stories circulating among those versed in a certain kind of desperation about how there was a place off Interstate 5, about fifteen miles outside Portland, Oregon, where someone with

nothing left but a car or a camper and a tank of gas could stay indefinitely.

Screened by thick stands of evergreens planted under Lady Bird Johnson's Highway Beautification Act, this back-lot settlement grew in relative isolation, its residents largely invisible to the outside world as they pursued the dystopian task of making a life in a place where no one was ever meant to stay. By the time I stumbled upon their community in October of 2009, they were a population of fifty, give or take. No formal census was ever attempted—or deemed necessary, for that matter—since they all knew perfectly well who they were and the myriad ways they passed their time. Seniors waited on social-security checks. Shift workers slept. Alcoholics drank. A single mother knocked on truck cabs. A one-eyed pot dealer trolled for customers. Others sat locked in their compacts, fingering sobriety tokens.

"We call each other Baldockians," said a woman who introduced herself to me as Jolee.

Jolee had been at the rest stop for going on three consecutive years when we first met, though she had lived there off and on for much longer, using the location as a winter retreat when it became too cold to pitch a tent in the foothills. When she was growing up, Jolee's dad had taken her to elk camp each year, taught her from the time she was just a little girl how to survive on her own in the woods. "And then he's all pissed off that I take that knowledge and use it to live like I do," she said. But in recent years, she had grown tired of testing herself for such long stretches, of being at the mercy of the elements, and so she and her boyfriend were residing at the Baldock in a rusting van that ran only occasionally and that periodically needed pushing across the parking lot to a new spot in order to appear in compliance with the rest stop's posted rule that a vehicle remain parked on the premises for no more than twelve hours at a stretch.

Jolee took it upon herself to keep an eye out for the strays, like me, people who needed the Baldock explained to them. Strays were different than visitors, like Jolee's kids, who came on Mother's Day or her birthday and sat for an hour with her at a picnic table, the grandparents who raised them waiting nearby in a running car. Strays were those who drifted into the community's territory by accident, but once they'd become aware of the Baldock's existence, they couldn't stop thinking about what they'd seen. The residents of the Baldock were used to strays, preachers, social workers, strangers with extra cans of kerosene and bags of groceries in the backs of their flatbeds, who kept coming back with questions and concern, but who never stayed.

I first came to the Baldock in an old school bus driven by a man whose job it was to bring hot meals to people living in the region's more rural areas, people for whom it is not an easy matter simply to drop by a soup kitchen or food pantry. I was a reporter at the time, working on a story for the local paper, shadowing the man's efforts. When he told me that our last stop of the night would be at a rest area, I could only imagine that he meant we would be taking a break, or perhaps offering food to down-on-their-luck drivers. But then we parked, and a crowd began to gather, and Jolee appeared. "Let me show you our home," she said.

And that's how I became the accidental chronicler of the Baldock's last days. In truth, it seemed as if they'd been waiting all along for someone to take an interest.

"People normally look right through us," Jolee told me. "Or they might ask, 'Where are you from?' like how people make small talk, and if we say, 'We're from right here,' they'll get this scared look on their faces, and then they'll rush away."

The access they gave me didn't seem to depend on my being a reporter, on any perceived authority that might have granted me; and, in fact, soon after I met them I signed paperwork accepting a voluntary layoff from that job. Instead, I suspect, they were judging me by a more subtle rubric, reading me for clues that would help them gauge my capacity to understand.

I came to learn that the orientation of all permanent arrivals was typically left to a

> Instead, I suspect, they were reading me for clues that would help them gauge my capacity to understand.

man everyone called "The Mayor." I could never get a fix on just what it was he had done to earn this title, whether it was due to a general sense of grudging respect for the fact that he was said to have once let a gangrenous toe rot in his boot because he was too cussed to see a doctor or the rumors that he kept a pistol in his RV. Either way, The Mayor saw it as one of his principal duties to greet the incoming residents: "I don't have money, booze, or cigarettes to give you, and don't give me any shit. But I always have food to share. Ain't no one out here gonna starve."

Baldock etiquette discouraged questions, and this allowed most people to maintain a presence as blurred and unfixed as the reflections cast by the bathroom's unbreakable mirrors. No one asked about the swastika tattoo that crept just above a collar's edge. Or why a police scanner rested in the pocket of a car's door where insurance papers were sometimes kept. In his own more talkative moments, The Mayor liked to remind anyone who cared to listen that "you meet all kinds here, the bad and the good. Mostly good. Still, best advice I can give is to look out for yourself. Don't trust anyone." What he meant was that all the residents of the Baldock, himself included, had versions of the truth they preferred to keep to themselves, maybe even from themselves.

Sometimes he would bring up wives, children. "Buried," he said, in a voice pumiced by all the years of smoking.

In Jolee's opinion, the most important person any newcomer could meet was the man who lived in a 1970s Dodge Vaquero motor home. "This here's Dad," she said as she motioned to a man of ashen face and hair who was trying to chase a tiny tawny-colored dog back into the battered rig. "Sweetpea, Sweetpea, come on now, sugar," the man coaxed as the dog jumped and nipped at the air, trying to catch circling flies with her teeth.

Addressing me, Jolee said, "I call him Dad because he's done the most to help us out here. He shared his knowledge about how things work, explained everything we need to know. He looks out for people."

What she meant but did not say, I would learn, was that Dad had once pulled her aside and pressed $100 in her palm. *Use it to leave him*, was all he said. And that had been the last of it. He never brought it up again and Jolee never told her boyfriend, who wandered over to the Vaquero every morning to suggest a run to the convenience store to get more beer. And Dad always obliged him.

Dad's name was Ray, and he seemed pleased that Jolee had mentioned him so prominently, over The Mayor. For as long as any one at the Baldock could remember, Ray'd been saying he had six months to live, smoking his days away beneath a sign that warned oxygen tanks were in use, while Sweetpea splintered bones on the floor of his motor home. Ray was born in Kentucky, he said, but moved to Oregon when he was fifteen or sixteen and over the years had felled trees and labored as an auto mechanic. Somewhere along the way he had done irreparable damage to his lungs and now had emphysema. "All that asbestos in those brake pads," he figured.

Sometimes he would bring up wives, children. "Buried," he said, in a voice pumiced by all the years of smoking. But it was never clear what he meant by this, whether he meant them or his memories of them.

Sometimes he said he had fought in Vietnam. Other times he said he'd never been. He had lived at the Baldock for going on fifteen years. Twelve. Thirteen. He didn't seem to know anymore, one day so much like all the rest, mornings with the paper, coffee on the hot plate, and then when the shakes set in, a nip or two, on through the day, until his voice feathered at the edges and his eyes bobbed and pitched behind his glasses.

"It's not that we want to be here," he told me the night we met. "It's just we can't get out of here. I'm sixty-eight years old. I get $667 a month in social security and some food stamps. That's all I've got except for what I can make panhandling or rolling cans. Everyone here's the same, figuring out how to get by on less than nothing. But I'll tell you, I don't know how much longer I can make it. Last winter was a bearcat. It was hot dogs on Christmas. I was snowed in for three days. Icicles from top to bottom." He pulled out a pouch of tobacco and some papers and rolled a cigarette as he talked. "I'm too damn old for this anymore."

He'd been of a mind lately to light out for the coast—he was sure he could get a job as a park host somewhere—and so he was rationing gas, trying to save some cash. He'd even picked a day for his escape: "First of the month, I'm fixing to be gone."

He said this in October 2009. He said it again in November and in December and in January and in March and in April.

He was, in fact, among the last to leave the Baldock.

Jack was among the last to arrive, driving in the night after the Fourth of July, his gas gauge near empty, the trunk of his little white Ford four-door loaded down with what he had managed to take while everyone was gone, as his wife had asked him to do, so the kids wouldn't see: a Route 66 suitcase packed with clothing, including his good church suit; an old camping cooler; a pile of books; a sleeping bag; a tent; and a scrapbook his wife had made that contained the boys' baby pictures and photos from the barbecue they threw in the backyard the day he got his union card.

He'd told himself he'd leave the rest stop come morning, but the truth was he had nowhere else to stay, not on $206 a week in unemployment, not with his wife and kids needing money whether he lived with them anymore or not and the debt collectors lining up. None of his family would take him in, and for a long time, he felt it was no less than what he deserved for what a fool he'd been. He'd known, after all, as someone who'd been raised in a strict family of Jehovah's Witnesses, and who had married a committed convert, that secret strip-club visits and hours of adult movies downloaded from the Internet rank up there on the list of the faith's most grievous sins, right along with lying about it all, repeatedly. Still, he couldn't stop. According to the church elders, who referee such matters, excommunication was the only fit punishment. "Disfellowshipping," they call it. And while a part of Jack wanted to believe that maybe it was a bit out of proportion to the offense, he did, as he put it in his more contrite moments, "regret the crap I put my wife through, and I really did put her through crap—it's not as if I was an angel, and then got kicked out." And so he accepted the elders' pronouncement of his exile, if only because he did not know of any other way to express his sense of humiliation appropriately, other than to make himself disappear.

At first, he pitched a tent at the state campground, but at fifteen dollars a day, the campsite fee added up quickly and he was left with less than one hundred dollars a week. It was there, in passing, that another man mentioned the Baldock.

He resisted the idea initially, but then, one day, driving along Interstate 5 on his way to a job interview, he decided to pull off at the rest-stop exit. He was stopping only to use the bathroom. That's the reason he gave himself. But when he still had some time to kill before his appointment, he found himself following the man's directions, guiding his car past the rows of mud-spattered semis and the volunteers dispensing Styrofoam cups of grainy drip coffee, until he reached the invisible line separating those who were simply passing through from those who had nowhere else to go. He sat for a few minutes and watched through the windshield, his engine ticking. He watched the dogs, running and rucking the earth beneath the trees to which they were tethered. He watched the people hunched around the picnic tables, sunburned and knotty-limbed. Their laughter, loud and muculent, beat against the sealed windows like birds' wings.

It took three more days for his resolve to build, then take. His first night, he parked as far as he could from all the other cars, which were gathered close, fin to fin, as if in a shoal. For much of the night, Jack sat bolt upright, certain he could hear voices, the jangle of dog collars outside his door. But in the morning, he couldn't think of anywhere else to go and he wanted to conserve what little gas he had left. And so he'd remained there, just sitting in his car, in the oppressive heat, and tried hard to look as if he wasn't looking. He could sense everyone was looking at him, too, though not in an unfriendly way. Sometimes someone would wave. Or nod at him, like an unspoken acknowledgement of something shared. It made him uncomfortable, the way they seemed to recognize something in him before he saw it in himself. At the time, Jack didn't yet feel he had anything in common with anyone at the rest stop; he still believed he would be there only temporarily.

No one else thought he'd be long for the Baldock, either. "I get the feeling this place is going to blow his mind," Jolee told me. "Short-timer," Ray predicted. "You mean he's not another volunteer?" a visiting social worker asked me one night. Jack worked hard at cultivating the appearance of normalcy, or what passed for it in the world beyond the rest stop, anyway. His clothes looked freshly pressed, though he had no iron. "If you take them out of the dryer and fold them just the right way while they're still warm, you can make it look like you've creased them," he later explained. He spit shined his shoes. Although he had only a high school equivalency degree, he regularly worked through stacks of books and in careful handwriting filled pages of a journal.

The childhood Jack described, when I asked about it, sounded isolated. Few friends. A life that revolved around the family's faith. At some point, though, he'd become possessed by the idea that he would like to live in a world that offered experiences more expansive than those he'd known. After years of working variously as a pizza delivery man and a swing-shift worker at the local dairy, he decided it might be wise to learn a trade, like carpentry, and had been fortunate enough to apprentice out just as a condo-building boom swept through Portland, industrial

Jack didn't yet feel he had anything in common with anyone at the rest stop; he still believed he would be there only temporarily.

wasteland giving way to "planned urban communities." Suddenly, he was framing walls in million-dollar penthouses with Mt. Hood views.

He recalled how once, during that time, he had taken his wife to a restaurant near a development in downtown Portland that he was helping to build. Up until then, he and his wife had only gone out to places like Applebee's and, months later, Jack still remembered the white tablecloths, the white flowers, the way the food came out on white plates, "like paintings." Looking back, he realized it was the first moment he had allowed himself to think he might be different, that all along he had been living the wrong life. But then his work started slowing. Then the housing bubble collapsed completely, and the condos men like Jack had been working on were left to stand empty, their interiors an expanse of white.

The layoff came not long after he and his wife bought their first house. In response, Jack thought it made sense to enroll in school again, to learn another trade, like driving a truck, so he'd have something else to fall back on. The school told him he could take out loans, and he figured if he found work quickly he could pay them back before long. He graduated with his CDL at the time gas prices spiked and trucking companies started slashing their fleets. He'd added another $5,000 in debt to his name. Soon, they had to let the house go, the minivan, too.

Now, at the rest stop, he read Dave Ramsey's book *The Total Money Makeover* by flashlight at night, marking passages that seemed particularly relevant. On Ramsey's advice, Jack had started to portion his unemployment money into envelopes that he marked "bills," "gas," "savings," "fun," and "allowance" for his two boys, even if it was just a couple of singles. Later, he would make an envelope for "child support." By the time we met in October, he had been out of work for six months and had been living at the rest stop for three. He was thirty-six.

He carried copies of his resume in the front seat of his car, in case an opportunity arose to hand one out. Once, he flagged down a maintenance crew working at the rest stop and pushed a sheet in their hands, but that failed to yield any leads, as did the applications he filled out through the unemployment office. He did not have a criminal record or a problem with drugs or alcohol, though he had joined a twelve-step group, hoping, as he put it, it would help him "fix whatever's broken in me." He'd even tried to continue going to services at the Jehovah's Witness Kingdom Hall in the nearby town of Aurora, although, in keeping with what is expected of the excommunicated, he sat in the back and did not speak to anyone.

In the context of the Baldock—where a convicted pedophile with a habit of luring little boys into his vehicle, driving them to out-of-the-way places, then forcing them to have sex at knifepoint, happily lived out his last days; where, a few years ago, the decomposing body of a fifty-six-year-old man believed to have been murdered was found in the underbrush not far from where vehicles parked; and where, more than once, the grip of a pistol could be glimpsed peeping out from under a seat—Jack, with his resumes and scrapbooks and savings envelopes, seemed remarkably naïve, impossibly good, even. "Just a baby," Ray told me.

Of course, it all depended on your perspective. Jack knew his parents and his in-laws and, most importantly, his wife had plenty to say about him and what he'd done. Or not say. Sometimes when he called, they hung up on him. Once, his mom took a few whispered seconds to say that she shouldn't be speaking to him, not after what he'd done, that those were the consequences of his excommunication, and he shouldn't call again. And he couldn't argue with the opinion his family now held of him. He was everything they thought he was. He was nothing. He had tried to come up with a list of good things

> "The day I pay taxes is the day I know I've made it back to the mainstream. That's what I want, to feel normal again."

about himself in his journal. He wanted to be honest.

Finally, he wrote, "I am alive."

They had their own ways of measuring time. One month had passed when the medical delivery truck arrived to drop off a new set of oxygen tanks at Ray's Vaquero. It was fall when the school buses came to fetch the children. Saturday when the church group came round, offering pancakes and prayers. Thursday when the bus from St. Vincent de Paul pulled in with its onboard kitchen and cafeteria tables where the seats should have been, a place out of the cold where they could eat plates of fettuccini and turkey melts. Night when the jacked-up pickup came through the lot, its driver tapping his brake lights, waiting for one of the semis to wink its high beams back, the signal that he should park and climb inside to name his price.

They marked the persistence of loneliness by the frequency with which a knackered blue van appeared, groaning its way through the parking lot, the driver waving gently like a beauty queen on a float. It was Everett and his cat. A local social-service agency had managed to get him into a low-income apartment complex that allowed pets before he and the cat had to face a nineteenth winter at the Baldock. Still, the van coasted past nearly every day. "Too quiet in my new place," Everett would explain and then launch into his latest theories about the causes of unemployment and homelessness to anyone who stood outside his window long enough to listen—NAFTA, globalization, illegal immigration. He never required any kind of acknowledgment, except to be heard, engine idling, cat perched unblinking on the passenger seat.

Soon, they felt the weather turn, winds wailing cold out of the Columbia River Gorge and turning the condensation that accumulated inside their windshields while they slept into streaks of ice. Mornings, they followed each other's footprints through the frosted grass to the restrooms, where they washed and shaved beneath the industrial lights.

On one of those cold nights, after most of the other residents had retreated to their cars, Jolee stood with me in the wind by the picnic tables with an insulated coffee cup in her hands, watching the receding taillights of cars bound for the freeway on-ramp. "All any of us want is to get back over there one day," she said, her eyes following each car as it left. "We want to be over there with them, doing normal things. Like paying taxes. I'm serious. The day I pay taxes is the day I know I've made it back to the mainstream. That's what I want, to feel normal again."

By mid-November, she was gone. She gathered her things from the floor of the van and stuffed them in a backpack, then walked over to Jack's car to borrow his cell phone, which she pressed against her bruising cheek. "I'm sick—I need to go somewhere to get better," she said. Her boyfriend watched silently from the open door of the van with the dogs, his own face welted and swollen. Eventually, Jolee's father's pickup appeared and she climbed inside the cab. When it disappeared onto the freeway, her boyfriend got up and walked over to a sign directing patrons to the restrooms, and he drove his fist into the metal as hard as he could. Finally, he spoke. "Time to go to the store," he said. "Who's going to give me a ride?"

He went on a bender that lasted days, stumbled around in a fog. He accidently locked one of the dogs inside the van, the pit-bull mix who'd loved Jolee, and by the time he remembered and opened the door, the dog had torn the stuffing from the two front seats, shredded all the clothing strewn about, then snapped at his reaching hand. No one knew what to say, and one of the cardinal rules of the Baldock was that no one was in a position to judge, so they all kept quiet, and let him go on saying that the tears he wiped from his red eyes were because of the dog.

Jack for his part had given up his silent visits to the Kingdom Hall and had stopped talking about one day reconciling with his wife. He felt embarrassed when he thought about his uneasiness that first night at the rest stop, how he had imagined he could somehow hold himself apart. After four months at the Baldock, he'd seen enough of "what people do to survive" to realize that he had been deeply misguided ever to presume he'd known what it was to endure. Like the woman who often left her ten-year-old son alone in their motor home while she visited the rows of parked semis—and even the rigs of her neighbors—creeping back

hours later, sometimes with what looked like bite marks on her chest. Or the people who stood by the low wall near the rest-stop bathrooms, which they called just that, "The Wall," flashing signs made from the cardboard backs of empty half racks at all the weary travelers emerging from the cocoons of their cars, road tired and bladder full, hoping to part some change from them. They organized their panhandling in shifts in an attempt to maintain some kind of order and equity, but there were often fights when they tried to chase off anyone who didn't live at the rest stop, the tweakers who had homes or hotel rooms, but who would parachute in just long enough to beg money off tourists for a hit. In the hierarchy of the Baldock, those who came to beg but who had somewhere else to stay were openly disdained, cursed as cheats and liars, not because of their habits, but because they presented themselves as homeless when they had somewhere else to go.

As a rule, the police tended not to bother the rest-stop residents, unless someone called in a specific complaint. Although officials had long been aware of the community living there, and the local district attorney's office certainly made its position on the matter clear when it began referring to the Baldock as "Sodom and Gomorrah," the unspoken policy, at least on the ground, appeared to be one of benign neglect, so long as the residents kept themselves out of the run sheets.

But then, one day, a particularly ambitious state trooper came through and ticketed a number of vehicles for lapsed tags, and rather than watch their homes disappear on the backs of tow trucks, those residents quickly disappeared. The whole scene had struck Jack as unbearably unfair, and he couldn't stop thinking about it, like a pawl clicking over and over again into the grooves of a gear. He sat at one of the picnic tables for hours, trying to organize his thoughts. Finally, he got in his car and drove to the local community center. There, in front of the public computer, he began to type.

Baldock residents often spoke about how much they feared breakdown—as in, "My car's broken down on me twice now and I don't know what I'll do if it happens again." Impounds were an altogether different matter, however, and represented perhaps the most frightening possibility of all for someone whose car was his final vulnerability, the one thing left tethering him to any illusions of stability. Losing a car to impound almost certainly meant losing that car for good. Or as Jack wrote at the computer that day: *How can we afford to get them out? . . . (W)e cannot pay for towing or impound lot fees. Even if we pull all our money together, this is an expense we cannot afford . . .*

He typed: *We have a very difficult time paying auto insurance, gas and food. Many of us are looking for work, and have to travel long distances in search of employment. Gas prices are high and food stamps are good but not enough people receive them. None of us can afford a home, an apartment, hotel or even campgrounds . . .*

He typed: *We are homeless!*

And he typed: *All we seek is a safe place to live, until we find better options. The rest areas provide us a place to sleep, help each other out and have access to the rest rooms 24 hours a day . . .*

He kept going until he'd filled the whole page. He imagined it would be a letter of grievance, written on behalf of the entire community. He ended with the line *Thank you for your support.* Later, Ray read a copy at his dinette, holding it close to his glasses. "Boy can write!" he said, speaking as if Jack was not standing next to him. "Fancy. There's even semicolons!"

For Jack, the biggest declaration in the whole letter had come down to a single word.

We, he had written.

It was a word drawn from the nights they made communal meals, pooling their ingredients to stretch emergency food boxes and food-stamp allocations. Someone would always fix up plates for those who slept during the day and did shift work at night, balancing leftovers and thermoses of coffee on the hoods of cars for the drivers to find when they woke. From the way they bought each other presents from the Dollar Store, socks and singing cards (*Wild thing, you make my heart sing*). From the time they climbed onto

As a rule, the police tended not to bother the rest-stop residents, unless someone called in a specific complaint.

Ray's roof to fix the leaks that soaked his bedding, or when they helped Jack change his oil, or lent one another cooler space or propane. But also from the moments when the dogs wouldn't stop barking, and someone was screaming for them to shut the fuck up, and when the trash cans overflowed with all the garbage they'd dumped, and yet another person was asking if he could get a ride to the Plaid for more beer and smokes and only offering pocket change to cover the gas, and from the old-timers who would grouse about how the young had no work ethic, just wanted to smoke dope and have everything handed to them, and then they'd ask if they could take a shift at The Wall. It was Ray, pawing women's asses, braying and frothing at The Mayor that he was nothing more than an imposter, that he, Ray, had more right to appoint himself sovereign of the Baldock. And the boy who spent his nights alone in his motor home, waiting for the sound of his mother at the door—he did not go to school, but no one said anything, just as no one said anything about the abrasions on his mother's chest that turned purple, then green. In a single word, Jack had written himself into the Baldock, and he'd meant it unequivocally—the whole kind, desperate, resourceful, ugly truth of it—without denial or defense.

Thanksgiving marked the turning, the point at which time and memory began to pull away from them, though no one recognized it as it was happening. They were all too preoccupied with the planning of a Baldock-wide turkey feast; a list had been drawn up of ingredients to procure, and while everyone seemed to agree on mashed potatoes and gravy, some people disagreed over the value of stuffing and yams.

People decided to lose themselves in holiday preparations rather than focus on a disconcerting little story that had begun knifing its way through the populace. Apparently, a few days before Thanksgiving, one of the rest-stop cleaners told someone who told someone else that as of the first of the month, the Baldock would have a new landlord, and this one was not likely to be tolerant of the current laissez-faire living arrangements. Rumor had it there were all sorts of plans to spruce the place up—artist demonstrations, fancy coffee, solar panels, nature trails (Ray had harrumphed over this one: "Nature trails, my ass; if there was any nature to find here, we'd have killed it, gutted it, and eaten it by now, had a big old barbecue").

But disbelief gradually gave way to paranoia. Whether it was the maintenance-worker-cum-informant who was the first to mention the possibility of police sweeps and mass banishment, or it was the result

> Thanksgiving marked the turning, the point at which time and memory began to pull away from them.

of the residents' own grim future casting, soon the rest stop was frantic with speculation of an impending eviction. And so it came to pass that the inhabitants of the Baldock found themselves in a curious and unexpected position: after telling themselves for as long as they could remember that they couldn't wait to leave this place, they now realized they wanted nothing more than to stay.

They tried to talk about other things. On Thanksgiving morning, the early risers crammed into Ray's motor home, downing cups of coffee and taking turns putting the soles of their shoes on the propane heater until they could smell the scorched rubber, savoring the burn of their numb toes. "You know what I love most about Thanksgiving?" Jack said. "Football. It's been months since I've actually seen a game on a TV, not just listened to it on the radio." Everyone nodded and they talked about how luxurious it would be to sit on a sofa again, stupid with turkey, tasked with no other concern than whether to flick between the college or pro games. It struck them all as the height of decadence, of insanely good fortune.

And then the man who looked like a gnome and hardly ever socialized knocked on the motor-home window, face flushed. "Did you hear they're going to kick us out?" he shouted.

"You're late to the party," Ray barked through the window. "We've been hearing that for days now. All bullshit. Just scare tactics. They want to make the panhandling stop. I've been here for thirteen years

and this one always makes the rounds, but it's all show."

He raised his cup of coffee to his lips, but his hand was trembling.

"Anyway, I'm leaving. Come the first of the month, I'm outta here. I'm sick of all the drama. The doctor tells me I got six months to live and gotdamned if I'm gonna die at the Baldock."

His face was red and the cords of his neck had stretched taut, and no one spoke for fear of winding him up even more. He reached down, took a beer from the case he kept under the motor home's dinette, and poured some into his coffee as though it were cream.

And at this, the day began its slow slide into drunkenness for everyone except Jack, who didn't complain when he was asked to make a run to the convenience store when provisions ran low. He came back with five dollars' worth of Powerball tickets, bought from his "fun" envelope. The jackpot had reached nearly $200 million. "I figured if we won, we could all buy houses, maybe even the rest stop," he said.

Eventually, the main rest area, which had been heaving with holiday travelers, slowed to a few scattered cars. Afternoon tipped toward evening. The food remained uncooked, the air inside the motor home brackish with smoke. Ray, who had been brooding over his mug for some time, finally spoke. "Some people would say they wouldn't be caught dead living like this, in this nasty old RV," he said. "But you know what, I consider myself so fortunate to have this. Because when you've had nothing—and I've been there—living like a no-good dirty bum, low as you can go, in the streets, and people won't even look you in the face, like you're an animal or something and you don't have shit, you're thankful for whatever you can get. Let me tell you, I've never been so thankful."

He jabbed his face with his fists, trying to hide the tears.

"I don't know what I'll do if I lose this. I can't live like that again."

No one spoke.

Abruptly, Ray collected himself and motioned for another beer. "You know, when I leave here on the first, I won't miss a single one of you fools, stuck in this place. Now if you'll excuse me, I need the pisser."

The dreaded December 1 arrived without incident. Outwardly, at least, each day resembled the next. Ray's Vaquero did not budge. The blue van traced its lonely revolutions. Jack dropped money into his envelopes. He had finally found a job, working the graveyard shift at a manufacturing plant for $9.30 an hour, making "plastic injection molded components." And while at first he was relieved to be receiving a paycheck again, he had been doing the math and it had dawned on him that it would never add up to the kind of money he needed to move into even a modest apartment, first, last, and a deposit. He'd toured a complex in Wilsonville—"They had microwaves built into the cabinets, it was beautiful; I'd give anything to live in a place that nice"—but they wanted to see proof of income of at least $1,400 a month. He made just under

that. "It's like a merry-go-round you can't get off," he said. "I don't know how I'm going to get out of this."

So he continued to sleep in his car at the rest stop and hoped each day that it would not be his last. Everyone did. Some people urged a discussion of contingencies, the way some families speak of fire-evacuation plans or designated meeting places following natural disasters. What about forest-service land? Was there a remote wooded space where they could all caravan? Too cold this time of year, the pessimists argued. Think of all the food and propane and water you would need to stockpile.

Others, like members of any neighborhood group upon hearing rumors of possible planning changes, turned to the public computer at the community center for reconnaissance. As a result, they now knew the name of the new landlord: Oregon Travel Experience, a semi-independent state agency, as the online literature put it. It had been granted the go-ahead by the legislature to take over the operations of five rest areas that had previously fallen under the purview of the Department of Transportation. And though none of what they could find was written in what one would call plain, unadorned speech, one phrase in particular, about helping the rest stops achieve their "full economic development potential," seemed to them to translate as having something to do with money—be that making money or saving it. Either way, it was not a concept that they suspected would live comfortably alongside homelessness. Intuition told them that much.

Then one day, a woman appeared in the back lot. By the pristine condition of her vehicle, they knew she wasn't a new arrival. As it turned out, she was the new landlord, head of the OTE. Her name was Cheryl, she said. She'd stopped by because she wanted to personally reassure everyone that OTE was not just going to kick people out of the rest stop, but they should know things were going to change at the Baldock. She had been talking to people from the community center where many of them received assistance, and she hoped that over the next few weeks they all might be able to work together to find a way to help everyone move on to something more stable.

"We're not stupid," Ray said later, after she had left. "It was just a different way to say the same thing: you're out of here."

Jack was not ready to embrace Ray's cynicism. He wanted to believe that the promise made to them had been sincere, that no one would be kicked out of the rest stop until he or she had somewhere else to go. But where would that be? Whenever he tried to trace a clear path out of the Baldock for any of them, it always came out confused, occluded, unmappable. No sooner had he considered a possible exit route than his mind would throw up a fact that directly contradicted this option,

She wanted to personally reassure everyone that OTE was not just going to kick people out of the rest stop.

and so it went, fact upon fact, one after another, like a thicket of construction barricades choking all conceivable ways forward.

Fact: There's not a single homeless shelter in this particular county.

Fact: What if you have a criminal record or are living with someone with a criminal record? What if you have an eviction in your past? No one rents to you.

Fact: Most RV parks won't rent a spot to rigs ten years or older, yet that's what most people at the Baldock owned.

Fact: Most one-bedroom apartments in the area rent for $750 a month.

He rehearsed his arguments on me, and on anyone else who would listen, and when there was no one to listen, he repeated them to himself, until he was losing sleep. It had reached the point where he was reporting for his graveyard shift bleary, his thoughts smudged, sluggish. He blocked his car windows with sunshades to keep out the daylight, but still he winced and churned at the sounds of his neighbors, who seemed to be tuning their voices to a pitch that matched the collective anxiety level.

They grew irritated with each other. It was easier to cloak fear with anger. Ray, for one, announced that his motor home was henceforth off limits to any more coffee klatches. He locked himself inside and did not speak to anyone, though they could see him, glowering at them all through the blinds. He should have been happy. The Mayor had abdicated, putting the Baldock in his rearview mirror. As it turned out, he was not homeless, merely restless, prone to long cooling-off periods when confrontations arose at home. After carefully considering his options, he'd apparently found the idea of returning to the missus preferable to gutting out another day in the uncertain climate of the Baldock.

In this way, they welcomed spring, agitated and aggrieved. Finally, in March, a meeting was called at a local church. Cheryl from the OTE promised to be there, along with the man she had recently appointed the rest stop's new manager, as well as local politicians, a deputy district attorney, a trooper from the state patrol. A good number of people from the Baldock showed up, even a few people who no longer lived there, including Jolee, whose new home was a camp trailer on her parents' property, and Everett. Ray had said he would boycott it.

"Ornery old fart," Jolee said, and she called him on his cell phone until he relented and showed up late, smelling of drink, his face gray. Jolee pressed a mint on him.

They sat at tables set with tablecloths and formal place settings for lunch and bouquets of lilacs and bulb flowers and bowls of pastel-wrapped candy. Someone had set up a whiteboard at the front of the room. The Canby Center, the social-service agency that had worked most closely with the residents over the years, had organized the event, and the center's director at the time, a woman named Ronelle, spoke first.

"We're here so that you can have a chance to speak," she said. "Please be frank about the obstacles and the barriers you face so that the people here can understand what you are up against, and what might help you. "

But how to make it all fit on a whiteboard?

They each tried to tell a corner of the story, but it came out fractured, a chorus of elisions:

"A lot of places won't let you have animals and animals are part of our sanity."

"I had to sell my house and move into my motor coach."

"Your *motor coach?*"

"SHH!"

"You have no idea how scary it is trying to imagine where to go to next."

"I never thought in my life I would panhandle, but I've flown a sign to raise money for my tags, my insurance."

"A lot of us have jobs, but they aren't very stable or we don't have enough hours to make what it takes to get back in a place. I make just above minimum wage, and I have child support to pay too."

They each tried to tell a corner of the story, but it came out fractured, a chorus of elisions.

"Some of us just slipped through the cracks. We don't have alcohol problems, medical problems, or a mental illness. There seems to be no help for us."

"I've had times where I've worked double shifts, and then I need to catch up on my sleep all at once. I might sleep twelve hours straight in my car. I need a place where I can do that, so I can keep my job."

"You know, if you move us, you aren't going to get rid of us. We just go hide."

"We used to have movie nights in the summer. Jack had this portable DVD player and he'd set it on one of the picnic tables, and we'd all pretend like we were at a drive-in . . ."

Ray said nothing.

Finally, Cheryl rose and spoke. "We understand you're a community, a neighborhood." She respected that very much. She knew they were afraid, but she wanted to reassure them a "transition plan" was being developed. "We promise to keep you informed every step of the way."

So much said, and yet, in the end, it would be silence that told them the most. The phrase they most hoped to hear—*you can stay*—went unspoken and there was only the scrape of chairs all around, the rustle of skirts and suits departing.

It was time to go, but they dawdled. Everett shook the remainder of the candy into the front pocket of his overalls. Jolee went with her boyfriend off to a quiet corner to talk, their heads close together. And Jack stood off to the side, rehearsing one last speech: "What if I did some maintenance work for you, strictly volunteer.

Could you let me sleep there during the day?"

Maybe, in those last days, if they had been different people, more like the people they saw on the other side of the rest stop, those so seemingly certain in their slacks and sedans, counting down the miles to home, maybe then they might have known how to reassure each other, how to spin this into a good thing, a fortunate thing, to be given the chance to leave this place and pretend it had never existed. Wasn't that what they had wished for all along? As it was, they hid their faces under propped hoods, screwdrivers clenched between their teeth, cussing recalcitrant old engines into cooperating for the drive ahead.

Proffers had been extended to each resident, elaborate relocation plans crafted by a committee of representatives from the county and state, police officers and social workers and housing specialists, assembled at the request of Oregon Travel Experience.

For Jack, and seven others, immediate slots in a six-week class offered through the county that would help him land low-income housing. For the more complicated cases that eluded immediate solutions, prepaid spots in campgrounds and motels. For one man, detox. For others, help navigating social-security applications and untangling veterans' benefits.

For Ray, a stall had been secured in an RV park willing to allow his old motor home, but he wasn't having it. "It's nothing but a drug den. Place is full of meth heads and thieves. Sweetpea and I won't go." He was convinced that everyone who agreed to leave the Baldock was just being set up for a fall. "Once they get you alone," he said, "you just become a number. We should hunker down, like a family."

He was still refusing to budge, right up until the last day in April, when everyone was asked to caravan to Champoeg State Park, where a block of adjoining campsites had been booked for the weekend, after which everyone would head on to whatever was next. True to its word, Oregon Travel Experience had not kicked anyone out, but now that all the residents had been offered someplace else to stay, that promise no longer held. From this day forward, anyone who remained at the rest stop, or who returned, was subject to trespassing charges should he violate the twelve-hour rule. Or as Ray translated it: "Once you leave, you leave. They've got you."

As the others made their last-minute preparations, packing and replacing flat tires and loading squirming dogs into cargo holds, Ray hunkered down in his Vaquero. "This is gonna get nasty," he promised through the blinds.

His standoff lasted less than two hours. By late afternoon, he'd pulled into one of the empty berths at the state park, next to Jack, who stood shrouded in tent fabric. "Can someone please help me with the poles?" he called. This was the campground where Jack had first stayed when his wife kicked him out. It also marked the first time in nine months he did not have to sleep in the seat of a car.

The sun warmed the leaves of the ash trees and, together, they sat at one of the communal picnic tables, watching the dogs skitter through the underbrush and admiring the trailers of their new, if temporary, neighbors. It was a nice campground, everyone agreed, though they would never venture farther than their assigned row. They would not go where there were birding trails and pet-friendly yurts, or to the field reserved for disc golf. They kept close together, to what was familiar, working their way through their coolers, telling each other this wasn't so different from the Baldock, but then worrying all the while that their new neighbors might think them too loud, too uncouth ("DON'T PEE AGAINST THAT TREE!"), shushing the dogs, trying not to think about the checkout dates recorded on their receipts, when they would all head off into whatever it was that waited for them after this, alone.

Once, long ago, this had been a pioneer settlement, the last stop for those who had set off across the plains, drifting west until they couldn't drift anymore. Now, on special occasions, volunteers in period garb demonstrated for park visitors the difficulty of life for those who had once tried to settle on the frontier's edge. Each year, in "a celebration of Oregon's rugged pioneer roots," the curious and the masochistic could attempt the skills those pioneers acquired for daily survival, such as wheat threshing, butter churning, and wool carding. This particular weekend, however, happened to mark the occasion of Founder's Day, when, nearly one hundred and seventy years ago, the settlers had gathered and voted to establish a provisional government. The land where the park now sat was to have been its capital. Already, in preparation for the festivities, men in boots and braces were rigging draft horses to plow furrows in the earth as minivans puttered past.

Such re-creation was all that was left of what had once transpired there. Eighteen years after the historic vote, the nearby river tongued its banks, then surged. The settlement vanished beneath seven feet of water, and the pioneers scattered. They never rebuilt. Twelve miles away, for the first night in more than a decade, the back lot of the Baldock stood empty, like a stretch of back shore licked clean by the tide.

Ray disappeared first, pulling out of the campground in the middle of the night. No one heard from him for months, and everyone started to wonder if he might really be dead.

The rest of them tried to forget the Baldock as they moved into rent-assisted apartments and bought plants and hand towels and carefully positioned throws on the backs of donated sofas, where they sat, absorbing the quiet. Some of them found jobs, and some of them lost those jobs when they failed the drug tests. Those who had not been visited by their children in their car days practiced unfolding hide-a-beds, stored plastic cereal bowls in the cupboards.

They called each other, until they didn't. Months passed.

They did not see the workers bent over the long-neglected flower beds of the Baldock, planting local bulbs of peony and iris.

Then Ray finally surfaced, alive, but rigless and grieving. "I did a dumb thing," is how he said it to me. "Had some drinks with a friend, drove off, cops stopped me. I'm not gonna lie, I had beer on my breath, so they gave me a DUI, took the motor home and I couldn't get it back."

He had been looking for a place where he and Sweetpea could stay—how he hated to beg—and for a while the joke was it looked like a Baldock reunion, because it was Jolee who offered to help. She had a couch of her own now—she'd managed to get a little rent-controlled apartment in Oregon City that she shared with her boyfriend, though since he'd left the rest stop, he was no longer being called a boyfriend but a fiancé—and she told Ray he was welcome to the living room. Just like old times, they'd said, and crammed into the little apartment. And it was true that it was just like old times, but that wasn't always good. Ray grew restless— "can't stand being cooped up"—and took to walking Sweetpea around and around the apartment complex, until one day he slipped on a patch of ice and shattered his

Ray hunkered down in his Vaquero. "This is gonna get nasty," he promised through the blinds.

hip—"broke the socket clean through"—sentencing himself to forty-five days in a hospital bed.

"I've got nothing," he said upon his release. "I'm seventy years old and not a damn thing to my name." He'd left Sweetpea with Jolee and he hoped to buy a van "come the first of the month, something less than $750, if I can find it." But even if he found a new vehicle, he had no idea where to go. He insisted he had no desire to return to the Baldock. "That's all in the past. Gone now. Buried." But the way he said it sounded as if he wished it wasn't true.

Jack was the one who went back.

"Yes," he'd said, and then he hung up the phone and set it on the coffee table of his apartment, where he now kept his journals and scrapbooks in a neat, angled stack. Then he'd picked it up again to quit his job at the manufacturing plant.

On his last shift, his colleagues presented him with a sheet cake. They had scribbled a message onto the chocolate frosting. "Good luck Jackass!"

He pulled back into the parking lot of the Baldock on New Year's Day.

It was January 1, 2011, and he had stayed away from the rest stop for a total of six months.

They set him to work mowing the grass and emptying trash and erasing the graffiti that erupted in the bathrooms. He pruned the trees where the dogs once howled and paced. He made it his special project to tame the overgrown spinneys that romped the edges of the property, only to unearth in his sculptings a decade's worth of discarded liquor bottles, tattered condoms, needles, all carted away like evidence of an obscene archeological dig. He worked until no signs of the old settlement remained.

Also among his duties was to tend to travelers who might be stranded, who needed a jump or a tire changed or some gas. Sometimes, he gave directions. For all this he made ten dollars an hour and received benefits better than those he had known when he was with the union. It was the happiest he'd felt in a long time, but also, strangely, the loneliest.

For company, he sought the continued counsel of Dave Ramsey, who strongly advised a second job if one hoped to shed debt more quickly. And so, on his days off, Jack returned to the manufacturing plant and his cake-giving colleagues of the graveyard shift.

The borders of his life had now contracted to a simple triangulate: work, his boys, and the garden apartment where he hung his sons' framed school photos on the wall and taped a flier for a one-bedroom house for sale at the end of the road with an asking price of $129,000 to the refrigerator. He had been adding figures endlessly in his head, and although he was so tired he sometimes found his mouth refusing to form whole sentences, he was certain that, if he could keep this up and his car did not break down on him, he would be debt free within the year, maybe even build up an emergency fund.

Sometimes rumors reached him about his former neighbors at the Baldock. Ray had disappeared again and no one knew where he had drifted to this time. Jolee had lost her apartment and was briefly sighted living with her fiancé in the bushes at the confluence of the Willamette and Clackamas Rivers, where, according to the local parks and recreation department, "the beaches attract both the sun worshipper and the nature lover with sun, water, nature paths and wildlife!" A notice in the classified section of the local newspaper had recently announced the auction of all the possessions in her storage unit due to lack of payment.

Mostly, though, Jack lived in silence, quietly and deliberately tracing the same route each day, from rest stop to apartment, and at the end of it, the sound of his key in the door, then dinner at a small pine table with a single place setting and his manager's first review of his work at the rest stop, which he reread as he ate: "Keep up your consistently good attitude and strong work ethic and you'll do fine."

You'll do fine, he tells himself and tries not to think about those days at work when a car pulls into one of the rest stop's parking stalls, belongings strewn in the back, and how he prays it'll leave before he has to be the one to knock on the window and tell whoever's inside it's time to go.

FICTION

The Worm

Donald Ray Pollock

In 1917, just as a sticky June turned into a blistering July along the border that divides Georgia and Alabama, Pearl Jewett awakened his three sons with a guttural bark that sounded more animal than man. They arose silently from their particular corners of the one-room shack and pulled on their filthy clothes, still damp and stinking with the sweat of yesterday's labors. Moonlight funneled through gaps in the chinked log walls and lay in fading milky ribbons across the dirt floor. A black rat scuttled up the rock chimney, knocking bits of rotten mortar into the cold grate. Their heads nearly touching the low ceiling, the young men gathered around the center of the room, and Pearl handed them each a bland wad of flour and water dabbed in cold grease for their breakfast. There would be no more to eat until evening, and then they would each get a share of the sick hog they had butchered in the spring, along with a mash of boiled spuds and wild greens scooped onto dented tin plates with a hand that was never clean from a pot that was never washed. Except for the occasional rain, every day was the same.

"I seen two of them niggers again last night," Pearl said, taking a bite of biscuit. "Out there in that tulip tree singin' their songs. They sure do like that thing." He swallowed and stared slack-jawed for a minute or so out the rough-cut opening that served as a window, then wondered aloud, "What you 'spose would happen was we to cut it down?" The last tenants of the shack, a family of mulattoes, had all died of the fever several years ago and were buried out back in the weeds along the perimeter of the now empty hog pen. Due to fears of the sickness lingering on in a place where black and white had mixed, the owner of the land, Captain Tardweller, hadn't been able to convince anyone to live there until the old man and his boys came along the previous fall looking for work. Lately, Pearl had been seeing their ghosts everywhere. The morning before he'd counted four of them.

"Don't sound like a bad life to me," Chimney said. "Laying around playing music." He was sixteen and the youngest. "What you figure happened to them other ones, Pap?" He grinned at his brothers, Cane and Cob. "Think they ran off to town lookin' for a jug?"

The room went quiet. Pearl drew his slumped shoulders back and tightened his drooping mouth into a grim smile as he slowly turned toward the boy. All three of his sons resembled their mother, with their squarish chins and pale blue eyes and dark hair, but Chimney had yet to grow the scraggly beard and hard, expressionless look the others wore. Because he reminded Pearl of his dead wife the most, the old man usually chose to ignore him, but now he leaned closer and studied Chimney's face intently, as if he were peering into a smoky portal to the past. His breath reeked of stomach gas and rancid drippings. A solitary bird began to twitter from somewhere close by. The boy grew nervous, glanced over at his brothers, took the last bite of his biscuit. Without any warning, Pearl's hand whipped out and caught him by the throat. "Spit it out, damn ye," he growled. "Spit it out." Chimney tried to break away, but his father's grip, seasoned by years of plowing and chopping and picking, was like a vise. With his windpipe squeezed shut, he soon ceased struggling and managed to spew a few wet crumbs, which stuck to the hairs on Pearl's wrist.

> **With his windpipe squeezed shut, he soon ceased struggling and managed to spew a few wet crumbs.**

"Pap, he didn't mean nothing," Cane, the oldest said. "Let him go."

"I'm tired of his mouth," Pearl said through clenched teeth. He snorted some air and tightened his hold even more, seemingly bent on shutting the boy up forever.

"I said let him go, goddamn it," Cane repeated. Grabbing the old man's other arm, he wrenched it back with a rough twist and a loud pop filled the room. Pearl let out a piercing howl as he shoved Chimney away and broke free of Cane. The boy coughed and spat the rest of the biscuit onto the floor, and the brothers watched in the gloomy half-light as the old man ground it into the dirt with his shoe. Nothing else was said. When he was done, they all followed Pearl out of the shack single file. Cob stopped at the well and drew a pail of water, and they carried it, together with their tools—three double-headed axes and a couple of machetes and a rusty, leather-handled saber with a broken tip—along the edge of a long green cotton field. Just as a red, swollen sun, looking like the eye of a debauched Cyclops, crested the hills to the east, they came to the swampy patch of woods they were clearing for Captain Tardweller. Cane took off his ragged shirt and spread it over the top of the canvas bucket to keep mosquitoes from laying their eggs in it, and another day of work began. By afternoon, with nothing but warm water sloshing around in their guts, all they could think about was that sick hog hanging in the smokehouse.

Not long after sunrise, the last of the worm slid from Lucille's mouth and dropped upon her chest with a soft plop.

Chimney had just turned three years old when his mother took ill. Pearl had a farm of his own back then in North Carolina, just a few acres, but big enough for a man to get by on if he was willing to work. Life was as good as an illiterate farmer with no inheritance could hope for in those days, and Pearl made sure to give the Almighty credit for that. He did without tobacco to pay for a pew in the First Baptist Church near Hazelwood, and every Sunday morning, no matter what the weather, he and his young family walked the four miles there to worship. Pearl was especially proud that his wife was the only one in the congregation besides the minister who could read the lessons. He had quickly volunteered her after the last lay reader backslid and ran off to Charleston with a business partner's money, disregarding the fact that Lucille was so shy she had a hard time looking even him in the eye. Every week he had to coax and threaten her into walking up to the front of the congregation, telling himself that it was for her own good. And so, when she first started staying in bed on the Sabbath, complaining of feeling weak and light-headed, he couldn't help but think she was faking it, and several months passed before he became convinced she really was sick.

By that time, Lucille had lost a considerable amount of weight and her sagging skin had turned the dreary color of a rain cloud. Taking out a lien against the land, Pearl sent for doctors. One of them bled her and another prescribed expensive tonics in brown bottles while a third put her on a diet of curds, but nothing seemed to help. Then the money ran out and all he could do was watch her slowly wither away. What struck her down remained a mystery until the night of her wake. As he sat alone keeping her corpse company in the dim, flickering light of a single candle, Pearl noticed that the tip of her tongue was beginning to stick out from between her lips. Leaning over to set it right, he saw a slight movement. *My God*, he thought, *can it be that she's still alive?* Just then a worm, no wider than a ring finger and no thicker than a few sheets of paper, pushed forward several inches out of her mouth. Pearl lurched back and knocked the chair over in his rush to get away from the bed, but then stopped himself at the doorway. He stood for several minutes listening to the frantic pounding of his heart and the soft breathing of his sons in the other room. With a shudder, he thought of some words he had heard Lucille read the last time she was able to do the lessons: "Where their worm dieth not and the fire is not quenched." Though he couldn't recall any more of the passage, he was certain the minister had explained in his sermon that it was an apt description of hell. He debated what to do. He couldn't bury his wife with that thing inside her, but he had no idea how to go about removing it other than to cut her open, and he couldn't bear the thought of that. Stepping forward with the candle, he saw another two inches emerge, and the blind head rose up and moved slowly back and forth as if testing the air. He paced around the room, fighting the urge to crush it. The only thing to do, he finally decided, was to wait it out, and so he sat back down near the bed and spent the next few hours watching the creature slowly work its way out of her.

Not long after sunrise, the last of the worm slid from Lucille's mouth and dropped upon her chest with a soft plop. Pearl looked out the window and beyond the yard to his fields, barren of crops and overgrown with weeds. Lucille's dying had started in the spring and taken up the entire summer. Soon, the man from the bank would be coming for his money and Pearl didn't have it. He stood and said the words aloud: "The worm dieth not and the fire is not quenched." He studied on this for a while, then turned to the bed and gathered up the worm like a spool of wet rope and carried it outside, past his still sleeping sons. Spreading it along the ground, he pulled it tight and pinned each pulsing end of it down with stones he took from the border of one of Lucille's flower beds. Two peahens, all that remained of his livestock, darted out from under the porch and started pecking at it. He grabbed them up, one in each hand, and bashed their heads against a fence post. Then he went back into the house and drank a cup of cold coffee and shook the boys awake. By noon, they had buried Lucille in the spot under a poplar tree where she used to sit in the shade and shell beans. For the next two days, Pearl ate chicken and watched the scalding Carolina sun dry the worm into a silver, leathery strip. Then he stuffed it into an empty coffee-bean sack and sewed it shut; and ever since then, he had used it as a pillow to rest his head on at night.

After he lost the farm, Pearl and his sons wandered with empty pockets across a harsh, dirty South devoid of prospects, and his luck turned from bad to worse. He couldn't understand it. He prayed to God to smooth the way a bit, but no matter how hard they worked, the best the four of them could ever do was stay one step ahead of starvation. Sitting by the fire in whatever meager camp they had managed to make that evening, Pearl supped on parched corn and moldy bread and went back over his life, trying to recall something he might have done that would justify such a curse. He knew that he had sinned on occasion, yet no more than most, and certainly not as much as some. Pride had always been his biggest problem, and forcing Lucille to read the lessons had been a vain and selfish act, but still, wasn't God supposed to forgive? If not for him, at least for his sons? Though his faith had always been strong, doubts began to enter his mind, and that worried him even more than where the next meal was coming from.

The years passed without any letup, and by the time Pearl met the man along the Foggy River, the worm had turned to powder in his pillow. He was sitting on the bank half-asleep while his boys tried to catch a fish with their hands. They hadn't eaten anything in two days, but he didn't have the strength to help them. An occasional sparking sound that had started in his head not long after Lucille died had recently turned into a constant sizzle, as if his brains were being sautéed in a skillet. The man came out of the woods and sat down beside Pearl without a word, as if they had known each other for years. Suddenly aware of a presence, Pearl roused himself and looked over, saw a bent and misshapen stranger carrying a rod made of ash and wearing nothing but a grimy, ragged sackcloth. On his forehead, a red and black canker the size of a silver dollar seethed like a hot coal. Pearl was reminded of a picture card he had once seen in the First Baptist Church of a heathen who had lived his whole life chained to a tree sitting on a pile of his own slops, his eyes turned to black bubbles from staring into the sun. A pockmarked missionary just returned from some foreign land had passed it around while grubbing for donations. Pearl wondered if he was dreaming. "Looks like you been on the road a long time," he said to the man.

The stranger nodded. "See that yellow bird sitting over there in the cypress?" he said, pointing with his rod.

Shading his eyes from the sun with his hand, Pearl looked across the river. "Yeah, I see him."

"I been following him for ten years now. He takes me wherever I need to go."

Pearl thought about that for a minute, then asked, "You some kind of preacher?"

"God speaks to me from time to time," the man said with a shrug, "and I follow His bird. Not much else to it."

Before he realized it, Pearl began telling the man the story of the worm and the ill fortune that had come after. He confessed that he was beginning to wonder if God even existed, for why would He treat one so badly and let another off the hook completely? It didn't make sense. After Pearl finished, the man sat quietly for a while stroking his matted and mangy beard. Then he looked down at his callused feet. He leaned over and tugged at one of his big toenails with his knotty fingers. Without so much as a wince, he tore it off and held it up for Pearl to see.

> "Friend, you and them boys of yours could drown me in that river there and it'd be the most blessed thing ever happened to me."

"You got it all wrong," the man said. "The truth is you been chosen. God's giving you the chance for a better resurrection. Without you taking hold of some of the misery in the world, there can't be no redemption. Nor will there be any grace. That shouldn't come as no big surprise if you study on it. Look what He did to His own son. Most of us got it damn easy compared to that. But what they call 'preachers' these days don't want to tell people the truth. Ol' Satan's tricked them into teaching there's an easier way. Why, some even go around claiming that God wants us all to be rich. That's hard to believe, ain't it? They might as well lead their flocks to the gates of hell and shove 'em in. No, you got to welcome all the suffering that comes your way and then you be redeemed."

"You really believe that?" Pearl asked, staring down at the man's bloody toe.

"Friend, you and them boys of yours could drown me in that river there and it'd be the most blessed thing ever happened to me."

"I don't know, mister," Pearl said. "Going a little hungry from time to time ain't no bother, but we 'bout starved clear out."

The man smiled. "I ain't et nothing in over a week except a few tad-poles and the creatures I've found in this beard of mine. I wouldn't want no more than that."

"But what is it I get for all this redeeming you talkin' about?" Pearl said.

"Why, one day you'll get to sit at the heavenly table," the man said. "Won't be no scrounging for scraps after that." He went to toss the toenail away, then thought better of it and slipped it into his mouth.

"So you saying that them that has it good down here, they don't ever get into heaven?"

The man chewed for a moment, then swallowed. "Their chances are slim to none, I reckon. Too many spots on their garments, too many wants in their hearts."

"Well, what about this noise I got in my head? I'd give the rest of my life for one night without it."

Scooting closer, the man put his ear against Pearl's. He held his breath and listened. From a distance, they looked like two spent lovers cuddled against each other watching the water pass by. A dragonfly hovered above their gray heads, then darted off into some cattails. "Mercy," the man finally said, "sounds like you gettin' ready to hatch a star in there."

"You figure it will ever go away?"

"Oh, I expect so," the man said. "Everything does eventually." Then he glanced over at the cypress and reached for his rod. "It's been nice talkin' to you, brother, but I see my little scout is ready to move on." Just as he stood, a loud commotion started down at the edge of the water and Cane whooped and slung a large catfish a few feet up onto the muddy bank. The man shook his head as he watched it flop around in the dirt. "Best ye tell him to throw that thing back in," he said.

"Preacher, I can't do that," Pearl said. "That's their supper."

"Mark my word, you let them eat that cat, before long them boys will be wanting everything the easy way." Then the man stepped down into the river and made his way across to where the bird was waiting on him.

No sooner had the man disappeared into the trees than the sizzle in Pearl's head spluttered to a stop. He entered briefly into a complete and profound silence, and in that glorious minute, he began to see God in a new light. If life was going to be hard, at least the preacher had provided a good reason for it, even a great one. From then on, Pearl seemed to follow intentionally the road that promised the most misery, and the only thing that satisfied

him was the worst that could happen. In the hopes of replicating that per-
fect moment again, he plugged his ears with sawdust and red clay and peb-
bles and chunks of wood, but the outside world always seeped through. He
even considered piercing the thin drums with a thorn, but he worried that
God might look upon such a selfish act as the desecration of a holy temple.
Slowly, after various experiments, he came to realize that he wouldn't
know the great silence again until he went down into the grave. That
moment by the river had been just a preview of the eternal peace to come
if he stayed the course and didn't weaken. "I will be redeemed," he kept
repeating to himself. "I will be redeemed."

I WANT A LOVE

At a certain altitude it was the man over me over the couch
A paperback flopped open to an insignificant page as the basement leaked

Water a study of scales study of want study of my hair on his chest
His chest breathing his password of night the moon a lacquered nail its

Insouciance trickling white sound in my brain the village a limp hand
Mindlessly open as in sleep as in death he is sleeping I am sleeping

Overpeopled but I want a love as simple as a peacock feather brushing me
A peacock feather boasting eyes and black cry against this tin crack of earth

The planet buckling its new gait a bomb renting a crowded bus but
I called this a city a place to store my men and wives a place for talking

Fucking under a handsome sun the men string fish from the harbor bury
Chicken feet in the sand all this oil embossed in our eyes dredging us

Billions of legs wrapped around billions of legs I want a love to remove me
From all countries from Sangiovese cocoa cow be reversible the village

Stacked over me patting my bare spine I want a love to tell me I am responsible
Let me stop us I want a love to sleep with my women sneak abortions

Record my seven billion promises to dirt and steaming plates instead this man
In the village he turns me on my side he sings my singular love gets swallowed

FICTION

Turtleface

Arthur Bradford

We were paddling our canoes down a remote, slow-moving river, a full day's travel in either direction from the nearest road, when Otto decided to do something spectacular and stupid. Around a bend we encountered a sandy cliff rising up out of the water. Otto announced he would climb the cliff and then run down its steep face. We could all take pictures as he descended in long Olympian strides. At the end of his run, as he neared the base, Otto explained, he would launch himself into the river, a downhill running dive. It was late in the afternoon and we had all been drinking beer and whiskey.

Otto and I paddled to the cliff's base and he got out. Then he climbed. It was tough going due to all that loose sand.

"How's this?" he shouted down. He was about halfway up.

"Higher!" I shouted back. I was excited about the stunt and reasoned that greater height would maximize the effect.

I was feeling envious as well. Sheila and Maria were in the other canoe, watching intently. They wore cutoff blue jean shorts over their swimsuits. Sheila was a photographer. She pointed her large-lensed camera up at Otto. Maria, my girlfriend, was a nurse and on the verge of dumping me for a number of legitimate reasons. At that moment I wished I possessed Otto's imagination and daring.

There was one other person with us, a cousin of Sheila's, named Tom. He was a large fellow who had joined the trip at the last minute. He couldn't, or wouldn't, paddle because he had broken his thumb. Instead, he declared he would be in charge of doling out the beer, and he spent the day sprawled in the center of the women's canoe doing just that. His skin had turned from pale white to dark crimson over the course of our journey. Maria had warned him about the dangers of exposure to the sun but he dismissed that advice with a wave of his cast-bound hand.

"I'll be fine," said Tom.

Otto reached a point on the cliff where he could climb no higher. The terrain above him was too steep. He was perhaps a hundred feet above the water now, clinging to exposed tree roots for support. Clods of dirt tumbled down the slope and bounced into the water in front of us.

"Do it!" shouted Tom. He threw a half-full can of beer toward the cliff where it landed without a sound in the sand.

"Are you going to pick that up?" asked Maria.

"Nope," said Tom.

"I'll pick it up," I said. I paddled my canoe back toward the cliff.

> He was losing control, legs scrambling, barely able to keep up with his downhill momentum.

"Are you ready?" shouted Otto.

"Yes!" I shouted back.

"Where should I dive?" asked Otto.

I could see that Otto was having second thoughts. But the cliff shot straight into the river and the water below it was dark and deep. It all seemed fine to me.

"Go to my left!" I shouted back, pointing to a general area.

"My steps are going to be so long, man!" shouted Otto. "Watch this!"

Otto gave a halfhearted whoop and leapt into the air. He took one huge stride, and then another. He was right about those long steps. He covered a tremendous amount of ground with each leap, such was the pitch of the terrain. The sun shone down and sand kicked up behind him, creating an impressive, superhuman image.

Sheila clicked away with her camera and said, "Oh wow." Maria nodded appreciatively.

Admiration and envy swelled within me. I should have come up with this, I thought, or at least climbed up there and done it with him, a tandem performance. We could have shared the glory. The women would have rubbed our backs around the campfire that night while recounting our heroics. Otto's body pitched forward as he neared the river's edge. He was losing control, legs scrambling, barely able to keep up with his downhill momentum.

"Ahhh!" he cried.

He dove forward, flying out toward the water, and hit the surface with a smack.

Ouch, I thought.

"Whoa, fuck!" said Tom, slapping his knee with his one good hand. "Damn!"

The women were silent, unsure whether to laugh or be concerned. I moved closer to where Otto had landed. His body floated up in an awkward manner, facedown, arms splayed out from his sides.

"Turn over, Otto," I said out loud.

Maria yelled at me, "Get him, Georgie!"

I sloshed forward and flipped Otto's body over. His nose was smashed. Something was wrong with his lip, too. Otto took a huge gasp of air. He was alive, a good sign. I recall thinking, *Oh, this isn't so bad.*

Blood began to spill from Otto's nose and mouth. Sheila was right. I had been too optimistic.

"He's okay!" I called to the others. "He's alright."

"No, he's not," said Sheila.

Blood began to spill from Otto's nose and mouth. Sheila was right. I had been too optimistic. He wasn't okay at all. Where was this blood coming from? What was wrong with his face? It was punched in. Jesus, how did that happen? It was just water.

We hoisted Otto on board Sheila and Maria's canoe. Tom got out begrudgingly to make room in the center. He stood next to me in the river while Maria, the nurse, attended to Otto's face.

Sheila kept saying, "Oh Lord. Oh my Lord."

Tom opened a new beer and together we scanned the water where Otto had landed, looking for the rock or tree limb that must have caused the damage.

Eventually Tom said, "There's your culprit."

He pointed to a dim, submerged object spinning in the current just below the surface.

"What is it?" I asked.

We watched for a moment as the object rose up, wiggled a bit, and then sank down.

"It's a turtle," said Tom, almost chuckling. "He hit a fucking turtle."

"Oh God," I said.

It was a small snapping turtle, the size of your average pie. It was injured, too, and struggling to remain upright in the water.

I waded over and fished the creature out of the river. Its shell was cracked and I could see tender insides through the gap.

"Oh no," I said.

"Tough day for him," said Tom, shaking his head.

Over in the canoe, Otto coughed and moaned.

"What happened?" he stuttered. "What?"

"We need to get him out of here," said Maria. "We need a hospital. A helicopter, something."

Of course, there was no hospital or helicopter anywhere nearby. Our cell phones had lost any kind of signal long before we had even put the boats in the water that morning. I thought about shouting or blowing a whistle, but it really was no use. We'd simply have to paddle Otto down-river as fast as we could.

Our plan, before this happened, had been to camp out on a sandbar and reach the road crossing early the next day. From there one of us would hitchhike back up to the vehicle we'd left at the starting point. It was a plan hatched by a group of people in no particular hurry.

We fastened Otto down as well as we could. He was conscious, but dazed and in shock. The only lucky element to our situation was the presence of Maria, the nurse. She tended to him with improvised bandages and ice from the coolers. Even if there really wasn't much that could be done for Otto right then, we all felt better knowing that someone competent was involved.

Because Maria was occupied with her patient, that boat needed another paddler. I took her spot in the stern and Tom, broken thumb and all, was given the task of paddling the second boat solo.

"I can't do this," he protested.

"Jesus, Tom," said Sheila. "This is an emergency."

We shifted most of the gear into Tom's boat to make room for both Otto and Maria in the middle of ours. As we readied to leave, I made a spur-of-the-moment decision. I fished the injured turtle out of the river. Then I emptied one of our coolers and placed the turtle inside it, with a little bit of river water.

Tom watched this procedure with disdain. "What the hell are you doing that for?" he asked me.

"I'm taking the turtle with us. We can't just leave him here," I said.

"We sure can," said Tom.

"We need to go," said Maria.

Sheila and I set out at a frantic pace and nearly capsized the canoe right at the start. It would have been proverbial salt in the wound, dumping poor Otto into the water just then, but we managed to keep upright and soon hit our stride. It wasn't long before we had left Tom far behind us, cursing and swirling about in the current. He was in for a long, rough trip, paddling one-handed all by himself, but we didn't have time to worry about that.

We paddled past lush pine forests and stunning rock outcroppings, hardly noticing the landscape in our haste. The wild surroundings had seemed pristine and magical that morning, but now it all took on a desolate air, especially as the sun dipped lower and cast long shadows in the canyons. I kept hoping we'd meet up with another group or pass some lonesome cabin equipped with a radio, but there was nothing. At one point we startled a moose.

"Moose," said Sheila as we cruised past it.

"Wha?" said Otto.

"Shh . . ." said Maria. She had been talking to him throughout our journey, gently waking him from time to time to be sure he didn't slip into a coma.

"How's he doing?" I asked.

"Stop asking me that," said Maria.

"How's the turtle?" asked Sheila.

"Not so good," I reported. I held the cooler steady between my feet. The turtle lay still, listlessly sloshing about in the water, retracted inside its cracked shell.

Night fell and still we hadn't reached the road. Maria pointed a flashlight ahead of us so that it cast an eerie beam across the water, and we forged on. My hands were blistered and my shoulders numb. Sheila could barely lift her arms. She puked over the side of the canoe and collapsed. I felt a wave of admiration for her then, paddling so hard her body gave out on her. She hardly knew Otto, by the way. They had been dating for only about a week before embarking on this trip. We pulled over and Maria gave Sheila water and massaged her arms. Then they switched places. Maria placed a cool, wet bandana over Otto's face.

"Don't lift it up," said Maria as she took the bow.

We made good time with Maria's fresh arms and reached the bridge crossing around midnight. This felt like progress, except we soon found that there were no cars traveling the road at that hour.

"Fuck," said Maria. "We should have paddled faster." This comment seemed directed at me, since Sheila had clearly done all she could.

We dragged the canoe onto the shore and left Otto inside it. Maria grabbed a cell phone and ran down the road looking for a signal. Sheila and I stayed behind with Otto, both of us too tired to run around the wilderness on such an errand. Otto kept at it with his raspy wheezing and intermittent coughing fits. Awful as he sounded, the noises offered a bit of comfort. When he was silent we worried that he might stop breathing altogether.

Sheila and I fell asleep in the dirt next to the canoe and woke up hours later to the sound of a truck engine. It was nearly dawn. A logging rig had picked up Maria several miles up the road. They'd managed to contact the state police and a trauma unit was on its way in a helicopter.

It was a gruesome sight, hardly recognizable as a face. Something had shifted, or disappeared.

I woke Otto up and told him help was coming.

"Help?" he said. "What's the matter?"

"Do you remember what happened?" I asked him.

Otto was silent. I pulled the bandana away from his face and let a bit of light from my flashlight shine upon him. Maria had done a good job cleaning things off, but now the swelling had set in. It was a gruesome sight, hardly recognizable as a face. Something had shifted, or disappeared. *Where is Otto's nose?* I thought.

Finally Otto said, "I'm in a canoe."

"Right, right," I replied.

"And you told me to run," he said.

"Well, no, you decided to run," I pointed out. "You were on a cliff."

"And you told me . . ."

"No, you had made up your mind . . ."

"Stop bothering him," said Maria.

"Okay," I said.

I got up and approached the loggers who had picked up Maria. They were standing beside their truck smoking cigarettes in the dim light.

"Our friend is hurt," I told them.

"We know that," they said.

"Do you have any tape?" I asked. "Strong, sturdy tape?"

"Duct tape?" said one of the loggers. "You want duct tape?"

"Right," I said. "Duct tape."

The logger reached inside his truck and pulled out a dirty silver roll.

"Like this?" he asked.

"Yes," I replied. "I'll give it back."

I took the roll of tape and found the cracked turtle in the cooler. I placed a strip of tape carefully over the break in its shell, as much to keep things out as to keep them in. The turtle's head and legs remained retracted and it was difficult to tell if it was even alive. Maria watched my efforts with disdain.

> I watched the turtle in the cooler. Toward noon his little nose poked out cautiously and my heart jumped. He was alive!

"When this is all over you and I need to have a talk," she said to me.

"Okay, sure, I know," I said.

The sunrise brought a fresh round of blackflies and we swatted them away until the helicopter finally arrived. It hovered over the dirt road spraying dust and rocks in every direction. Three men jumped out with a stretcher and suddenly the place was bustling with activity. With crack precision they loaded Otto into the chopper and it was decided that Sheila and Maria would go along. I stayed behind with the canoe to wait for Tom.

The helicopter lifted off and things grew quiet once again. The loggers turned to me.

"You mind if we depart now?" one of them asked. "We're late already."

"Go ahead," I told them. I gave them back their roll of tape and they left.

It seemed as if Tom should have arrived by then, but I figured he must have stopped somewhere when it got dark. He was probably sleeping in, waiting for the problem to get solved before he arrived back on the scene. I washed the blood out of the canoe and settled in to wait.

I watched the turtle in the cooler. Toward noon his little nose poked out cautiously and my heart jumped. He was alive! I dipped his body into the cool river and cleaned him off as best I could.

Tom showed up that afternoon, wet and angry. His canoe was half full of water and all of the gear was gone.

"Where the hell is everybody?" he asked me.

"A helicopter came," I said. "They went to the hospital."

"A chopper? Here? Aw, fuck." Tom held up his hand. The cast over his thumb had mostly rotted away.

"I think I'm going to need a doctor too," said Tom. "They should have waited for me."

"Otto was in bad shape," I pointed out.

"Yeah, but . . . look at this," said Tom. He motioned toward his swamped canoe. "I could have died back there. You assholes abandoned me."

Tom was drunk. Although our gear was gone, he had managed to save a few beers. He offered one to me.

"Thanks," I said. The beer tasted terrible and I felt immediately dizzy since I hadn't eaten anything since the day before.

Tom peered into my cooler, looking for booze, and saw the turtle, cleaned off and wrapped in duct tape.

"Well look at this," he said. "You're a regular Doctor Dolittle."

"He's still alive," I told Tom.

"He's not going to survive."

"You might be right."

"Oh, I'm right. You know what we're going to have to do?"

"What?"

"Eat him."

"The turtle?"

"Right," said Tom. "It's the proper thing to do when you mortally wound an animal."

"I'm not going to eat that turtle," I said.

"Look," said Tom, "it's more respectful than letting him die in vain. That little fella was doing fine until you and Otto decided to fuck up his day. Now you just want to tape him up and flee the scene. Show some respect, Georgie. It's the least you can do."

"Hold on," I said. "What do you mean by 'you and Otto'? It was Otto's decision to run down that cliff. I was just there to provide support. We all were."

"I had nothing to do with it," said Tom. "I wash my hands of the matter. Except this turtle here. I'll help you make a soup if you want. I'm hungry as hell and the meat will go bad if we wait much longer. It's the law of the jungle, Georgie. Eat what you kill. Leave no trace."

I had no response for this logic except to say that we were not going to eat the turtle and the matter was no longer up for discussion. About an hour later we caught a ride to our car in the back of a pickup truck. I held the cooler with the turtle on my lap, trying not to let it bounce too much on the dirt roads. Tom held on to his broken thumb and moaned.

Back at home I took charge of the turtle's rehabilitation. I visited a veterinarian who offered a grim prognosis.

"It won't survive," he said. "The wound is too severe and infection has set in. I don't know why it's still alive, to be honest."

Against his advice I paid $800 to have an antibiotic IV inserted into the turtle's small veins. I also learned that it was a female turtle, not a male, as I had for some reason assumed. I named her Charlotte, after an elderly woman I once knew who sort of resembled a turtle. I purchased a plastic children's wading pool and filled it with rocks, water, and moss-covered tree limbs. This I placed inside my small apartment to provide a habitat for Charlotte. If she was going to die, I reasoned, it would be in relative comfort.

Otto was laid up in the county hospital for nearly a month. They treated several infections, brain swelling, and did their best to reconstruct his face. The doctors and nurses there kept commenting on how lucky he was to be alive.

"I'm not lucky," Otto would tell them. "I ran into a turtle."

I visited Otto often during his recovery, a gesture meant to be kind-hearted, but somehow interpreted as an effort to ease my own guilt.

"Ah, so you're the accomplice," remarked one of Otto's attendants upon my arrival.

"I wouldn't call it that," I said. "I was just there at the time."

"You told me where to dive," said Otto, sipping on a blended fruit shake.

"When I told you that, there was no turtle in the water."

"Well, how could you know?" said the attendant, smiling in an odd placating manner that I've come to believe is taught at medical institutions.

The swelling in Otto's face had subsided, but what was left now was an unsettling tableau not unlike one of those big rubber masks you sometimes see kids wearing on Halloween. His nose had been rebuilt into an odd nub and remained shifted off to one side. He was missing a cheekbone, or something, below his left eye, so that side of his face was sunken significantly. He'd lost several teeth as well and now spoke out of the side of his mouth. It was an odd sensation, watching Otto heal up in the hospital. At times I felt jealous for all the attention and care he was receiving. He was the hero who had braved the cliffs and survived, albeit scarred. I was just the petty coward accomplice, the one who had watched from below and directed him toward the invisible turtle. I knew it made no sense to envy a man with injuries such as Otto's, but I did.

A wealthier, better insured person would likely have had more options for reconstruction than Otto. As it was, he had no insurance at all, and once his condition was considered stable, he was given a mix of prescription pills and asked to leave. I was the only one there on the day of his release.

"Where's Sheila?" asked Otto.

"She's not here," I told him.

"Great. Fantastic."

As I mentioned before, Sheila and Otto's relationship had extended only a week before his accident, and throughout his stay at the hospital I could see her performing an awkward calculus in her head. How long must she stay with him? I guess she had determined his release date was as good a time as any to move on, and I couldn't truly blame her.

You will not be surprised to hear that Maria dumped me as well. She had come to visit me in my apartment and gazed disdainfully upon Charlotte, resting in the pool I had set up for her.

"This is ridiculous," she told me.

"She's doing better than expected," I pointed out. "She's begun to eat the food I give her."

"Your best friend is in the hospital," said Maria, "because of this turtle."

"Otto is not my best friend," I pointed out.

"That's not the point," she said.

"And it wasn't Charlotte's fault," I continued. "If anything, she's the victim here."

"That's not the point either," said Maria.

I had thought Maria might be impressed with my rehabilitation of the wounded turtle and see that I was indeed capable of compassion and competence, but that was not the case. She pronounced the whole situation disappointing, and left.

Once the paperwork was complete, Otto and I departed the hospital and located an organic food shop, where I bought him a fruit smoothie.

> I knew it made no sense to envy a man with injuries such as Otto's, but I did.

He sipped it and gazed at the hustle and commerce on the street outside. You could see people walk by and do subtle double takes when they saw Otto's face, startling as it was.

"I guess everything just moved along without me," he said.

It was true. In fact, Otto had been evicted from his small home while he was laid up as well. Apparently he had fallen behind in rent long ago and his crafty landlord seized upon his absence to move his belongings to the curb.

"Can I stay with you for a while?" asked Otto. "While I figure things out?"

I said yes, of course, though my place was small, and already made more cramped by the presence of Charlotte and her pool. I had meant to tell Otto about Charlotte before we arrived, but it was a hard subject to broach, and so he simply came upon her when he arrived.

Otto was not a good roommate. He snored loudly and was up at all hours, pacing about and muttering to himself.

"What the fuck is this?" he asked me.

"That's Charlotte," I said.

Otto moved closer and saw the ridgeline on Charlotte's shell where the crack once was. It was a vicious scar, but few would have guessed at the sorry state she had been in. Charlotte was quite recovered at this point and, seeing Otto and the turtle together, it occurred to me that despite her smaller size she had fared better in the collision. Although it was also true that she was now confined to a plastic wading pool as opposed to living free in the wild. I suppose a sound argument could be formulated for either conclusion, now that I think about it.

"Is this the turtle I think it is?" asked Otto.

"Yes, Otto," I said. "It is."

"You kept this thing?"

"She was going to die out there," I pointed out. "Tom wanted to eat her."

"Eat a turtle? Like in a soup? Is that what he wanted?"

"I don't know. Yes, I think he mentioned making a soup."

Otto reached into the tank and pulled Charlotte out. He held her high in the air as her stubby legs flailed about.

"Careful," I said, "she might bite you."

"I ought to chuck this reptile out the fucking window," he said.

"Please don't do that," I said.

I moved toward Otto and he held Charlotte away from me, his damaged face twitching in anger. We stood there in an uneasy standoff as the water bubbled gently in the pool beside us. Charlotte retreated into her shell, ready for yet another shock to her system at the hands of my friend Otto. But he didn't have the stomach for such cruelty in the end. He flipped Charlotte back into the pool, where she landed upside down, and I quickly righted her.

"It wasn't her fault," he admitted nobly.

Otto was not a good roommate. He snored loudly and was up at all hours, pacing about and muttering to himself. Whereas he had once been a great outdoorsmen, he now preferred to stay inside most of the day. On the few occasions he did venture outside, people could not help staring at his odd features. I even caught myself staring at times, such was the severity of his injury. Every so often someone would approach me privately and ask what had happened. The story was always met with such incredulity that I took to simplifying it greatly.

"A diving accident," I would say.

On the rare occasion that someone asked Otto directly, he would usually answer, "a hockey fight." This explanation was always accepted without question.

Sometimes I would return to the apartment to find Otto deep in conversation with Charlotte. He would whisper things to her, observations about the TV show he was watching or snide comments about my housekeeping habits. Otto's injuries required him to blend up most of his food and he expected me to maintain a steady supply of fruit and yogurt as well as clean up the mess he made preparing his shakes. As he drank down his meals he would sit beside Charlotte and gloat.

"No, Charlotte," he would say. "You can't have any of this! Turtles can't eat citrus."

These conversations would go on at all hours, sometimes becoming so heated that I feared for Charlotte's safety. But for the most part it was just companionship. Where Otto had once seen Charlotte as the agent of his destruction, he grew to view her more as a comrade in arms. No one else understood what they had been through. I sometimes felt that they were forming an alliance against me, despite all I had done for them. We rarely spoke of the accident, but when we did Otto would always be sure to centralize my role in encouraging him.

"We all know why you took Charlotte home and nursed her so carefully," Otto explained to me. "Because of what you'd done."

"She needed help," I said. "If anyone should feel guilty it's you. You landed on her."

"Ha!" laughed Otto. "I should feel guilty? Look at me. Do I look like I should be feeling guilty about anything?"

Throughout this period Otto ingested vast amounts of pain medication and I began to suspect that he was playing several doctors at once for prescriptions. Meanwhile, preposterous bills relating to his hospital stay showed up in the mail.

"One hundred and forty thousand dollars!" screamed Otto. "How do they expect me to pay that?"

One of the bills suggested Otto call a helpline to discuss his situation, which he refused to do. I decided to call the number myself one afternoon. It turned out this wasn't a financial helpline, as I had thought, but rather a connection to some kind of support group for people who had experienced traumatic injury. I signed Otto up for one of their meetings and told them I'd bring him there myself.

"Why would I want to attend some shit like that?" asked Otto, after I told him what I had done.

"It might be helpful," I said. "You stay in the house all day long. It isn't healthy."

"Healthy? What does that even mean, 'healthy'?"

Otto retreated to the corner near Charlotte's pool, as was his wont. He stared at her and whispered something I could not understand.

The next day Otto fashioned a small leash for Charlotte and announced he was taking her outside for walk. At first this idea seemed ridiculous to me, but it turned out regular constitutionals of this sort are recommended for captive snapping turtles and the practice proved to be enjoyable for both Otto and Charlotte. Of course, the walks were anything but brisk, and the two of them together presented an odd tableau, eliciting even more attention than Otto had when he'd ventured out on his own. But Otto clearly took comfort in Charlotte's companionship, and I was thankful for the time alone in the apartment. Around town, Otto became known as "Turtleface," a moniker I did my best to hide from him.

When the time came for the first support group meeting Otto put on his coat agreeably, then casually picked up Charlotte and wrapped her in a thin blanket.

"She's coming with us," he said.

"Okay," I consented. It seemed a small price to pay for progress.

The meeting was held in a classroom at the local community college. Otto and I walked in late and scanned the room, a semicircle of wheelchair-bound amputees and various examples of disfigurement. One man had a leg swollen up the size of a barrel.

"Oh fuck," said Otto, "would you look at this?"

"You're one to talk," said the man with the swollen leg. "And what's that, a turtle?"

Otto covered up Charlotte with his coat, a protective gesture.

"It's my turtle," said Otto. He seemed to think the man wanted to take it from him.

"Actually the turtle belongs to me," I pointed out. "I was the one who nursed it back to health."

"We share custody now," said Otto.

"Why don't you two sit down?" said a small woman named Nadine. She was the facilitator. We sat down and joined the semicircle.

> Around town, Otto became known as "Turtleface," a moniker I did my best to hide from him.

Although they were in compromised physical shape, the people before us seemed to be a fairly well-adjusted bunch. They told stories and laughed at their wild misfortunes. One woman had been mauled by a chimpanzee at the zoo.

"It was my own fault, really," she said, showing us the scars on her neck, back, and shoulders. "Everyone knows how strong a chimp can be when it's angry."

Another man had a mental affliction that compelled him to dump scalding hot liquid on himself whenever he discovered it was within reach. The coffee machine was kept in another room on his account. His face was shiny from all the burns and much of his hair was gone.

Otto had no sympathy for this person. "Well, I can tell you how to solve this problem," he said. "From now on don't pour any more hot water on yourself, okay? Just stop doing it."

The burned man looked Otto up and down. "Suppose I told you to stop running into turtles," he replied. "Would that help?"

Otto pulled Charlotte out of his coat and handed her to me. "Hold her," he said. "I'm going to kick this guy's ass."

Nadine stood up and expertly talked Otto down. Apparently this sort of confrontation was not uncommon when someone new entered the group.

"You seem angry," she told Otto.

"Of course I'm angry," he said.

Afterward, I felt that the support group had done little for Otto, but the next day he told me he had experienced an epiphany overnight.

"I've come to the conclusion that we need to return Charlotte to the wild," he said.

I was resistant to this idea at first. I liked Charlotte and had imagined that when Otto finally left my home the two of us would lead a contented existence together. Perhaps you are aware that snapping turtles have life spans nearly as long as humans and as such make for good long-term companions.

> I woke up in the morning, naked, holding on to Sheila, who was naked as well.

But Otto laid out his plan and I couldn't deny the simple logic of it. We would return to the location of their misfortunes. Charlotte belonged back in her homeland now that she was well. And the journey would be cathartic for us all, he claimed.

Maria wanted nothing to do with such an endeavor, but we managed to persuade Tom and Sheila to join us for the trip. It was late fall, and chilly, by the time we got everything together and set off. Tom brought a cross-bow along with him because he claimed it was bow-hunting season and he hoped to shoot an animal of some sort.

"I'd be more than happy to dress and cook it for everyone while we're camped along the river," he said.

"No thanks," said Sheila. She was a vegetarian.

Tom refused to apologize for wanting to eat Charlotte back when she had been injured.

"It would have saved us a lot of trouble," he pointed out. "Though I do support returning her to her natural state since the resources have already been wasted bringing her back to life."

"She was never dead," I pointed out.

"Close enough," said Tom.

Otto was stoic throughout the journey down the river. He spoke softly to Charlotte, who rode in a large cooler beside him, pointing out the sights along the shoreline.

Tom and I took to drinking whiskey from a tin flask and by the time we reached the sandy cliffs where Otto had crashed months before, I was feeling sick. We had gotten a late start that morning and the days were shorter now, it being late autumn so it was nearly dark.

"We'll camp here," declared Otto, "and release Charlotte in the day-time. She might get disoriented if we let her go at night."

"I'm going hunting," said Tom. He donned a headlamp and smeared mud on his cheeks. "I'll go get us some dinner."

Tom stumbled off into the woods and that was the last I saw of him.

I helped Sheila set up the tents and then passed out inside of one of them. Outside, I could hear Otto making a fire and chattering away with Charlotte. He was full of energy and kept calling out for Tom. At some point Sheila crawled inside my tent and said, "I'm cold. Can I sleep with you?"

I woke up in the morning, naked, holding on to Sheila, who was naked as well. My arms and head were freezing, having been exposed to the cold all night. Sheila shivered and huddled further beneath our blankets. She felt wonderfully soft and warm and I tried to remember what we had done together.

Eventually I wandered out of the tent and found the fire still smoking. The other tent was empty and one of the canoes gone. On Charlotte's cooler I found a note. It said:

"WENT LOOKING FOR TOM—OTTO"

The sun rose and things got warmer. I made myself some coffee and began to feel quite good. I splashed some of the cold river water on my face and looked around for signs of Otto and Tom. It was all trees and wilderness. Sheila and I seemed to be the only humans for miles.

Up above me loomed those tall sand cliffs. Sheila was still sleeping and I decided Charlotte had been left in that cooler long enough. It was my understanding that Otto wanted to make some kind of ceremony out of releasing Charlotte back into the wild, but I overruled him. I placed the cooler in the remaining canoe and paddled across the river to the cliffs and the spot where Charlotte and Otto had collided earlier that summer. It was difficult to determine the exact place, but when I'd gotten close enough I opened the cooler and dumped Charlotte in the river. She landed sideways and spun about, bewildered at her new surroundings. She paddled up to the surface and poked her hooked snout into the air. She stayed there for a moment, floating, that sealed-up scar still visible on her bumpy shell. I imagined the other turtles would wonder at it, and perhaps she'd tell them of the strange land she had visited and the strange behavior of her caretakers. Readjusted now, Charlotte sank down below the surface, swiftly paddling her sturdy legs, and disappeared into the murk and sway below.

I turned my attention once again to finding Tom and Otto. I thought I might climb the cliff to get a better vantage point. From there I could call out for them and see the lay of the land. I fastened the canoe to a nearby tree and began to climb up the sandy slope, just like I should have done earlier that summer when I had meekly watched Otto from below. Stopping several times to catch my breath, I eventually ascended even higher than Otto had, until my feet were scratched and sore and my chest heaved from the exertion. I stood there gazing down at the ribbon of river beneath me and tried to steady my breathing.

I called out, "Hey Tom! Otto! Tom! Otto!"

But no one could hear me up there. The river down below was just a whisper. I pictured Otto standing near this spot, trying to discern the directions I had called out to him. It wasn't my fault. It had all been his decision, of course. I could see that plainly.

Far below me I saw Sheila emerge from the tent, stretch her arms, and gaze about. She was stark naked, a female beauty in the wild. I felt like a god, or a ghost, peering down upon her, unseen at this great height.

And I thought I might do something daring then, something a little spectacular, and unexpected. I launched myself forward. One, two, three, four, five . . . giant long jumps down the mountainside. I cleared thirty, forty feet per stride! I was a monster, a freak of nature, hurtling toward the water.

"Hey Sheila!" I called out, glancing her way, trying not to land on my face as I hurtled down the cliff side.

She looked about her, started.

"I'm over here!" I shouted. I was nearing the bottom now, carrying impossible speed. I leaped out, shooting into the water, sleek like a dolphin, waiting for the pain.

A crashing noise filled my ears and then coldness walloped me from all sides. Fuck, the water was so cold. A sharp, aching pain shot up my genitals and I struggled to the surface, gasping for air. The current carried me downriver and I kicked a rock hard with my foot. I sputtered to the shoreline and flopped myself into the canoe, wheezing, unable to fill my lungs with enough oxygen. My big toe had been cut open by the rock when I'd kicked it and now it started to hurt, and bleed. I'd cracked the toenail and my head ached as well.

I heard a voice, Sheila, calling out to me. "Georgie! Georgie! Are you alright?"

"I'm okay," I said, holding up my hand, waving it above the gunnel so that she could see it. "I'm all right."

A moment of time passed during which I imagined Sheila standing there, still naked on the shoreline, worrying about me. I wondered if she'd even seen my great feat, that perfect running dive into the cold water. Again, I raised my hand up, and again I said, "I'm all right. I'm fine."

"I'll make us breakfast," called out Sheila. "Vegetarian sausage and eggs."

"Thank you," I called out. "I'd like that."

I stayed down there, lying on the canoe floor, not wanting her to see me just yet. I lay back on the bottom of that canoe and I listened to the water flowing underneath me and I began to feel damn good indeed. 🛡

Rosalie Moffett

RE: GRAND THEFT AUTO 2

How do i get to the country redneck places in gta II, i die and i can't find it anymore.
—RECENT QUESTIONS, *GTA.WIKIA.COM*

Sex, your shadow, a really good
tangerine—some things are forever
lost when you die, though not the rednecks.

Drive NW and you'll find them in Redemption.
Their pickups are parked outside of Disgracelands,
that Elvis bar where the jukebox flips the days over

like pancakes, and never takes requests. You'll realize
after a while that the music just plays in a loop.
A dog in Argentina has visited his master's grave

every day for six years now, and no one knows how
he even found the cemetery. But that's real life, it was
in the news. Somewhere else

is the dog's master, looking around
from the top-down, 2-D game view. Life seems to go on
in the hereafter—but it's different. He's still trying to learn

the new controls for his car. He doesn't know yet
that it doesn't really matter if he crashes,
if he crashes over and over. So he drives carefully.

Sometimes he tries the ESC button, just to see. If you see him,
you should tell him that he can go to the mobile home park
where the rednecks run the car crusher, or to the church

where the neon sign flickers from *JESUS SAVES* to *U SAVE*
for a re-up on life, but he can't go home, and he should stop
looking for the edges of the game.

Heart of Darkness

Illustrated by Matt Kish

Every illustrator, no matter what the project, is confronted with choices. In considering how to approach *Heart of Darkness*, I had to make a lot of choices, and they were never simple. What struck me while illustrating *Moby-Dick* was just how vast Melville's novel seemed. It is an enormous book that, to paraphrase Whitman, contains multitudes. It contradicts itself in style and tone in gloriously messy ways and it's strong enough to carry the weight of the visions of dozens of artists, from Rockwell Kent to Frank Stella to Benton Spruance to Leonard Baskin to, well, me. What I'm saying here is that with Melville, there is room.

Conrad is something entirely different, particularly when it comes to *Heart of Darkness*. There is a terrifying feeling of claustrophobia and a crushing singularity of purpose to the story. It's almost as if the deeper one reads, the farther down a tunnel one is dragged, all other options and paths dwindling and disappearing, until nothing is left but that awful and brutal encounter with Kurtz and the numbing horror of his ideas. Where *Moby-Dick* roams far and wide across both land and sea, *Heart of Darkness* moves in one direction only, and that is downward.

While it could never have been an easy task to take a well-known piece of classic literature and breathe some different kind of life into it with pictures, the inexorable downward pull of this black hole of a story—this bullet to the head—made demands that I couldn't have imagined. Poe wrote that "a short story must have a single mood and every sentence must build towards it," and I knew that in order to let Conrad's ideas knife their way inside, every one of my illustrations had to carry this downward mood and build toward that ending. But what to exclude? What to leave out? Which path to go down? How to take this story of white men and black men and Africa, this filthy horrible business of ivory and slavery and greed and murder, and show it, really show it, in such a way that this mood would be visible?

Begin with the title: *Heart of Darkness*. One would think, initially at least, that here is the first visual clue. Darkness. Blackness. Inky swirls of ebony on murky pages. That seemed too easy to me, entirely too obvious. But there was another reason why I knew immediately that this was not the right choice to make. In college, as an undergraduate, I took an introduction to poetry class. A very basic thing, really, just an overview of Western poetry hitting all the proper and expected notes. The professor, though, was not at all proper or expected, and her almost embarrassing passion for poetry put us on edge and made our minds scuffed and raw enough for the poetry we studied to leave a few scars. At some point, while discussing "Requiem" by Christina Georgina Rossetti, the professor devolved into another of her oddly personal narrations

exploring the poem and its significance to her. It involved her brother, his murder, and her as a young woman in college attending his funeral on what she called the warmest and sunniest day she could remember. At first she was outraged but gradually she broke down—apparently at that funeral, then again in front of the stunned class—when she realized that murder could and did take place under the bright and shining sun, where everyone could see. It was folly to think that terrible things happen only in the dark. That experience stayed with me and informed the first choice I made. Conrad's Africa, the scene of so much death, so much killing, so much horror, would not be a dark place in the literal sense. The sun would shine there, in my images, as brightly and hotly as it does on the happiest of days and that would be the right way, the best way, to look unflinchingly at what Conrad is putting in front of us. Immediately, the world of the novel began to take shape, a place filled with bright acid greens, the patterns of leaves and the shadows of trees, a sickly diseased yellow sky rotten with the kind of sunlight that casts everything into a sharp and lacerating clarity. The first choice had been made.

While *Heart of Darkness* is set in Africa during the rape of a continent and at the height of what amounted to a racially and economically driven genocide, what disturbed me the most is that these things are hardly confined to that part of the globe or even that period of time. Our history is stained with what Conrad so aptly described as "just robbery with violence, aggravated murder on a great scale, and men going at it blind." I knew that in order to illustrate this book truthfully, I had to find a way to show that what happens in *Heart of Darkness* is horrifyingly universal. That it doesn't end there and will probably never end. That this isn't just the story of Europeans in Africa; it is the story of humanity, wherever we may go. I needed to find a way to show that at the bottom of it all, we are all complicit in this. We have all profited from it. To do that, I had to take these pictures and pull them away from reality, away from what the viewer might be able to connect to a specific time or place or thing, and make them something so odd that they could literally be anything. Only then would the names "Africa" and "Europe" and the concepts of "whiteness" and "blackness" fall away so that the reader could see it for what it is—"robbery with violence" and "aggravated murder on a great scale." Conrad's Europeans became grotesqueries. Pale, bloated, fleshy monstrosities with gaping, slavering mouths, huge brutal hands, and intentionally symbolic heads. Their victims, while perhaps marginally less monstrous, are gaunt and spectrally black. Shades of death, no strangers to superstition, hatred, and violence themselves, lurk furtively in the hidden spaces of a nightmare-green landscape overrun with conquerors, fanatics, and opportunists quick with the gun and the lash. The second choice had been made.

Though I had read *Heart of Darkness* several times in the past, never before had I followed so closely, so uncomfortably, in the footsteps of Marlow. And never before had I felt the death grip of Kurtz so profoundly on both my waking thoughts and my troubled dreams. But, thankfully, it ended. Looking back on this body of work, this step-by-step journey to the heart of darkness and, hopefully, back again, I can see its shape better. I can see how each image was designed with one singular mood, and how that murderous intent was carried through and delivered upon. This book is for me, personally and artistically, a long and slow road through the kind of hell that never ends and never changes. It is a travelogue of our history as human beings and even now I am not sure quite how to feel about it all. Of *Moby-Dick*, Melville wrote, "I have written a wicked book, and feel spotless as the lamb." Of this *Heart of Darkness*, I cannot say the same. I feel changed. I feel older. I feel tired. I feel more wary. I feel, at times, less hopeful. The sunshine seems sometimes be a lie. To return to Conrad one last time, in order to understand these images you must "imagine the growing regrets, the longing to escape, the powerless disgust, the surrender, the hate."

But while I may not feel spotless, I don't feel ashamed. Conrad wrote a crucial book. It had to be done, and it must continue to be read. Hopefully, in showing this tale in a new light, I have added something to that. It had to be done. And I hope you will look.

5

"And this also," said Marlow suddenly, "has been one of the dark places of the earth."

37

"They were dying slowly—it was very clear. They were not enemies, they were not criminals, they were nothing earthly now, nothing but black shadows of disease and starvation, lying confusedly in the greenish gloom.

81

"Going up that river was like traveling back to the earliest beginnings of the world, when vegetation rioted on the earth and the big trees were kings. An empty stream, a great silence, an impenetrable forest. The air was warm, thick, heavy, sluggish. There was no joy in the brilliance of sunshine. The long stretches of the waterway ran on, deserted, into the gloom of overshadowed distances."

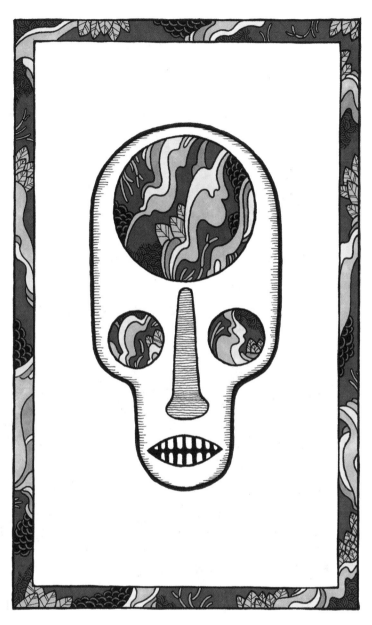

89

"The mind of man is capable of anything—because everything is in it, all the past as well as all the future."

101

"Besides that, they had given them every week three pieces of brass wire, each about nine inches long; and the theory was they were to buy their provisions with that currency in riverside villages . . . unless they swallowed the wire itself, or made loops of it to snare the fishes with, I don't see what good their extravagant salary could be to them."

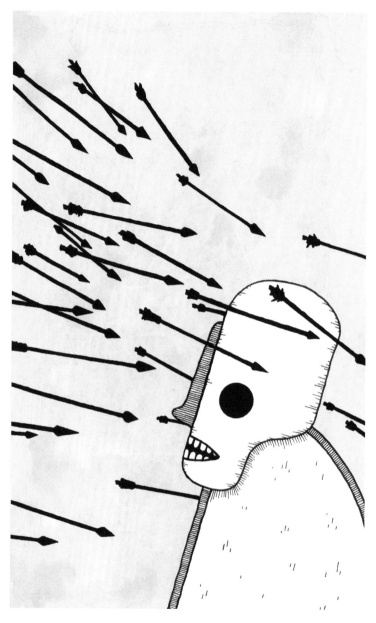

111

"Sticks, little sticks, were flying about—thick: they were whizzing before my nose, dropping below me, striking behind me against my pilot-house."

121

". . . it had taken him, loved him, embraced him, got into his veins, consumed his flesh, and sealed his soul to its own by the inconceivable ceremonies of some devilish initiation. He was its spoiled and pampered favorite."

129

"Then without more ado I tipped him overboard. The current snatched him as though he had been a wisp of grass, and I saw the body roll over twice before I lost sight of it forever."

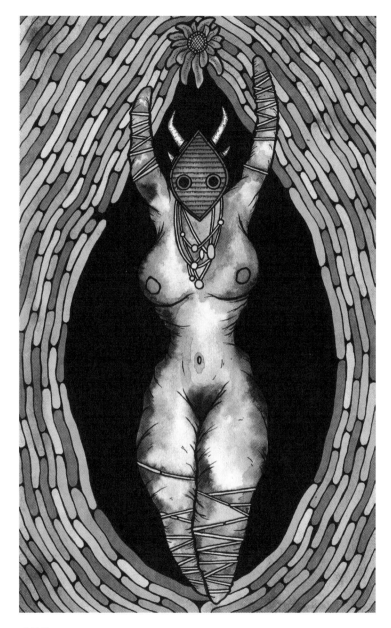

155

"She walked with measured steps, draped in striped and fringed cloths, treading the earth proudly, with a slight jingle and flash of barbarous ornaments . . . She was savage and superb, wild-eyed and magnificent; there was something ominous and stately in her deliberate progress."

179

"'The horror! The horror!'"

Albert Goldbarth

MAPPED

How deft we are at making it all
about the me. The ambulance

that bears a man in artificial
cardiovascular pumping to his mysterious fate:

an overkill mnemonic for the baby aspirin
you forgot to take. The child's

surgery: one more excuse for you
to shine . . . all night, you were awake

with her; the sponges and the call button!
We can't help it, we can't fight the way

the brain is mapped around a central image
of itself around an image of itself. . . .

When the visiting curate swallowed his toast
in a talky, wrong-way gasp, his host

—eureka!—Charles Darwin fled the table,
wholly Charles-minded, to the alcove

where the earthworms turned in their jars,
and he spent the next half-hour thinking

about the mechanics of soil aeration,
while Emma was left to tend to the air

their visitor needed to breathe more calmly.
Where would we be, if Newton didn't heed

his self-set gravity, or Rosa Parks
the inward moral weight that kept her

sitting? Last week Katt and Tayvon
came to town. You'd think the swordfish begged

to die for the honor of being lifted
to his lips. The weather?—an ornament

to her beauty; in other moods, a rebuke.

JUNG / MALENA / DARWIN

A man could stumble into the consulting room
with werewolf all around him. A woman
would swear she flew. Another, spectral meetings
with emissaries from outer space. It isn't surprising
Jung believed that everyone bears
a "shadow self," an extraextensional
him or her; nor should it be surprising
I believe *him*, I agree: another
possibility-field is furled inside us and,
at some chance cue, will opportunistically
open. Only that explains where N goes to,
when W's asleep. Tomayto /

tomahto. Malena is synesthesiac; "o"
is black for her, so "orange" isn't really
orange—her two incompatible hers
in sibling rivalry. Orange reminds me:
Florida. Amazingly enough, in 2003
the aurora borealis was visible
as the water-skiers stopped inscribing their esses over the water
and the orange pickers halted in a grove,
with an almost religious glaze to their eyes,
as somebody else's sky grew superimposed
on theirs. When N drags home in the wee hours,
W's still asleep: and dreaming of L. When Darwin

thought to test sonic responses of earthworms,
he requested that his children serenade
his soily jars of them: and, dutifully, an orchestra
of whistle, bassoon, and piano began
concatenating the night away in the billiards room,
its air alive with tremble and skreek,
low-blown moan and high-pitched tootle, so
racketing you'd think the row of dead wrens
and the barnacles might rise up and start capering.
The worms appeared deaf to the music; nor,
I'll bet, does this concert sound like a day
in *your* world—though it's *of* your world.

DETECTIVE / WOODY / SCI-FI

One clue in the mystery novel is that the husband
is drawn to young boys. The darkness
separating him from them is like the outer space
between two planetary systems that are likely
to collide with fatal results. And yet he really does
love his wife. Well, most lies aren't that
disastrously convoluted; and yet, as we can verify
from any one day in our own familiar worlds, it's
never quite up front and easy. Woody Allen says
"The heart wants what it wants." Although
the head isn't always informed of this. Life is always
a "mystery": the books shelved thus are merely us

times us; they take their power not from difference
but resemblance. That's what love is, in a novel:
it's your neighbor-boy's unraveling ménage à trois; and Inga's
congruent loves for her children and for most any guy
with a baggie of crack and jail tatts; it's Jesus duking it out
in you with Buddha; and it's never, ever free of complication.
In a science-fiction novel, a starfaring alien race
evolved from plants is searching for a new home
solar system: their sun is dying, and so their instruments
are tuned to identify chlorophyll-friendly planets.
Earth, for instance. Their intent is to destroy us.
Their hunger is innocent: light and sugar.

ESSAY

COMPANY TOWN

Ginger Strand

Va-Va-Vegas

The Searchers

When we got there, Vegas was littered with girls. A confetti of wallet-sized nubility carpeted the Strip: Akiko wearing nothing but a gold necklace, Heather in only a headband, Gina tugging down red panties, Julie with tiny white stars pasted over her nipples. There was Brit, naked and doggie-style; Diana with a finger on her tongue; and athletic Sandy with one leg thrown over her head. Vicky had shoved her shirt up over her fulsome breasts, but they were nothing compared to Tawny's. In fact, the sidewalks were awash in breasts: Linda's close together, Amiana's small but pert, Susan's pointing outward, Sunny's a bit droopy, and Alisha's such perfect half spheres they screamed *boob job* from a block away.

Jocelynne's breasts looked real. It's not just that they were live, right there in the Love Ranch living room, as opposed to an airbrushed ad. They were gravity bound, a little floppy. There was a small C-shaped stretch mark on the right one. Periodically, a boob would escape from her blue bikini top and she'd calmly tuck it back inside, the way a waitress at the pickup counter might absently stick a stray french fry back on a plate.

"To be successful with this takes a lot of strength," Jocelynne said. "You have to know who you are." Which makes sense for a woman who spends long periods of her life living under an assumed name.

Jocelynne and I were sitting in the living room of Dennis Hof's Love Ranch South in Crystal, Nevada, one of a handful of legal brothels within striking distance of Las Vegas. It wasn't a bad room, the vibe sort of down-market ski resort: a big fireplace, some taupe couches, that low-pile carpeting that's one step above indoor-outdoor. We were drinking cranberry vodkas—full disclosure—bought by me. At the Love Ranch bar to our left, Dallas and Cherry, the other prostitutes on duty, were chatting up a couple of guys, probably locals. Contractors, maybe, or prison guards. My driver and I had passed two correctional facilities on the way there and that was about all we had passed. I was tired, so the vodka was hitting me hard. I had spent the day with the photographer Susan Meiselas, seeking photographable signs of the illegal sex trade in Vegas, which was why, though it sounds odd, I had come to a brothel. I was looking for something physical, some corner of the Vegas skin trade that actually involves real skin on skin. Because in all its over-the-top marketing of sexy, this town seems to have completely lost sight of sex.

I was in Vegas on an experimental road trip through the Southwest with five photographers from the Magnum agency:

Susan, Jim Goldberg, Paolo Pellegrin, Alec Soth, and Mikhael Subotzky. Magnum called it "Postcards from America." We were traveling from San Antonio to Oakland in a huge RV with two assistants and about a half million dollars' worth of computers and cameras, but other than that, we were no different from all the other photographers who had made this trip: Robert Frank, Stephen Shore, William Eggleston, Lee Friedlander, and, before that, Walker Evans, James Agee, and Dorothea Lange, on assignment for the Farm Security Administration. All of us were trying to do the same thing: what FSA director Roy Stryker called "introducing America to Americans."

And yet today, America needs no photographic introduction, to Americans or anyone else. Instagram, Flickr, Tumblr, Picasa, Twitpic, et cetera ad nauseam: the Photobucket runneth over. What does it even mean to be a professional photographer in this world? Or a writer, for that matter? Why dedicate your life to crafting something that used to be considered art, or documentary, but is now just a cheap commodity called *content*? At Microsoft, I'm told, the product is known as *dog food*. It would be nice to consider this the tech sector's pathology, but the Web has blighted us all. We're all dog-food pushers now.

Such were my gloomy thoughts as we trudged around Vegas, when Paolo told me he thought I should go to the Love Ranch. He had been there the night before and photographed several women, but he didn't think the pictures were enough. He suggested I go and get stories. Also, he had forgotten to get model releases—could I do that? After a week on the road with five camera-toting maniacs, it sounded great to me. I was tired of looking; I wanted to get back to talking.

In other words, I was like most people who drive the eighty miles of black desert between the Love Ranch and the Strip. I didn't expect authenticity. But I was searching for something that might at least feel real.

Maverick

Jocelynne came to Vegas on a lark. A friend of hers was headed there to work as an erotic dancer. Jocelynne agreed to go along, help her settle in. When they got to town, her friend applied for a work card and immediately landed a job. Jocelynne went to the strip club on her friend's first night. Watching the girls on stage, she thought, "I could do that." She had never worked in the sex industry before, or even considered it, but the next day she got her work card and started dancing. Within a week, she heard that the state had legal brothels, and that she could make even more money there. She'd had no idea there were legal brothels in the United States. The next week, she was working in one.

Up to that point, the story sounded like a vaguely improbable morality tale about the corrupting effect of Sin City. One week

> I was looking for something pysical, some corner of the Vegas skin trade that actually involves real skin on skin.

from lap-dance virgin to happy hooker? But here's where it got truly hard to credit: according to Jocelynne, she had been married at the time. Her husband, a dentist back in Texas, supported her in her double life. Even when she continued to go to Nevada several times a year, to put in stints at the brothel. Even after they had two kids.

"If I was home you wouldn't have any idea I had ever done this or would even think about it," she said. In Texas she was a normal soccer mom. She joined every PTA committee, made cookies for the Little League team, had dinner on the table by six. They had a dog, a Labrador mix. It was all perfectly respectable. In fact, her daughter had just started college at Texas A&M. She had hoped for Baylor but didn't get in, which kind of bummed Jocelynne out. Talking about her daughter's college rejection was the only time I saw Jocelynne's vivaciousness flag. But then she switched to her son's passion for baseball. At home, she was a different person: her kids were her thing.

"Do they know what I do?" she said. "Absolutely not." And she had no plans to tell them. When she made the ten-hour drive from small-town Texas to Crystal to put in a two-week stint at the Love Ranch, she would tell them she was visiting her ailing mother.

"There's no reason to tarnish what's already there," she said.

Jocelynne insisted that she worked as a prostitute not out of need, but desire. She called it the result of "desperate housewife syndrome." Her normal life was good, but it didn't give her everything she needed.

"I love attention, and here I get it," she said. "I'll be the first to admit it; this is where I get it. I feel special, I feel picked above somebody else, instead of just 'what's for dinner' . . . Sometimes when you're married for a while, they forget that all you need is 'God damn you look good.' You can find it in an affair. I found it in something that pays me."

The payment part was important too, because, Jocelynne confessed, she likes things. She likes bags, and sunglasses, and jewelry. Especially watches. Sometimes with a client she eggs herself on by thinking about what the money will buy. "'It's the new Chanel, it's the new Chanel,'" she laughed. "That's what's going through my head."

Her marriage ultimately broke up, less because of her work than because of her compulsion to shop. Out there in small-town Texas, her husband couldn't understand why she had to have a matched set of Louis Vuitton luggage, or ten pairs of designer shades. She insisted their split was amicable. Her ex would watch the kids when she came to Nevada to work. He was one of the few people in her life who knew her not just as who she was at home, but as Jocelynne, too.

> Jocelynne insisted that she worked as a prostitute not out of need, but desire.

"It wasn't done out of need or necessity or rock bottom," she said. "I think that's why I can deal with this better than some girls. This is not my last resort; this is like a resort to me."

The sentence had the hollow ring of a tagline but she delivered it well. I had to give her credit: so far, it was as if Jocelynne had read my mind. She was painting the picture of the sex trade I had come to find: the well-balanced, self-actualized woman who happens to like sex, and money, and has no problem blending the two.

A while ago, she said, she had stopped working. She figured she was retired. But then a friend called her from Nevada. Dennis Hof had bought one of the shoddy old brothels outside Pahrump. It was a place alternately known as the Cherry Patch Ranch and Mabel's Whorehouse, but the women working there called it Pussy Prison. It was tacky and run-down and the management had made some bad decisions. But Dennis Hof was going to change all that.

Hof is currently Nevada's most famous sex-industry entrepreneur. Unlike most brothel owners, he loves the limelight. He's equally himself with porn freaks, shock jocks, and earnestly grave reporters from NPR. The HBO soft-porn "reality" series, *Cathouse*, filmed at his swank Moonlite Bunny Ranch, had made semi-celebrities of some of the women who worked there.

Now Hof was going to work his magic on Pussy Prison.

"You gotta come out of retirement," Jocelynne's friend told her. The women were sure they were going to rake in the bucks, because the Love Ranch South, as Hof renamed it, was about an hour from Vegas.

Lust in the Dust

Vegas used to be about treasure but today it's all about booty. The strip clubs are booming: Olympic Garden, Cheetah's, the Spearmint Rhino, Club Paradise, Treasures. The famous ones pack in tourists: Larry Flynt's Hustler Club has four stories and six hundred dancers on staff. The largest club, Sapphire, has three to four hundred dancers at any given time working its three main stages; its 71,000-square-foot space has tables, VIP booths, and "skyboxes." And it's not just all for men. There are nights with male dancers at the big clubs and shows for women, like the Plaza's "American Storm," the Excalibur's "Thunder from Down Under," and the bachelorette-party classic, Chippendale's. Many casinos have added erotic entertainment to their amenities. The Flamingo presents "X Burlesque," the Luxor offers up "Fantasy," the Stratosphere has "Pin Up," and Planet Hollywood puts on "Peepshow" along with a class for women called "Stripper 101." For those who want more than just a show, there are swingers' bars like the Red Rooster, the Green Door, and the Fantasy Swingers' Club, and countless massage parlors and reflexology salons around town whose advertising implies there's sex sold inside. Even the Cirque du Soleil has gone porno. Clearly, the marketing minds behind "What happens here, stays here" are on to a new reality: Sin City is now about boning, not betting.

That's what the photographers and I decided to hunt down on the Postcards trip: the Vegas sex machine. Almost as soon as we had checked in at the Golden Nugget, Mikhael arranged to meet and photograph an escort. Paolo headed for the Love Ranch. Jim and Alec waded into the wilds of the Strip. And Susan and I started looking for signs of the illegal sex trade. Of all the photographers, Susan's process is the most like my own. Her work is also research based and often involves long interviews with her subjects. She tries to push beyond the image and is fascinated by the unseen, the deeper story under the surface of things.

That night, a guy named Aaron gave us a sex-trade tour of town. He was a cab-driver Susan had lined up and he seemed disgusted by much of what he saw. Prostitution, contrary to popular belief, is illegal in Vegas: state law bans it in Clark County. This means there's a lot of streetwalking and escort rings run by sleazy pimps. A notorious hot spot for street soliciting is a truck stop called Wild Wild West. We cruised by it but there wasn't much to see: trucks, lined up and idling in a dark lot.

From Aaron we learned that much of what supposedly happens in Vegas is fake. The clubs and massage parlors and reflexology salons that make all kinds of salacious hints, he told us, are classic clip joints. They give cabbies like him kickbacks—anywhere from ten dollars to a hundred—for dropping off gullible tourists looking to get laid. The marks are plied with liquor and teased until their money runs out. They almost never get sex.

Susan and I walked the Strip the next day. By mid afternoon, it was crammed with Mexican and Guatemalan workers wearing T-shirts that screamed *Girls! Girls! Girls!*, aggressively handing out business cards emblazoned with naked women. The tourists took them and dropped them. What the cards were advertising was vague: they said things like "Vegas Finest Models" or "Totally Nude" or "Private and Personal." The most explicit promise was "Full Service Adult Entertainment." All the cards declared that a woman could be in your room in twenty minutes and that billing would be discreet. It wasn't clear if they were offering a legal private lap dance as a cover for sex or offering sex as a cover for what would turn out to be just a lap dance.

With us was Ashley, one of the dozens of college photography students who had volunteered, via social media, as drivers for the Postcards trip. Ashley told us that a friend of hers had once found her own face on an escort business card, her online profile photo pasted onto a stranger's naked body.

There her friend was, being handed out on the Strip like an evil twin. As soon as she told us that, we could see that some of the cards we'd picked up had been made the same way, the heads just a bit too large or small for the body, or cocked in an anatomically improbable way. Sometimes there was a disconcerting mismatch: airbrushed softporn body with girl-next-door face. Which is, of course, about as perfect a fantasy as a MILF who likes sex and handbags so much, she moonlights as a hooker.

By nightfall, the sidewalks had vanished under a carpet of 866LVGirls and 5StarVegasEscorts and CandyAppleGirls and HotAssEscorts and LasVegasGirlsGirlsGirls. And in fact, this seemed partly to be the cards' purpose—less advertising a service than providing local color. Everyone, it seemed, expected Vegas to be crammed with hookers—and the female tourists dressed to fit in. While the men toted drinks and acted bro-ish, the women tottered along in cheap platform heels and a catalog of unflattering fetish wear. It made the real escorts easy to spot in hotel lobbies; they were the ones who apparently weren't trying to look like whores.

There was something bovinely spectatorial about the tourists herding down the Strip, cell-phone cameras held high. They seemed less interested in sex than in a staged and codified show of sexiness, the theme-park version of vice. And that's what they were getting in "Fantasy" at the Luxor, owned by MGM Resorts; or in "Pin Up" at the Stratosphere, owned by an affiliate of Goldman Sachs; or in "Jubilee!" at Bally's, owned by Caesar's Entertainment, which is owned by Hamlet Holdings, which is owned by a troika of private equity firms. Sex has gone corporate in Vegas, which means it's not transgression, but an imagineered simulacrum of it. The Strip is now to vice as a ride on Disney World's Jungle Cruise is to a safari in Africa.

Once Upon a Time in the West

Vegas was built on vice. A former Mormon fort turned dinky supply town when the railroad came, the town's population waxed and waned with the fortunes of nearby mines, never getting beyond a few thousand souls. Then, in 1929, the federal Bureau of Reclamation began construction of the huge Boulder Dam (later renamed Hoover Dam). Concurrently, it started building Boulder City, a company town for the project's workers.

Nevada, like the rest of the West, was full of company towns. They were necessary to feed and house workers in remote places. The government or corporation would build, own, and manage everything—homes, schools, parks, hospitals, stores. Some company towns operated on company scrip, requiring workers to purchase food and other necessities at inflated prices from the town's owner. Most were segregated. All had strict rules of behavior,

banning alcohol, gambling, and prostitution. Naturally, the workers went looking for all those things outside the company-controlled setting. And the closest town to Boulder City was tiny Las Vegas.

In short order, Vegas was booming, and its population increased sixfold by 1930. The two towns' symbiotic duality was typical in the old West, the sin city and the company town were binary planets orbiting a money sun. Although counterposed, they weren't opposites: company towns were locked down, but even the West's sin cities were far from rollicking free-for-alls. "Wild West" has come to be shorthand for an amped-up orgy of free marketeering, but in fact, the real Wild West was highly regulated. Nevada built its reputation on license, but vice was really an issue of licensing. The state may have allowed boozing, gambling and whoring, but it subjected them all to detailed regulation—especially prostitution. City ordinances designated certain blocks as red-light districts. Nevada state laws passed in 1887 and 1903 banned brothels within four hundred yards of schools, churches, and principal streets. In 1913 the state forbade brothels to advertise and attempted to eliminate pimps. Ten years later, the state began to require counties to license brothels.

Yet the highly regulated vice was exactly what made the West, especially in Nevada,

> "Wild West" has come to be shorthand for an amped-up orgy of free marketeering.

seem wild. Writers and photographers have always upheld the West's image as a rough-and-tumble frontier, built on unconstrained appetite. You couldn't have the Wild West without hookers, whiskey, and cards any more than you could dispense with cattle, cowboys, and Indians. It wouldn't feel real.

"Vice flourished luxuriantly during the heyday of our 'flush times,'" wrote Mark Twain in his 1872 travel book, *Roughing It*. "The saloons were overburdened with custom; so were the police courts, the gambling dens, the brothels, and the jails—unfailing signs of high prosperity in a mining region." This freewheeling image was kept alive by journalists, dime novels, Western movies, and photo essays featured everywhere from the *Saturday Evening Post* to *Ladies' Home Journal*. The first issue of *Life* magazine in 1936 included a story called "Franklin Roosevelt's Wild West," about the rollicking shantytowns springing up around the federal Fort Peck Dam project. Margaret Bourke-White's photographs played off the old West idiom, showing packed bars, ramshackle homes, and used-up mattresses stacked outside a bordello.

None of this was new. The American West had been spawning images of itself since the arrival of the first settlers. After the Civil War, the West became what theorist Hal Rothman calls "the psychic location of the national creation myth." The impulse to mythologize the West only increased once Frederick Jackson Turner proclaimed the frontier closed. Americans looked to the West as the home of the authentic American character: individualist, physical, egalitarian, antiauthoritarian. It was, said British academic and politician James Bryce, "the most American part of America."

You couldn't have the Wild West without hookers, whiskey, and cards any more than you could dispense with cattle, cowboys, and Indians.

Ride with the Devil

It was probably inevitable that Susan and I ended up at church. On our second day in Vegas, one of us figured out there was a conference going on about the problem of human trafficking. We got into a cab and headed straight there.

We arrived in the anti-Vegas. The conference was sponsored by a Christian community group called the Dream Center. Its pastor, Aaron Hansel, had taken up the problem of human trafficking as a personal ministry. There were speakers from law enforcement, as well as outreach organizations like the Salvation Army. There was a buffet with coffee urns, pastries, and industrial-sized bottles of soda. The women, blonde, highly manicured and made-up, wore pantsuits or skirts and blouses with bows. At the entrance was a table laden with pamphlets promoting causes such as marital counseling, gambling awareness, and abstinence. At least half were antiabortion. I picked up one called "When Is It Time to Get Out?" It listed "What women want from a relationship" (love, understanding, and security) and "What men want from a relationship" (respect, peace, and sex). It wasn't clear why this was meant to be helpful, or for whom.

The speakers frequently reiterated their central point: trafficking is real and everywhere. They described how traffickers control victims by doling out love and abuse in equal measure. If the victims have family, the traffickers threaten to hurt them; if they have kids, the traffickers threaten to take them away. In the accompanying brochures, there was no distinction drawn between trafficking and prostitution, and the victims were always depicted as middle class and white. One foldout poster showed a highly attractive white woman in a red lace camisole with a scared expression. In screaming letters made to look like chalk it urged "Look Beneath the Surface!"

The celebrity speaker was a family court judge named William Voy. A big personality in an orange Hawaiian-print shirt, he stood at the Lucite podium in the Dream Center's place of worship and told the crowd, again, that human trafficking exists.

"It's there, I can assure you, because I see it," he said. Then he told a series of inspirational stories about the tough love he'd used to save women from prostitution: He locked a woman up in a detention center and threatened to leave her there. He took a new mother to a halfway house, telling her, "You leave this place, I am taking that baby." Referring to trafficking victims as "children," he explained that his goal was "a house where a child who wants to leave is told no. Where someone puts hands on that child and puts them back in the house."

I began to feel distinctly uncomfortable. It was growing difficult to tell the traffickers from the would-be saviors. They were all trying to control the same women. And the spectacle of the anti-Vegas was beginning to look too much like the spectacle of Vegas: a lot of sound and fury about sex from people who were neither selling nor buying it.

I decided it was time to talk about the sex trade with someone who was actually in it. So I conscripted Ashley to take me to the Love Ranch and ended up spending most of the night with Jocelynne.

A Fistful of Dollars

These days, at any given time, there are around twenty-five to thirty licensed brothels operating in Nevada. State law bans prostitution in counties with populations over four hundred thousand, but it's legal in most of the rural counties. Not all of them have it, however; brothels tend to be along interstates or clustered at the county lines closest to Vegas or Reno.

Nevada brothels do not employ prostitutes. Women work in them as independent contractors. They negotiate their own deals with clients, and the house takes half of their earnings. To work, women sign up for shifts—the minimum length is nine days—during which they eat, drink, sleep, and work on the premises. Few prostitutes live near the brothels where they work. Some live elsewhere in Nevada, but many are from out of state. They are responsible for getting themselves to their workplace. Jocelynne drives from Texas.

"I need that ten hours," she said, "to go from being soccer mom to being Jocelynne."

Once she arrives, she can't work until she gets her initial medical exam, which costs $65. While in residence she has an exam every week—a cervical smear testing for gonorrhea. Once a month, she is given a blood test for HIV and hepatitis. She must pay for those too. She also pays the $125 for the sheriff's card allowing her to work. This involves a background check: state law prohibits women with felony records from working in brothels.

In some cases, brothel workers are allowed to leave for limited times during their shifts, but in many cases they must stay on-site. This is known as "lockdown." Officially, it's in the interest of public health: it ensures that the women are not practicing unsafe sex off the premises. (Condoms are mandatory in brothels.) But it goes without saying that it also ensures the women aren't doing any outside deals with customers, depriving the house of its fifty percent.

The unpleasantness of lockdown varies with the comfort level of the brothel. The larger, more famous ones are almost like spas, with lounges, workout rooms, tanning beds, and housekeepers. Dennis Hof's Moonlite Bunny Ranch has horses that the women can ride. The Love Ranch South has pink bicycles for them. At all brothels, the women pay room and board—up to around $50 a day in the fancier ones. They must pay for their own drinks, if clients don't buy them; tip staff members, like bartenders and housekeepers; and buy their own sex toys and condoms.

"Even to walk in here," Jocelynne told me, "you're already in the hole."

Because brothels are remote and lockdown can make it hard to go to town, they have for sale things the women might want: snacks, cigarettes, toiletries, phone cards. The more exploitative mark those things up. The previous owner of the Love Ranch sold the girls $10 phone cards for $80. If they brought food when they came, he'd take it away and sell it back to them. The women assured me that had changed under Hof's management. They were no longer being overcharged. But they did buy extras from the brothel, things like mouthwash and hand wipes, which were nice to have. And periodically, traveling salespeople came to sell them shoes and clothes.

"They've got some cute stuff," Jocelynne said. In her room, she showed me the things she'd bought from the clothes guy the previous week: a pair of crotchless pink tap pants, a butt plug attached to a huge fake diamond ring, a pair of leopard-print platform heels. The heels still had a price tag on them: $82.50.

In a flash, I realized I recognized this economy. The brothel was indeed part of the old Wild West duality. But it wasn't Sin City; it was the company town.

One-eyed Jacks

In 1931, as Boulder Dam was rising and its workers were bringing home a combined half million dollars a month, Nevada's legislature decriminalized gambling. It was an undisguised bid for economic survival. The state's economy had been built on resource extraction. Now the gold was gone, the copper and silver were going, and the federal government would soon be done building dams. Most of the state was too arid for significant agriculture. Nevada had one industry left: tourism. So it adapted, with breathtaking speed, to a new economy based on selling an experience. And it was obvious what that experience would be: the old West.

Lacking a brand-name scenic feature like the Grand Canyon or Yellowstone, having no Spanish colonial ruins or dramatic Indian sites, Nevada's claim to Westernness was sin. The state's early promoters emphasized its history of free-flowing booze, unrestricted gaming, and easy women, building a tourist industry on the myth of the old West as playground. The first resort completed in Las Vegas was El Rancho Vegas, designed in rustic Western style. It was quickly followed by the Last Frontier, the Boulder Club, the Frontier Club, the Western, the Horseshoe, the Pioneer Club, and the Golden Nugget. Next to the Last Frontier was Last Frontier Village, a hotel and Wild West–themed town with a school, a jail, a post office, and a working train, all salvaged from Nevada ghost towns. Its Gay Nineties saloon included a bar taken from the old Arizona Club, one of the swankest brothels in the Vegas red-light district. Frontier Village was said to be the inspiration for Disney's Frontierland.

> The state's early promoters emphasized its history of free-flowing booze, unrestricted gaming, and easy women.

By 1935, Vegas was staging an annual Western festival. A host of writers arrived in Nevada and began touting the state as the place where the mythic West lived on. The trend reached a peak when society columnist Lucius Beebe moved to Virginia City in 1950 with his partner Charles Clegg and revived the *Territorial Enterprise*— the paper for which Twain worked in the 1860s. The bon vivant Beebe used his paper to promote Virginia City as a frontier free-for-all while also churning out magazine articles on life in a rough-and-tumble Western town and a syndicated column for the *San Francisco Chronicle* called

"This Wild West." While he lived there, Virginia City's only industry was tourism.

Ironically, even as the content creators were building the state's Wild West brand by trumpeting gambling, booze, and hookers, the casinos were working to criminalize prostitution. They claimed it detracted from the destination's family appeal and might scotch the lucrative convention trade. The Las Vegas Chamber of Commerce, having hired high-end ad agency J. Walter Thompson to promote the city, argued that prostitution would jeopardize the ad men's work. In 1949, the Nevada Supreme Court ruled that counties could ban brothels as public nuisances. Clark and Washoe Counties—which include Vegas and Reno—promptly did. Critics of the mob-run casino industry said the casino owners' real intent was to keep prostitution on the down low, thereby making more money through kickbacks and bribes.

The real change, however, started in 1969, when Nevada passed a law allowing public corporations to buy casinos. Organized crime began to exit the industry, and the corporations came in. Casinos were quickly rolled up into global hospitality brands. The newly powerful casino lobby revived the campaign to criminalize prostitution statewide. The rural counties, some of which received a majority of their revenue through prostitution licenses, fought back.

It might actually be more correct to consider tourism a subset of the sex industry.

In 1971, a compromise bill passed in the state assembly, banning prostitution only in counties with two hundred thousand people or more. Later, this became four hundred thousand. Even without this change it was clear that the law was a sop to the casino industry, designed specifically to ban prostitution in Vegas. Vegas belonged to the corporations now, and from the perspective of a brand like Harrah's or Wynn's, prostitution is just bad for business. It's more than an image problem. If you're having sex, you're not gambling or shopping. Corporations are only interested in experiences they can sell, or at least use to sell other things.

Heartland

In the decade between 1997 and 2007, Nevada was the nation's fastest-growing state. People have come to see the state as a model for how the United States will adapt to the new global economy. *Time* magazine declared Las Vegas the "New All-American City" on a 1994 cover. A 2008 Brookings Institution report called the Intermountain West the "New American Heartland" and

anointed Las Vegas its capital. What happens in Vegas, it seems, doesn't stay in Vegas at all. It's what happens next in America.

In pivoting to tourism, Nevada was quick to embrace the developed world's shift away from an economy based on manufacturing and toward one based on providing services. But the state also had, from the very earliest days, an understanding of exactly how the tourism industry would evolve. Nevada's promoters may have been the first to realize they were selling not things, not even services, but experiences. And since the main experience they were selling—the Wild West—had never existed, the first thing they had to do was fake it.

And why not? Tourism is the selling of experiences, and an experience, by its very nature, must be faked to be sold. The brothels had been cultivating a Wild West aura for years: it's one of the few prostitution models with popular appeal in a nation so ambivalent about sex. To this day, almost every brothel has a name evoking cowboys, cardsharps, and hookers with hearts of gold: Bella's Hacienda Ranch. The Wild West Saloon. The Kit Kat Guest Ranch. The Sagebrush Ranch. The Chicken Ranch. The Wild Horse Adult Resort & Spa. Big 4 Ranch.

Prostitution is often considered a subset of the tourism industry. But it might actually be more correct to consider tourism a subset of the sex industry. In our service-sector, experience-brand economy, leisure has become a product you buy. And when it comes to selling you an experience, prostitution got there first.

"This is a fantasy for everyone," Jocelynne said of brothel life. "It's a fantasy that you live in and men come into."

Some of the women, she admitted, take the fantasy all the way, lying to clients not just about their names, but about the kind of people they really are. They'd say they were educated and well traveled when they couldn't put two sentences together, or they'd say they were from small towns when they'd grown up in a ghetto. On brothel Web sites, the profiles exude the same level of veracity as copy on Match.com: "I'm just a fun-loving girl next door who can't wait to share my interests with you!"

"Of course we tell you what you want to hear, because that's what we do," Jocelynne said. "We're actresses." Which seemed in part to be a warning about taking her own story too seriously—the Texas housewife, the soccer mom who can't resist prostitution's allure. It was all a bit too *Belle de Jour*.

I asked Jocelynne how much her own desire plays into what clients she takes on, what parties she agrees to. One of the advantages of Nevada's system, she said, is that you never have to take a client if you don't want to. Negotiations all take place in private rooms, and although the house management listens in, they never have any say over whether a woman accepts a client or not. If the woman doesn't want to perform a certain act, or doesn't like a particular client, she can "walk" him—take him back to the bar, where he's free to start negotiations with somebody else.

"My out is, if I don't feel that person, I'm going to get the numbers up here. And if they agree to that, then, like, well, heck yeah," she said.

Most of the women have some things they would never do, or would price so high they'd be unlikely to have to. Jocelynne said she isn't a big fan of heavy S&M—too often she just starts laughing. But the one thing she really never does is GFE, the girlfriend experience.

"That's where they want the whole intimacy thing," Jocelynne explained. "They want to be able to kiss you. Use their tongue in your mouth, kiss you, hold you, and spend like an hour." She said it with a derisive tone, but GFE is clearly a popular option. Some Love Ranch propaganda even declares Dennis Hof originated "the real GFE." But for Jocelynne, it is off limits. "Some girls do it, some girls don't. I don't. That's turning into something I'm completely not. I mean, I don't even kiss my boyfriend. I think tongues are really dirty, disgusting."

I could understand this easily, because I once nearly took a job as a dominatrix. I was in school, living in New York City, trying to piece together a salary with various jobs. I taught, worked in a theater, transcribed sessions for a psychoanalyst, and temped as a secretary, and I was still broke. I answered an ad in the *Village Voice* because the job paid $100 an hour. No sex, but lots of spanking. The manager interviewed me at the house at ten at night. He explained that everyone had to start out as a submissive before graduating to dominatrix. It was easy, he assured me. I debated it with friends. In the end, I didn't take the job. I knew I could fake the dominatrix part. But the other—I was afraid it might feel real.

Increasingly, all of our jobs are blurring the boundary between real and faking it. The most extensive study of Nevada's sex industry is *The State of Sex: Tourism, Sex and Sin in the New American Heartland* (2010). The authors, academic sociologists Barbara G. Brents, Crystal A. Jackson, and Kathryn Hausbeck, see Nevada's form of legal prostitution as more than just a legal and cultural outlier. They point out that the global economy's shift to selling experiences, things like themed travel, preprogrammed adventure, or fantasy, has played into a commercialization of feeling. Flight attendants, sales clerks, baristas, even fast-food cashiers are all being scripted now, as global brands embrace the notion that they are not selling goods, but atmosphere and interaction.

"Welcome to Starbucks!" the clerks there say. "What can I get started for you today?" More and more jobs require workers to take on a fake persona, on top of providing service. The first wave of social critics to describe this trend saw it as a degradation of the real, a new millstone around the neck of labor. But Brents, Jackson, and Hausbeck, true to their postmodern convictions, don't. By now, they say, we have grown comfortable seeing our selves as multiple. We're one person at work, another on Facebook, another in bed with a lover. We spawn avatars as we move through worlds both real and online, with varying degrees of likeness to our "real" selves. In fact, there may not even be a "real" self at the center, just endless new versions, our personalities unpeeling like onion layers hiding an absent core.

Our selves, in other words, have become just another kind of content.

Leaving Las Vegas

These days, Nevada is trying to move away from tourism. With Indian casinos popping up everywhere and states racing to legalize gambling, Nevada no longer has a monopoly on games of chance. The state would like to become a high-tech center, a kind of Silicon Desert. But tourism is now the planet's largest industry; it's hard to see Nevada ever giving up on such a proven economic engine. Some folks are even arguing that since gambling is no longer unique, the right thing to do is loosen the restrictions on prostitution. Bring it to the larger counties, allow men to work as prostitutes. Nevada, they say, will never dissociate itself from its identity as a Wild West playground. The state has been playing the role for so long, that's the real Nevada now.

After we wrapped up in Vegas, I felt dissatisfied. The photographers felt much the same. No one had really hit the jackpot. The one person who'd made a picture he liked was Mikhael. He had trailed his escort for days, even gotten permission to photograph her with clients. But he wasn't satisfied. Eventually she told him that everything he was seeing was fakery, and that only the sex she had with her boyfriend was real. So they drove for hours and Mikhael photographed her with him. In the photo you see only her. Her arms are up, her head thrown back, her mouth an oval of black. Her chin is a tiny mountain with a cloudlike shadow on its side. It might be pleasure we're seeing, or it might be a pose. Even with no photographer in the room, we all fake something if we know we're being watched.

We got in the RV and went west. Paolo later confessed that when the trip was over, he went back to Vegas, because he felt that he'd never broken through its surface. I'm not sure he was satisfied even then. I'm not sure any of us were ever satisfied.

I tried to write about my encounter with Jocelynne for months, but other things kept getting in the way. The months rolled into a year. I never checked up on her story. I didn't really think it was important. To the extent that Jocelynne was lying, she was playing her role. What else did I expect? Her real identity was no more my business than it was that of her clients. But almost two years later, I listened again to my tapes. In one section, late in the interview, in a part I hadn't transcribed because it wasn't important, she unguardedly said her daughter's first name.

> Eventually she told him that everything he was seeing was fakery, and that only the sex she had with her boyfriend was real.

I got out my files. For some reason, I still had the model releases I had gotten the women to sign for Paolo that night. Jocelynne had signed only her first initial and had scrawled out her real last name in a nearly illegible hand. I could make out the first letter and a few possibilities for the next four. But if the daughter's first name was real and the Texas A&M story true, that might be enough. I went to the Texas A&M Web site and began typing in names. Within five minutes, I had found Jocelynne's daughter. I went to Facebook and there she was. She looked like Jocelynne, the wholesome co-ed version. She looked sweet. She had posted hundreds of pictures of herself, mostly wearing Aggie Spirit wear and posing with an arm around friends. Looking through her friends list, I found her little brother. She had recently written on his wall: "Congrats to my favorite Little League pitcher—you rule little bro!!!"

She was friends with her mother, so I found Jocelynne, too. Her name, obviously, was not Jocelynne. She was wearing normal clothes and sunglasses, but she looked the same. Her Facebook page was public too, so fifteen minutes in, I also had the name of her ex-husband and the names of her real-life friends. Not Cherry Pie and Exotique and Candee Gal but Lori and Chelsea and Jeanne. I was looking at pictures of the most normal family in the world: carving pumpkins, opening presents at Christmas, cheering at Little League games, striking goofy poses at the beach. I went on the Web and found her address, the books she was reading, the clothes and hairstyles she had pinned on Pinterest, the home decor she liked on Houzz. Her ex-husband really was a dentist. She really had a dog.

The whole story checked out. The desperate housewife, the soccer mom, *Belle de Jour*—it was all true. I felt sick. I wasn't going to do anything with the information, but it felt wrong even to possess it.

I went back through this story and changed all the names. I changed every identifying detail. It was hard; I'm not good at making stuff up; that's why I write nonfiction. But here it's all made up. Jocelynne is not from Texas. Her ex-husband is not a dentist. Her daughter never wanted to go to Baylor. She does not have a C-shaped stretch mark on her right breast. Her son does not play Little League, and her daughter never wrote on his wall. Her name that is not her name is not Jocelynne. The content, you see, is faked. But everything else, that's all real. 🛡

OUT OF THE WOODS

ON H. L. DAVIS'S

Honey in the Horn

URSULA K. LE GUIN

Writers west of the Mississippi are up against the eastern notion that everything west of the Mississippi, except maybe Stanford, is cactus. Many Easterners also hold that "regional" fiction is inferior and that a "region" is anywhere that isn't the East. You can't beat logic like that. It's amazing that H. L. Davis of Oregon won a Pulitzer, even in 1936. Lately, however, he's been so neglected, so lost to literature, that readers may be startled to recognize in his style and tone a model for Ken Kesey in *Sometimes a Great Notion*, Don Berry in *Trask*, and most other serious novelists of the West, including even the high-toned Wallace Stegner. Molly Gloss, in *The Jump-Off Creek* and *The Hearts of Horses*, is his true heir, the one I think he might have acknowledged as getting it pretty near all the way right.

Davis's prize-winning masterpiece was *Honey in the Horn*. Its protagonist, Clay, is a likeable, mule-headed, mixed-up boy of eighteen or so, who has already been through a good deal, but hasn't yet shut down in self-defense. His instincts are decent, but he falls in with an unlawful posse and takes enthusiastic part in hunting down and lynching his own worthless father, who might only be his uncle. His girl, Luce, the most vivid character in the book, is a wonderful mixture of forthright honesty and wary elusiveness. It's a good love story, always balanced on the high wire between possibility and tragedy. Clay and Luce are both quite capable of murder, which keeps the tension up. Both are ignorant, intelligent, young but already damaged, haunted by bad mistakes, pursued by past darkness, yet struggling to find a moral sense in the huge complexity of life. Of the wildly various people they meet or travel with, some have sunk contentedly into crime, many into futility, some are merely restless, and some, like Clay and Luce, keep groping vaguely toward a clearer standard, a better way to live—maybe just over those mountains there . . .

Clay takes a lively interest in the world, and through him, in a deceptively easy-going style, Davis gives us his own stunningly vivid perceptions of people and places. Here we're riding with Clay across a hardpan desert:

> In the big stretches the alkali reflected the exact dark blue of the sky, and that parted to right and left as he rode into it, so that he rode with the sky rubbing either elbow and washing softly back from the mare's feet as she advanced. There were places where spots in the clear air expanded with heat and magnified distant sections of scenery so

they seemed only a few feet away, and then they would go on expanding till they got gigantic, until a couple of sage rats cutting grass would look as big as colts; and then they would vanish as if they had been dissolved in water.

Davis was a generous, cross-grained man, who drank too much, as journalists and male novelists were expected to do. He wrote several fine novels and stories, including the unforgettable "Open Winter," all of them about the Oregon country and the people who worked in it. He said he wanted *Honey in the Horn* to contain an example of every job people did in Oregon in 1912. That statement itself takes us back to a far-away world of hard, skilled, physical, and infinitely various work—such as cowboying, or blacksmithing, or cooking for ranch hands, or fishing for salmon by dangling off a rope in a waterfall with a gaff in hand, or sewing grain sacks shut. The novel was written during the Great Depression, when work was something very much on people's minds. The time it describes is now a century ago. Given the rate of technological change, it's been the longest hundred years in human history. To some, Davis's picture will be meaningless, to others fascinating. In any case, it's worth considering that from the beginning of human culture until a generation or two ago, everybody lived in the work-world he describes; and it won't take much to put us back into it.

For all its vivid, vigorous language, its dry, teasing humor, its grand scenery indicated by a few easy strokes, and its crowd of cantankerous characters noisily causing trouble for themselves and everybody else clear across two mountain ranges, the essential feeling the book leaves me with is loneliness. Or what I think of as the American version of the word: *lonesomeness*. Lonesome people. That could be a strike against it. We may adulate the lone hero, but we don't want to be him. Lonesomeness is what the ever-present TV and cell phone and social media save us from. All the same, it's what a lot of people in the West came looking for—room, space, silence. We're social animals, but we crave solitude to make our souls. Americans cherish their opinions at least as much as their souls, and opinions allowed to take root where nobody's around to crowd them grow great and very strange. Davis takes a good deal of pleasure describing them.

He had some strong opinions of his own, including a low one of "developers," the people who turned the West into desirable real estate, filled alkali flats with little white stakes marking out unbuilt avenues and opera houses, and fooled the hopeful with talk of ten-foot topsoil, railroads certain to come, fortunes to be made, orange orchards in the sagebrush. Developers are loyal, active servants of capitalism, of course; possibly that explains his opinion of them.

The kind of super-respectful language used today when speaking of non-white peoples that white racists label "political correctness" was as unknown to Davis as it was to Shakespeare. He treats everybody exactly alike. Nobody gets any respect from him who hasn't individually earned it. He speaks of Native Americans not across a gulf of wishful thinking, but from a personal knowledge of difference so rare in fiction that it will shock people, these days (and may be part of the reason why *Honey in the Horn* has been dropped from the canon). The many Indian groups are clearly, vividly differentiated. In a sketch of a coastal village, he describes a tiny isolated group of Athabascans:

> There was a kind of hopelessness about that lost tag-end of a great people, stuck off in such a place without anything to use their brains on if any of them ever developed any, with nothing that they could ever amount to except to become chief of a shack town containing maybe six dozen human beings, with strange people and strange languages all around them so that there could be no chance of ever getting away.
>
> Not that there was anything mournful about it. They didn't want to get away, and they had stayed where they were for pretty close to a thousand years without the slightest suspicion that any place in the world could be finer or more interesting than their own twenty acres of it.

Davis omits the probability that this village, like many on the Oregon Coast, had recently lost eighty or ninety percent of its people to white diseases; and he was a desert man, who couldn't imagine liking the rainy coast. Otherwise, he mocks these people only as he mocks everybody—his picture of white settlers near this Indian village is just as unsparing. Disrespectful of conventional pieties but fascinated by and respectful of cultural difference, Davis can feel sympathy with the Indians without feeling obliged to share their view of life. What's more, he knows that his judgment of it is immaterial. Such fair-minded plain speaking is too easily silenced by the emotional rant of racism/antiracism. When *Huckleberry Finn* is banned, calumniated, and bowdlerized for using the word *nigger*, despite the fact that "Nigger" Jim is the moral hero of the book, how can any lesser book survive?

For all their failure to attain any goal or even do anything that makes much sense, the book's characters are fiery with life—absurdly tragic, painfully funny, ornery as all get out. Through the grand indifference of the Oregon landscape Davis sends a cavalcade of mavericks and loners, a crazy symphony of dissenting voices, a pilgrimage of obdurate souls. In them, with some reluctance, with some relief and even delight, I see my countrymen as they can be seen only from the farthest West, the farthest stretch of the extraordinary American experiment in how to be human.

Love, Death, and the Changing of the Seasons

NATHAN ALLING LONG

Although I lived on a rural queer commune in Tennessee back in the early '90s, I somehow landed a job teaching English part-time at the conservative state college nearby. I kept to myself, until one day in the hall I ran into Charisse, a petite, stylish, lesbian feminist professor. We got along so well that by the end of our conversation, we had agreed to coteach a course on contemporary gay and lesbian literature—the first of its kind at the college.

When we met next, we brought our lists of favorite books for the syllabus. On the top of mine was Samuel Delany's postmodern autobiography, *The Motion of Light in Water*. On the top of Charisse's was Marilyn

Hacker's *Love, Death, and the Changing of the Seasons*, an autobiographical sonnet sequence.

"That's quite a coincidence," I said.

"What is?" Charisse asked.

"Well, you know, Delany and Hacker used to be married. They met in school and were drawn to each other instantly."

Charisse blinked. "I didn't know that," she said. Then we both sat in silence a moment, the awkward parallels between their lives and ours fluttering around the room like a bat.

The class enrolled a respectable twenty-three students—seemingly every literary-minded queer person in a student body of over ten thousand. We started with James Baldwin's *Giovanni's Room* and Leslie Feinberg's *Stone Butch Blues* and ended with the anthology *Brother to Brother* and Sarah Schulman's *Empathy*, but the highlight of the course for me was discussing Hacker.

Love, Death, and the Changing of the Seasons centers on a one-year relationship Hacker had in the 1980s with a young female poet named Rachel (sometimes called Ray), seventeen years her junior. Hacker at the time was divorced from Delany and was living with her teenage daughter, Iva, in Paris and New York. Told through a series of witty, bawdy, literary, yet accessible poems—nearly all sonnets—the collection reads like a novel, narrating Hacker's obsessive infatuation, courtship, passion, and eventual heartache. Along the way, it reveals a great deal about love and lust.

In the opening poem, "Runaways Café I," Hacker describes a brief kiss goodbye after a drink with Ray, which ignites a "fire down below." She then offers us several lovely revelations about the complex workings of the love-struck mind:

> *I will not go to bed with you because*
> *I want to very much. If that's perverse,*
> *there are, you'll guess, perversions I'd prefer: . . .*
> *For you, someone was waiting up at home.*
> *For me, I might dare more if someone were.*

Right away we are introduced not only to Hacker's obsession for Ray but also to her keen psychological perception, recognizing how intense love—and loneliness—can make us more reticent and shy. This is the kind of insight Hacker offers again and again in this painfully introspective collection of poems. In "Lacoste IV," she reminds us that "Pleasure delayed is pleasure amplified," a phrase I still console myself with when I don't get what I want when I want it. In "La Sirène," she talks of "nostalgia for/ all kinds of things that haven't happened yet." And in "[Didn't Sappho say her guts clutched up like this?]," she confesses:

> *I'm alternatingly brilliant and witless*
> *—and sleepless: bed is just a swamp to roll in.*
> *Although I'd cream my jeans touching your*
> *   breast,*
> *sweetheart, it isn't lust; it's all the rest*
> *of what I want with you that scares me shitless.*

The drama of the narrative is in watching this elder poet enter the uncharted territory of courting a much younger woman.

At the heart of each poem is Hacker's endless investigation of the moment. While at times the poems border on neurotic, her brilliance and obsessiveness are tempered by a good dose of lust and humor, as seen in the poem "Runaways Café II," which describes their second encounter over a dinner out. Hacker says that she can't "concentrate on anything but [Ray's] leg against" hers as she tries to eat dinner and "impersonated an adult." They come to realize they are both drawn to the other, yet Hacker cautions them to:

> be circumspect, be generous, be brave,
> be honest, be together, and behave.

Those unfamiliar with Hacker will either bristle or laugh at her irreverent shift in language and diction, how she uses highbrow words like "behoove" and "circumspect," then gives us the last phrase, reminiscent of Divine's comic comment to her daughter in *Female Trouble*, "I have just two words for you, Taffy, *Be Have!*"

All of these poems are likely to be pastiche, mingling pop music lyrics, descriptions of French haute cuisine, swear words, a reference to Shakespeare or classical art, lewd street slang, and even—my favorite—a corny pun or two.

Hacker is so versatile she can't even resist writing a few mockingly bad lines. Two lovely examples are offered side by side: one poem ends "Your last few lines were fucking elegant./. . . I wish you all the fucking you might want." And the following poem finishes with this Ogden Nash–like couplet:

"Achilles hung out in his tent and pouted/until they made the *Ilíad* about it."

But in the next breath, Hacker is sincerely romantic, telling Ray, ". . . when you sing, your voice/is something like a path around a lake," and confessing, "Always is a long word I can pronounce" and "I'd like it, Rachel, to end when I die/at ninety-seven in the south of France;/to let it, to let us, get good and old/and bad." However, though Hacker is romantic, she is not naïve: she wants a stubborn love, something that can "be resilient/as crabgrass cracking the interstices/of paving stones."

Along the way, Hacker deals with a close friend's death, some gentle jibing by friends about Rachel's age and brief infidelity, and countless dinners and shopping trips with her young lover. Interwoven in this budding relationship, which jets between France and New York, is the story of Hacker's complex—and at times confusing—relationship with her daughter (Delany, known as Chip, hardly gets a nod). She confesses to Iva, "Things are going to be different than they were" with Rachel around, but tells her daughter, "I love you, you know, down to my last, best word." Yet as the year progresses, we see Iva taking second place, and the lines between being a lover and a mother blur.

At the end of one poem to Rachel, Hacker writes, "I wake up with a strapping blonde/in bed, but she's eleven, and not you," and elsewhere Iva seems more a confidant for Hacker, and a literary foil for Rachel, than a child properly guarded from her mother's consuming new love interest. Hacker even confesses at one point that she's "not at all certain what [Iva's] going through."

But such complex relationships are part of the delight of the book—following Hacker as she obsesses over her role as poet, mother, lover, and friend. While it's fascinating to witness someone's blind fixation on another human, and Hacker's earnestness and skill as a writer have us rooting for her, we can feel the impending end of the relationship pages before the breakup. Rachel withdraws; Hacker grows clingier, until she is so desperate she loses Rachel for good.

Hacker's honesty is brutal, sarcastic, and blunt, and her pyrotechnical use of words is enthralling. Yet what makes this book speak to me is how we come to understand, as she does in the last poem to Rachel, that

Not one word will make/you, where
you are, turn in your day, or wake/
from your night toward me.

It is in that silent rejection and in the recognition of the futility of words that we feel Hacker's pain and love most deeply.

As we discussed these books with the class, I couldn't help but reveal that I had a great affinity for Delany, who, like me, was queer, dyslexic, and wrote fiction. Charisse and Hacker had much in common as well: a love of French culture and food, an interest in writing poetry, and a quiet, painful desire for connection.

Charisse and I often felt awkward in the class because we were coteaching a new course for the first time, we had different teaching styles, and we were discussing issues that could stir trouble in a conservative college town. We also felt a little self-conscious that our literary crushes had been married to each other. And although the students said they enjoyed our debates in front of the class, working so closely together also brought up our differences. Perhaps if Charisse and I had met when we were sixteen, we would have become a couple, but our idols had already gone down that road for us.

ON ROSMARIE WALDROP'S
A Form/Of Taking/It All

EMMA KOMLOS-HROBSKY

As the daughter of a backpacking dad who used to saw the handle off his toothbrush to cut down on weight, I'm a firm believer in being properly equipped for any expedition. I love a good packing montage, the discerning assembly of a tool kit to see you through parts unknown: the tincture of antivenom for the adder coiled in the foot of your sleeping bag, the fountain pen that doubles as a tent peg. And so I found a kindred spirit in Alexander von Humboldt, one of the real-life adventurers at the heart of Rosmarie Waldrop's experimental novel *A Form/Of Taking/It All*. An explorer and light packer both, von Humboldt ships out for the Americas "on the mail boat 'Pizarro' with sextants, quadrants,

scales, compasses, telescopes, microscopes, hygrometer, barometer, eudimeter, thermometer, chronometer, magnetometer, a Leiden bottle, *lunettes d'épreuves* and a botanist, Aimé Bonpland."

A Form/Of Taking/It All sets its readers on a parallel trek into terra incognita. Waldrop's book is a strange new world, indeed, and one for which we seem at first decidedly underequipped. *A Form* splices historical and personal narratives. It shifts shape on the page and sends sentences careening without warning from the concrete to the abstract and on into the sublime. Appropriately enough, its very first section is entitled "A Form of Vertigo." I'd like to think I'm brave—or at least stupidly eager and fearless—in the face of the literary unknown. Yet each time I read *A Form*'s opening pages, I feel a little like a Boy Scout who's strayed too far from my pack, squeaking futilely on my safety whistle.

Waldrop wrote the book between 1983 and 1985 and first published it in 1990, in an era before Anne Carson's or Maggie Nelson's genre-blurring books transcended the realm of cult devotion to earn wider acclaim. But even today, when notions of textual hybridity are more familiar, *A Form/Of Taking/It All* still looks pretty wooly. The line breaks slashed into its title are the first sign that its structure and logic have more to do with poetry than with linear, novelistic storytelling.

What makes *A Form/Of Taking/It All* so terrifically audacious a text? It's not that the book lacks characters to ground it. It's got plenty of those. Waldrop's narrative

---

mostly orbits around Amy, a writer who struggles to orient herself while visiting a friend in Mexico City. Amy serves as a cipher for the book's author and reader both. But Waldrop also dips into the memories of Amy's not-quite-lover and counterpoint, Ada, or bounces across the scholarly interests of their circle of friends and refracts their stories through episodes from the lives of Montezuma and Beethoven and Cortez. Nor does the book's slipperiness lie in disconnection from time or place. Waldrop's characters move across the landscapes of precolonial Mexico and modern-day Boston and D.C. They climb sulfur-glazed volcanoes and wade through "birdlime and the biting smoke of their torches" past ghostly-pale cave plants in search of the unknown. Where other experimental novels are confoundingly abstract, Waldrop's book is daunting instead in the volume of material it enfolds and in its insistence on working with all this material simultaneously.

The first time I read the book, I found myself happy to be wheeling through It All but still a little iffy on the Form. Well-trained backpacker's daughter that I am, I decided what I needed was a map. I started keeping a list of the book's recurring motifs, and then, on graph paper, charted them out across two hemispheres. I began to see the totality of Waldrop's system: its transoceanic movements and conquests, its organization around ideas of the known and unknown, its twinned characters, and the twins of those twins once removed. The compass rose I drew was more of a dial. It rotated one way to show the flip of the book's pages and the other to show the spin of the Earth, a reminder of Waldrop's allusions to the vectors along which Amy moves even when the text's action is minimal.

The resulting map showed a dazzling, dizzying cosmology, a picture of the world as a sort of gigantic Calder mobile in which a motion in one sector reveals what set something spinning somewhere else. On the page, I could see how *A Form/Of Taking/It All* tells a story about learning to think across voids, in which the ultimate scientific instrument is metaphor. Here, to speak of any topic is always to speak of a million others, and one point can be known only relative to a counterpoint. The result is an ever-complicating web of connections, in which a name dropped on page one will be animated by a reference fifty pages later, or a blue hanky will find its parallel in a blue mountain range located on the other side of the world. Waldrop swerves sentences off their trajectories to land someplace that feels unexpected until you realize that when she said "oilbird" she meant also "Ada" all along.

When considering the work of daring women writers, the hideous question of what territory falls under their domain always seems to surface. Waldrop's answer here is a resounding *everything*. In style and scope, the book offers a big "fuck you" to constraining ideas of female domesticity. Waldrop tells a story that's at least partly about the interpersonal relationships of Amy and her supporting cast, but she places those stories on the same scale as Napoleonic conquest and the charting of the New World. But even more powerfully, Waldrop's book grants women writers permission to be difficult, to leave complications unresolved, to go bigger and wilder. *A Form/Of Taking/It All* endorses unruliness and complication and generative disarray. It's a work that absolutely refuses to sit still.

And true to its own word, just when you think you've got the mechanics of *A Form* all figured out, its paradigm shifts. In its final section, "Unpredicted Particles," Waldrop's words grow sparse on the page. The textual universe we've made sense of through metaphor is thrown into chaos by its collision with the logic of quantum physics. Waldrop riffs on Heisenberg, his notions concerning our inability to pin down both a particle's location and speed, to know where something is and where it's going. Waldrop destabilizes everything she's built. After teaching us to understand the world via metaphor, Waldrop strips away the possibility of making meaning any such way, leaving us with a kind of postquantum poetry. That map we just drew has been erased. We've washed up once more on the shores of a new world. But in destroying our map, Waldrop also grants us full permission to explore; where we go from here is up to us.

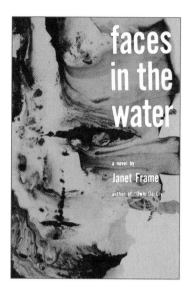

ON JANET FRAME'S

Faces in the Water

DAVID VARNO

I first read Janet Frame's novel *Faces in the Water* five years ago, when I was working for George Braziller, the New Zealand writer's American publisher. The book, according to passages in Frame's autobiography and some of her other autobiographical novels, is a fictionalized rendering of what she saw and experienced while being treated in a series of mental hospitals in her twenties. The narrator, a ferocious young woman named Istina Mavet, unleashes a kaleidoscopic battery of words that expresses not only her feelings but also those of her fellow patients, whose illnesses are more pronounced.

The book is raw with all the pain, filth, and helplessness one might expect from the practices of 1960s-era mental hospitals: the indiscriminate electroshock therapy, lobotomies, and general sadism. When Istina visits her family after her first stretch in a hospital called Seacliff Lunatic Asylum, where she was given shock treatment, she presents herself to them as a "sane person caught unwillingly in the revolving doors of insanity." Other narrators of madness might attempt to maintain a similar picture for their readers, but Istina doesn't spare us from the nightmare. She takes the "romantic popular idea of the insane as a person whose speech appeals as immediately poetic" and throws it out the window. When one institution fails to supply her with pants or stockings, she roams the place half-naked. When denied access to the restroom during mealtimes, she crawls under the table to "wet on the floor like an animal." These accounts confront us with the reality of despair, the breaking point where a troubled self may begin to unravel. Istina certainly was not well before she began her treatments, but for the most part the hospitals seem to make things worse.

In the weeks after I was hired to work at Braziller, I raced through other titles on their backlist before I read anything by Frame. George handed me Dalkey and NYRB editions of books by Nathalie Sarraute and Carlo Emilio Gadda that had first been published in the '60s and that he'd regretfully allowed to go out of print. I read them and several others, eager to feel that I could belong in the office and have something to contribute. I loved those books, but my experience with most of them was preprogrammed from hastily gleaning the flap copy or applying whatever George had to say about them, in the way an average literature student checks off what he needs to know for an exam. It was different with *Faces in the Water*, a book George felt strongly about but for which he shared few words.

There was a bookcase on the path between our desks with dusty first editions of the finest Braziller titles—Claude Simon, Sartre, Charles Simic, everything by Frame. Sometimes George would pick one out and pound it on the top of a filing cabinet with a grin or a glare, depending on his mood. But the day he pulled out *Faces in the Water*, his voice nearly cracked as he talked about how wonderful a writer Janet Frame was. At that time George was ninety-one, and Frame, who lived to seventy-nine, had died just two years before.

I took the book home knowing little about Frame aside from the fact that she was from New Zealand and George had published her books over a thirty-year period. I didn't know that Jane Campion had made a film adaptation of her autobiography, *An Angel at My Table*, which tells the harrowing story of her doctor calling off a scheduled lobotomy once news came that Frame's first published book had won an award. I didn't know about the playful magic realism in later books such as *The Carpathians* and *Living in the Maniototo* or the autobiography's knowing account of a naïve but intelligent young writer navigating her career. My point is that I had no context for Frame's work, which sometimes can make for the best reading experience. Every book that we open without knowing much about it takes us into an unknown space, but *Faces* is one of those books that preserves a sense of the unchartered even while we read. Frame teaches us how to navigate Istina's account along the way, without the signposts of a literary template.

Soon after the book's opening, Istina, who has just moved to Auckland to become a teacher, walks at night through the brightly lit city under the flashing tramlines. Here is how she describes the sparks pulsing from the rails: "[They] made it seem, with rainbow splashes of light, that I looked through tears." This stopped me dead in my tracks on a recent reread, and I remembered that it had the first time as well. I read it again and again, turning the image over in my mind like a child's jagged hand-drawn flip book, and marveled at how the landscape shapes her latent emotions, which in the writing are projected back onto that very landscape. This is the key to the book's unknown space; now I could see with Istina's eyes, or at least begin to glimpse what troubles her. Istina is forever on edge because she, like the other patients, like all of us, is running out of time. Death is everywhere in the hospitals. She describes them as a kind of purgatory, with "no past present or future." When a patient dies, there is just "the slight pause and panic that lie in the gap between heartbeats." Worse, the dread of shock treatment is repeatedly

compared to the electric chair: "Waiting in the early morning, in the black-capped frosted hours, was like waiting for the pronouncement of a death sentence."

Faces is a dark book, but it is not morose. There is sharp pleasure at the end of Frame's roiling sentences. She often eschews sequential commas, jamming words together with an urgency that hardwires us to a consciousness buzzing in overdrive. Her phrase "no past present or future" seems to account for this. Perhaps the no-comma technique is necessary, more than a stylistic tic. Istina is encouraged by her doctors to write, to let her madness boil over and get it all down so she can leave it behind. But despite their encouragement, the book is actually an act of defiance, showing us that she would rather keep what is hers.

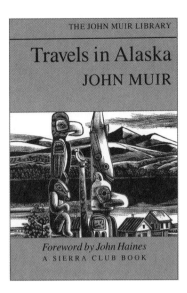

THE JOHN MUIR LIBRARY

Travels in Alaska
JOHN MUIR

Foreword by John Haines
A SIERRA CLUB BOOK

ON JOHN MUIR'S
Travels in Alaska

ASPEN MATIS

I grew up in a whitewashed room on a hedge-lined, suburban street. Blood-red geraniums and poinsettias in dark green plastic pots dotted our lawn, neglected in frequent rain. With the first frost each year, the flowers would freeze. The pots would crack open and spill the soil, black and sweet, that had sustained the plants through months of abandonment.

This was nature as I knew it in Newton, Massachusetts. Newton is called the "Garden City," yet in 1959 the town tore out the historic Mason School and its huge garden, bright with lilacs and buttercream roses, and poured into the new openness 2,178 tons of asphalt. This lot now offers central parking. The strip of flowers that remains, hugging the asphalt, allows the city to keep its name. Wandering these sidewalks, pacing this strip, I felt like a caged cub. I feared I'd be forever stuck in an artless world, until a slim old book I found banished that notion.

The paperback was *Travels in Alaska*, the little-read last thing John Muir ever wrote, published posthumously in 1915. It was both essay-meets-environmentalism-meets-poetry and a memoir of sorts. It exalted beauty and showed me where to see it: in icicles that shatter sunlight into honeyed kaleidoscopes on a spot of snow-blanked ground; in the vein-ridged wing of a common moth. It gave me permission to derail my life and leave the Garden City— first for Alaska, then to walk the height of America, alone, when I was still a teen.

I'd found it, brittle and browning, among flat basketballs and insecticide in my family's garage when I was seventeen, the 1979 trade paperback edition once priced at $5.95 but in this copy that value slashed and marked in pencil at just seventy-five cents. I opened it and it creaked. The spine cracked in two. I felt a swell of compassion for my parents to think that they had bought this wild old book. They had once fostered desire for something distant, something large—a seed they'd buried, abandoned. But neglected seeds— *wild* seeds—might still grow. I read the book in my bed that night in hopes of unburying something.

I was an unhappy teen. I felt blank, could not sit still. I had no friends. Inside my silent skull a whiteout, deafening and cold. As I read, I wondered what Muir's life was like before he set off on his adventures—was he once a misfit kid? Could he live at peace indoors? Was there a length of time during which Muir was trapped in a civilization rigid and unenlightened, unable to see through the crowds of factories outside his single, ruddy window? Had he once felt as I felt? Could I someday be as free and euphoric as he was when he was discovering Alaska for himself, skip-jumping over crevasses in America's most virgin spill of peaks, so consumed he would forget to *eat*?

Muir hiked and climbed and wrote and wrote and loved the air, the view, the whole moist and sunlit land. He was high on his new smallness. He would not sleep, couldn't—there were too many perfect snowflakes, too many unnamed peaks. And he had to write it here, now, while the blood pumped hot in his arms and his heart. He wrote: "When we contemplate the whole globe as one great dewdrop, striped and dotted with continents and islands, flying through space with other stars all singing and shining together as one, the whole universe appears as an infinite storm of beauty."

On my second day of my freshman year of college, before classes had begun, before I'd removed my colorful construction paper nametag from my dorm-room door, I was raped. I was broken into a spread of shards, sure I was not reconstructible. I dismissed my value. I was lost.

One night I did five shots of vodka back-to-back in my dorm room alone; I woke up in an argument with a nurse, lying in a hospital bed. Before that sad night, I'd never drunk more than two glasses of wine in a sitting. Then I joined an Internet dating site and went out with six people in six days and hated them all, and even met one in my room. I almost wished he were also a rapist and a killer and would at last end my seasickness that had no shore. I did not forget, though, Muir's words, the hope trails grant.

I rushed back to Muir, his books, maps of his treks. *My First Summer in the Sierra*, *The Yosemite*, *The Cruise of the Corwin*. I skimmed them for lines of places clean and gorgeous. I found strands of gems, glittering arrows, pointing to ridged peaks. In *John of the Mountains*, he told me: "In God's wildness lies the hope of the world—the great fresh unblighted, unredeemed wilderness. The galling harness of civilization drops off, and wounds heal ere we are aware."

In *Steep Trails*, he wrote to me: "Go quietly, alone; no harm will befall you."

I answered yes. Yes! I would go. I left school and went to the mountains.

Six months after I found *Travels in Alaska*, I was in Alaska. I had talked my parents into paying for the trip. Later that same summer, this time without their blessing and alone, I was hiking the 211-mile John Muir Trail through the High Sierra of California. The John Muir Trail is a segment of the mammoth Pacific Crest Trail, a lovely blip, meandering north. With the manuscript of *Travels in Alaska* in his rucksack, at the end of his life Muir boarded a train to Los Angeles, sick with pneumonia, hoping the urban doctors might revive him. They did not. He died there. His final ramble before he passed had ended in the desert of Southern California, the southern tip of the Pacific Crest Trail. Post-rape, newly a dropout, I traveled to that same desert and there began my long trek north into shimmering frost, silent glades, black and star-etched nights. I carried *Travels in Alaska* not in my knapsack but in my gut, my tent-snug legs, my will.

I was hiking alone, north from Mexico toward Canada on the 2,650-mile devastatingly gorgeous Pacific Crest Trail. On that walk I met rattlesnakes and bears; I forded frigid and remote rivers as deep as I am tall. I felt terror and the gratitude that followed the realization that I'd survived rape. I was not forever lost. I met myself, my future self, and Justin, the man who would become my husband. Our wedding invitations quoted John Muir: *In every walk with nature one receives far more than he seeks.*

A week ago, Justin found the old copy of *Travels in Alaska* I'd taken from my parents' garage. It had been wedged onto the tip-top shelf of the narrow cupboard in the bathroom of our Greenwich Village apartment between Mark Twain's *The Adventures of Huckleberry Finn* and Bonnie Nadzam's *Lamb*—two great American pilgrimage fictions. I was so excited to have it in my hands again that I reread it with a head-lamp through the night. In the morning, I called my father. I told him I had taken *Travels in Alaska*. I asked him where it had come from, what it'd meant to him and Mom. He said: "You have it?" He repeated back to me: "By Muir." Then he said he'd never read it, hadn't known they'd had it. He'd never even heard of it.

It turned out that *Travels in Alaska* had mysteriously and fortuitously appeared to bend the tracks of my life and direct me into the wild. 🛡

SYSTEM OF BECOMING QUITE

You have memorable hair, you own property
in Munich, which explains your blondish need
to be conventionally lit. I used to know
your anguish like the body of a fat fish I ate
and ate it. It is good to make a large thing
rompish inside you. When we were young,
once we were happyish people, we were
unrecognizable in our yellowish folds. It was
a pretty way to start. There are a thousand
atmospheres to try. If you beam you are
almost beaming. If it is brutal, then brutalish
is a way to live. Lovers never sufficiently love
anything. It's a wildish thing. It has always
astonished me, the way they are boundary with
their haves and half-wits. The way they claim
fantastically to know you from the darkish start.
Everything is becoming quite and not not.
Out here, a bridge is our god. We praise it
in a highish way. When I want you to stay
I tell you Munich is damn far away and we
have all this goldish light to contain. You are
becoming the considerable extent to which
I extend to. We are almost there. I'd happily
teach you a newish way to be here. Or on
your saddening days, dismantle your beautiful
bloomish and carry it utterly away.

SYSTEM OF DISMANTLING *BOMB*

If you were a blast I had I would not choose to
be you, would not choose to bristle or bow
no matter how bodacious your round. No
matter your super, your shell, your squad—
You are not God. You are a rhombic room.
I do not care where you've been – Dresden
or Damascus, Oklahoma – I would not bombard
a living city with my nuclear bits. Even zombies
know better than to mess with it. I don't
have a name for the sweetness of undoing,
but it looks like honeycomb it tastes like
a sombrero being tossed into the air. It's not
fair, everything you touch turns on; your fire,
your charge – every collision is a conversation
we've had, a combative kind of sad. It's hard
to render all your old tombs into a brand-new living
room. I'm trying to make this easier, not more
somber. If I were a tomboy I would have stayed
longer but my century is here and my dress is
barely there and we will never combine
our efforts into a worthy affair. My wombat,
this is my last little boom. The world will go
on without you, I've been too wrecked by your b-
eing. I promised I would never again swoon.
Look at you now: you're a comb, you're a womb.

FICTION

Leaving
the Sea

Ben Marcus

IT WAS BEFORE I DISCOVERED I COULD SURVIVE ON POTATOES AND salted water, before my wife started going for long walks into the thicket, before our house started leaning, started hissing when the wind came up after sunset, a house no different from a gut-shot animal listing into the woods, a woods no different from a spray of wire bursting through the earth, an earth no different from a leaking sack of water, soft in the middle and made of mush, when my children used their spoons to make a noise if I spoke to them, clashed their spoons in my face when I spoke to them, stood small before me using their utensils like swords, whether my words were hummed or sung or shouted, whether I was kind or cold of voice, which was before I felt the chilly finger hanging between my legs, a bit of ice high on my inner thigh, a patch of clammy coolness, instead of a hot and ample limb that could dilate if I so much as smelled her, when smell was a theft of wind, when wind was a clear blood leaking from trees, before my mother began saying it was so difficult whenever she tried to navigate so much as some stairs, a sidewalk, the doorway to a home, before I likened waking up to a car crash, equated walking to a free fall, working in the yard to grave digging, cooking food for the family to slathering glue on the walls, dotting the glue with beads, with jewels, when I likened weeping to camouflage, opening mail to defusing a bomb, when my wife began to say, "Only if you really want to," before I developed the habit of pretending I wasn't looking at her, when the eye was an apology hole, when the face was a piece of wood under the couch, when the couch kept the body from crashing through the floor and beyond, when beyond was something I had yet to think about at night, when unspeakable movies played through my head, before I went to such lengths in town meetings to cheat my face to show my good side to whomever might be caring to look, to anyone even accidentally looking my way, believing that if only my face was viewed from certain angles, then I would win something and something would come true for me and the words that broke the seal of saliva between my lips might mean something to someone and be actually usable, the way a shirt is usable as a barrier, the way a piece of wood is usable as a weapon, before I realized that my good side was competing fearsomely to duplicate my bad side, matching and maybe surpassing it, so that the bad side of my profile appeared to be on the rise, folding over the border presented by my nose and mouth and brow, taking over my whole head like a tide, when a tide did not refer to the advance of water, when most words had yet to wither, when their meaning was simply not known, before I flexed my arms if my wife happened to pay out the hug I sometimes still suffered to ask for when we encountered each other briefly in the hallway, and then noticed that she noticed me flexing my arms, yet hoped anyway that I could harden myself under her grasp and impress her with my constant readiness, when I tensed my stomach if she gestured to touch it, in case her fingers sank into me as though I were a dough, so that if she was ever near me I would contract, clutch, convulse, at first deliberately, then later out of habit, a set of twitches triggered first by her presence, then her smell, then just evidence of her person: shirts, purse, keys, photos, her name, seizure-inducing, threats to my body, when I had yet to conceal the terrible territory known as "my bottom" to anyone who might see it, including the children and adults and dogs of this world, whom I pitied by using big pants, even to bed, letting my shirts drape over my waistline to serve as a curtain for the area, when clothing served as a medical tent, an emergency service, before the phone started ringing one time only, the doorbell chiming off-key in the morning to reveal no one standing at the door, mail appearing with empty pages inside, little stones clicking against the window, then fast footsteps fading on the lawn, scuffling sounds, rustlings in the hedge, all of us

> I planted objects inside these people who were supposed to be my family, who had conspired to look enough like me to serve as a critique of my appearance.

always at the table, in our beds, our rooms, at the door, somewhere, unfortunately always locatable, lost-proof, when there was never any going below the radar or keeping off the map, every person and noise accounted for, before I could hear them swallowing the food that I made, could hear the corpse sounds their mouths made, as though they were eating a microphone, the food going into their bodies and dropping in the dark like stones, when I planted objects inside these people who were supposed to be my family, who had conspired to look enough like me to serve as a critique of my appearance, and these objects were not being digested, rather they were eavesdropping, spying for me as I positioned myself elsewhere, sitting on the couch with cookbooks or catalogs or magazines or books, when reading was the same as posing for a picture, modeling yourself for the book so that you will be seen as you wish to appear, when looking at pictures was the same as swimming underwater, before I discovered the flaw with my teeth that I confirmed every time a mirror was handy, checked as often with my tongue, whenever I needed a reminder that my chew pattern looked like footprints, discovered others checking it, their eyes never on my eyes but always pointed down at my mouth, confirming the flaws of my face, the vein in my nose that looked penciled in, the unfortunate curve to my fingers that blunted my hands and promised no hope that they could ever again keep hold of a cup, a bowl, a plate, some money, some hair, before my private limb was diagnosed as crooked, before I ever, as a regular practice, got down on my hands and knees, took myself out of the world of the standing people, surrendered my altitude, dropped down into table position, burying toys and letters in the yard, chipping at asphalt with a spoon, cleaning the hidden parts of the toilet, chasing my children on all fours outside in games featuring Daddy as a bear or dog, so that they could jump on me and ride on me and kick into the place where I would have gills if I were something better that had never tried to leave the sea, something more beautiful that could glide underwater and breathe easily, on my hands and knees at work looking for files or papers or reports, on my hands and knees crawling up to my wife in the bath, on my hands and knees in the closet, in the kitchen, in places like home, where the action seems best viewed from ground level, or where the action has ceased and a person can retire from view, right where the dirt starts and the air ends, the last stop for falling things, where things land and come to rest and get lost, on all fours as a strategy against vertigo, to be someone who has already toppled and can fall no farther, is already down, low, at sea level, but not yet underwater, so that someone could come up to me and accurately say, "Man down!," before it was safer to be a person, one who had to go by automobile to view the people known as his parents, before viewing times were established with respect to his parents, days of the week with certain times and restrictions, such as when the two of them would be sleeping, or priming their bodies for sleep, or dragging themselves out of bed for the purpose of sitting on their couch on display to my children, who could arrive at the location that contained my parents and examine them, a procedure that passed for a conversation, for play, for affection, a deep examination of these old people who were somehow, and dubiously, affiliated to them, which was well before the man came, before the man came, before the man came, knocking at the door one night, a tight report against the wood, letting himself in, sitting with us at the dinner table in the fashion of family, the man a smiler with a better face than mine, getting down from the cupboard a plate for himself, extracting his own place setting from the drawer, which was the first drawer he tried, walking right to it, too familiar, sitting with the kids, talking to the kids, whispering to the kids until they put down their spoons and laughed and used their faces for the man, before he brought his arm up under my jaw one night when I fumbled out of bed to pee, leaving me not even on my hands and knees but on my back, not gasping or hurt or scared, just disappointed to be on my back in my own house, so that nights thereafter when I groped over to the bathroom to pee even a drop, or stand there with closed eyes and wait until I discovered I had no muscle for the peeing my body was telling me I needed to do, I would raise my arms to keep from being struck, walked with my guard up, averting my head, waiting to be felled, when even in the daytime around the house I was ready with my arms to block what was coming at me, before I discovered him in my place in bed one evening upon returning from the bathroom, a successor where my body had been, holding on to my sleeping wife, when sleeping refined your argument against your spouse, and looking at me, looking at me, looking at me, from a face that once might have been mine, still well before our house felt thin, not wind-proof or light-proof or people-proof, but a removable thing that we could not weigh down enough, because, as the man said, we were hollow, though I might not have heard him, since this was still before I heard the airplane, before everything overhead sounded like an airplane, even when I could locate no airplane, just the most booming sound overhead, which stopped getting louder or quieter, as though an airplane was circling, but doing so invisibly, when invisibility indicated objects so close you felt them to be part of your own body, before I started hearing the big sound in the house when I turned on the faucet, the radio, the lights, when I opened doors or windows or jars of sauce to shush the white and gluey food I was offering everybody, and there came the sound, when everything I did seemed to invite more sound in, my motion itself a kind of volume knob, my body a dial, which if I used it would effect a loudness in the house that made life unsuitable, myself unsuitable, the world too loud to walk through, tasks such as walking, a loudness, washing, a loudness, speaking, a certain loudness produced by the machinery of the mouth, dressing for bed, a loudness like preparing for war, lying in bed, an earsplitting, terrible loudness, the noise of waiting for sleep, asking the children to be quiet, itself too much of a hypocritical loudness, my breathing itself, only my breathing, a loudness I could no longer bear, my breathing, my breathing, too loud for me to keep doing it. I was going to deafen myself if I kept doing it, breathing was going to render my head too packed with hard sound, it was too altogether terribly loud. Something very much permanent needed quickly to be done. A new sort of quiet was required. A kind of final cessation of breathing. A stifling. To be accomplished, no doubt, with those often out-of-reach weapons called the hands. 🛡

FORCIBLE TOUCHING

Flaying the blank. The crayon in a death grip, rubbing it in.
This coloring book, the Grief Counselor said, *will help. It is a good idea*
　　to never tell the child
　　the deceased went on a trip. Never tell the child
　　the deceased is sleeping. It is a good idea to

not be afraid. While the child colors Once upon a time
there was a happy little chipmunk named Chipper
　　who liked to play with his sibling *it is good*
　　to say it is normal and even. To stamp out fantasies.

The pound is by the petting zoo.
　　My first day, I do chambers,
　　the Animal Control guy said,
　　and his tongue was unAmerican.

　　Push animal in, close door, do switch.
　　I hear the gas, shh, shh.

　　We can hardly stand the wait, the Chipmunks sang in eunuch
　　harmony. Come on so. Another Lazarus memory,

winkling out of the cave in its graveclothes, vastated
by its visit to oblivion. You have to think of it
all the time because not to think of it means a moment
when the thought returns compounded, shocking as a defibrillator.
The heart. The clacking of that light percussion.

The clicking of beads on the reckoning frame. Abacus,
from dust. Coloring is a kind of bruxism. The gelding ground

his teeth, a rhythmic crunch. My sister was the one
with the beautiful touch. Light hands. The voice of the shuttle ==

as on a clumsy native loom she wove a brilliant fabric,
working words in red. *When the child colors* One day
  Chipper's mom told him his sibling
  had died *it is all right*
  to suggest crayons for the blotchy insides
  of the ears the blank circles in the eyes
  that indicate reflection. Unmellow Yell-
  ow Cool and Crazy Blue. The Animal Control

guy trembled in the one tongue
  that must do for all his days. *I hear animal soundings.*

  Cage cage scream scream. So pain.
  In this point I scared. I sad

  I'm gonna lose job here after.
  I was just pray to God. Sad you God

  help them die quick, sad hour
  farther. Dwell upon it always

or there'll be a whipflash, a concussed return.
I pushed the snaffle into his plush.
He was carrying good flesh. The voice of the shuttle is classic

tabloid stuff. Say her brother-in-law raped her
and cut out her tongue. How with shaking hands
she gathered up her tender vittles and comforters.
How there's a fund of talent in distress
and misery learns cunning.

When children color When someone dies
their heart and brain stop beating and
      thinking someone dead cannot speak
      cry laugh or eat *children may think something.*
      They might even feel == *Granny Smith*
      Screamin' Green Hot Pink.

Call Animal Control. *Sad you God*
      kill animals faster, hollow be their name.

      But when animals doesn't die quick, I sad
      gosh, gee, what's goin' on here, who ideas this?

Long poles with nooses. Jerk it along
while fending it off. Dwell on it always
or there'll be an awful dawning.
Curry with an over and over
oil for glow. The voice of the shuttle
is nectar and ambrosia. She wove her trauma into

a coat and sent it to her sister
who was the rapist's wife. And her sister ghastly
killed their son and cooked and served him
to her rapist spouse for lunch.
If the child colors special people

called Funeral Directors took care
    of Chipper's sibling's body in a pretty house
    called a Funeral Home *over and over*
    it is called Spooking in Place. It is Per-
    severing or Dwelling in the Gate.
Come on so. He tapped his watch

    and time leaked out. Abacus to dust.
    To chambers. So money. It take one minute for unconscience.
    Five minute for heart. For so long. For why?

So the memory won't come back blown up
every hour is that. The brain is beating
not the heart. There seems to be some frost
on the left ventricle. Give, I said and gazed into
the voice of the shuttle == harness and warp.
Selvedge, treadle, beader.

When the rapist learned about his shudder lunch
he chased the sisters and all three were turned to birds.
The gods were the ones with the terrible touch.
When children get frowny coloring When

the Funeral Director took Chipper into a special
        room where his sibling's body was lying in a very special
        box called a Casket *Do not be afraid to say Blizzard*
        Blue Midnight Blue Shadow Blue Surf's Up. Defib-
        rillate. Get rid of myths. Children may think
        something. Concealed in ivy. They made the person die.
        The person will return. It is quite surprising.
        Bound hand and foot with graveclothes!

Ask Animal Control. *So what you going to do*
        the long death coming? Shoot,
        burn, drown, freeze alive. Electrocute.
        Use decompassion. Needle in heart. So pain!

Think of it always. Not to means a moment
blasting back—shh, shh.
Sometimes I draped a chain over the tongue
as a control. The classics with their talking animals.
The voice of the shuttle == I've heard it
muttered for fifteen minutes afterwards.
Praying, they surmised. But they were not. Sure.

If a child draws word bubbles from the Casket
to the Chipmunktown Cemetery *sign*
        it is fibrillating. It is Twilight Spring
        Flesh Rose Dustbite.

Remove hard nubs like fleshbones
from the ears and the bad animal sounds fly back.
They become birds. Hoopoe, swallow, nightingale.

Coloring the grave may initiate a feeling.
If the child presses at the Cemetery
    some special words are said and the Casket
    with the body in it is buried in a grave *so hard the crayon breaks*
    or colors the page all silvery shades
    it is Milkshaking. Use clicker training.
    It is Granite Gray and Outer Space Gargoyle Gas Smoke Dirt.
    Children may resent you later for not being.
    They might even feel. There's a hole in the ghost. You will die
    and anyone sick will. Even the hospital will die.

Come on so. The voice of the shuttle is overness.
So many times I've cut out my own tongue. Never tell the child
vividvioletpurplehearttorchredatomictangerine.
When there's a story you cannot speak
you weave. It is too bright to rest your eyes on
but if you contort yourself your shadow will fall
    over it. It is a good idea. It is quite surprising.

RHUMBA

Rilla Askew

There's a snake in my boot!

Found a baby rattlesnake in the house when we got here last fall—not dead yet but dying, stretched S-like on the large glue board I'd set out to catch the scorpions and daddy longlegs that hold barn dances in our empty house while we're gone. This is my fancy about what the critters do in our absence: dozens of pale tan creatures, barbed tails arced high, sashay their long-legged partners across the living room floor, or lasso and ride the skittery six-inch black centipedes that sometimes scurry along our baseboards flaunting their wicked orange feelers. We find their desiccated corpses under chairs, beneath windows, laid out in the empty laundry basket when we return in the fall. My mind thinks: *What has exhausted them so?* A barn dance. A play party. A Wild West rodeo. More likely it's the poison I spray in the crevices before we close up the house to head north for the summers, but I enjoy the barn-dance fancy.

Our rattlesnake problem isn't fancy, though. It's fact.

"Watch out for the snakes," my husband and I tell each other when we go outside to walk or work. Our rock house sits on a rocky bluff in the Sans Bois Mountains of southeastern Oklahoma. Somewhere north on the ridge behind us is a winter den. If you've seen the rattler scene in *True Grit*, you've got the picture. This land where we live is the same country. The Sans Bois and the Winding Stair are twin ranges: rugged, low, humpbacked mountains slashing east to west above the plains, thick with hickory, oak, southern pine; they hold the same jagged sandstone bluffs and limestone caverns. When the days shorten, the rattlers come passing through on their way to that hidden crevice, where, until spring, they'll sleep entwined in great complicated knots, moil all over each other, crawl outside to sun themselves on warm days. A group of rattlers gathered together like that is called a rhumba, by the way. A rhumba of rattlesnakes.

One strangely warm November day in 2011, Paul and I watched a five-foot diamondback crawl out from beneath the ramp to our shed. The snake was beautiful, really, ruddier than most, and as thick around as my forearm, its rattles lifted high as it moved in no particular hurry but with clear purpose, down into a rocky drainage ditch, up again on the far side, continuing across the ridge in obedience to that den's siren song. I come from a people who will not allow any poisonous snake to live. My husband is a city guy from Boston with no family tradition of snake killing. Whether either of us could have brought ourselves to shoot that diamondback is a moot point, however. We didn't have a gun.

My dad has been mentioning this lack ever since we bought the place years ago. He took one look at the rocky ridge behind the house, the huge sandstone slabs that lie tumbled about the property like a giant's toy blocks—a thousand places for a rattler to love—and shook his head. "Y'all might want to think about getting yourselves a gun."

Okay, we'd think about it, we said.

And we did think about it. Talked about it, too. I leaned toward the notion of getting a gun. My husband did not. We have a mixed marriage, you might say. He's East Coast urban culture, where mainly just cops and criminals have guns. I'm rural Oklahoma culture, where pretty much everybody has one. Or several. My dad is a hunter. When I was a kid growing up, the full six-tiered gun rack on our den wall was as unremarkable to me as the swan-shaped lamp on top of the TV.

That first year we stayed here, I called Daddy and asked him to drive the thirty miles from his house to come kill the blacksnake in our wood box. Blacksnakes aren't poisonous, I knew that, but this one was *huge* and the wood box is *inside* the house, right next to the woodstove. When I opened it and saw those dusky looped-around lengths of muscular motionless body curled around stumps of last winter's wood, I dropped that oak lid with a thud and headed for the phone. "We can't be taking a chance on it getting out into the house!" I said by way of explanation to my Yankee husband as I punched in Dad's number.

He brought his magnum pistol and a five-pronged frog gig and ended up using the gig and a shovel. No sense firing a gun if you don't have to. He chased the snake outside into the yard, then pinned it to the ground with the sharp prongs while he got in a few good whacks with the shovel. "If you're not going to get a gun," Daddy said, "at least get you a good frog gig."

Which we did, not long after. We still have it, fifteen years later, stored in the garden shed where that five-foot rattler crawled out from beneath the ramp. We've never used it to kill a snake.

My sister Ruth and her husband own both gig and guns. They have a rifle, a shotgun, and a handgun Daddy gave them to shoot snakes with. They raise cattle across the pasture from Mom and Dad's house on our family's hardscrabble land east of Red Oak, where livestock deaths from coyotes and bobcats are common. Raccoons attack their laying hens at night—a ruthless, bloody slaughter, and only the hens' heads are eaten. Copperheads hide in the weeds beneath the water trough. In the creek beyond the pasture, thick brown water moccasins swim along the top of the water. There are reasons why people here kill poisonous snakes.

That baby rattler we found inside our house was a diamondback, its markings as clearly etched as the top of a matchbox. It could've been the offspring of the rust-colored one Paul and I watched crawl out from beneath our shed ramp the year before. If the glue board hadn't caught it, one of us could have stepped on it in the dark. We always put on slippers when we get up in the night, because of the scorpions, but soft slippers are no protection from snake fangs. Baby rattlers are born dangerous—they'll rear back, whip around, strike repeatedly if they feel threatened. Unlike a grown rattler, a young one

> The snake was beautiful, really, ruddier than most, and as thick around as my forearm.

has no ability to limit the amount of venom it injects. When I went to discard the glue board, the baby rattler moved. I jumped back about ten feet. The poor thing was nearly flat from starvation, it had probably been caught there for weeks, but the moment I came near, it began slowly, painfully writhing. I grabbed some long cooking tongs to carry the glue board outside, laid it on the stony ground, and ran over it with the car. You can't get sentimental about baby rattlers. Any rattlesnake, really.

I wrote a story once about a fellow who liked to drink in bars in southeastern Oklahoma with a young rattlesnake coiled under his hat—he'd sweep off his hat to reveal the baby rattler, just to shock and impress the ladies. That fiction was based on a true story my dad told about a cowboy snake wrangler from Heavener who did such things, and died from it. When I was researching the story, I learned a few facts. Rattlesnakes can strike two-thirds their own length and get back to coil so fast the human eye can hardly see it. They have medium-to-poor eyesight, a perfected sense of smell through that constantly flickering tongue, and excellent motion detectors via bones in their jaws that can feel the tiniest mammal footfall. They have acute heat sensors in the pits between eye and nostril—that's what gives them the name "pit viper." When a rattler strikes, its fangs pierce the flesh, instantaneously injecting venom as if through a hypodermic needle. *Venom* is the correct term, of course, not *poison*, although locally we still, and probably always will, call them *poisonous* snakes. In humans, a rattlesnake bite is horrifically painful. Symptoms include swelling, hemorrhage, lowered blood pressure, difficulty breathing, increased heart rate, fever, sweating, weakness, giddiness, nausea, vomiting, intense burning pain. If left untreated, death can come within hours.

Most species of rattlesnake—the velvet-tail, the ground rattler, even the eastern diamondback—when disturbed, will try to withdraw. Not the western diamondback: it will stand its ground. It may even advance to get within better striking distance. Western diamondbacks account for the majority of snakebite deaths in the United States. They account for most of the rattlesnakes we see on our mountain. Two weeks after the shed-ramp rattler, we encountered another. This time the whole family was there to witness.

Thanksgiving Day, 2011—another weirdly warm afternoon in November, the Sans Bois bluffs bathed in southern winds and amber sunshine, and everybody gathered at our house for dinner. In the after-meal lull, with the older folks all sitting around the front room dozing or talking, my four nieces and their little dog set out for a walk to the east pond.

Western diamondbacks account for the majority of snakebite deaths in the United States.

Nineteen-year-old Faith comes in the door after a bit, hunting her camera. "There's a snake coiled in the yard," she says, her voice remarkably calm. Little eight-year-old C.C. marches to the living room, stands in front of my snake-phobic mom, and announces: "There's a big snake in the yard, Grandma. We think it's a rattling one."

Daddy is up from his easy chair and out the door like a shot. I hurry around trying to locate my phone to take pictures while the rest of the family troops out to see it—except for my mother, of course, who wouldn't go out there on a dare.

By the time I reach the porch, the rattler has uncoiled and begun crawling away from the house toward a flat nest of sandstone slabs and boulders beside the pond path. I catch a glimpse of it gliding rapidly through the dead grass, its diamond markings mottled, but distinct. Its size is almost beyond belief: even winding S-like that way, the rattler is longer and thicker than any I've ever seen. What's even more unbelievable is the sight of my eighty-six-year-old dad following fast behind it with our frog gig—the one my husband has just helpfully fetched from the garden shed. I can see my dad's back, his bony shoulders hunched as he trails the snake quickly across the yard, and then Daddy's right arm arcs high, the gig handle gripped in his fist like a harpoon as he makes a great downward jab, and everybody gasps, or shouts,

Be careful! Watch out! But those small, sharp, metal prongs, designed to pierce a frog's vulnerable back, just bounce off the rattler. No way can they pierce that tough snake-skin. Before Daddy can try again, the rattler disappears into a hollowed-out crevice beneath a giant boulder.

In the pause that follows, we hear the rattles in the dark under the rock, still sizzling. Daddy frowns, bending over to peer inside the crevice. Young Faith, in denim skirt and soft mukluks, circles the rock with her camera. She's a city girl, an aspiring photographer, smart and fearless, at least where animals are concerned. She has no idea of the danger. "Faith!" I call out. "Keep your distance, hon!" She retreats a little ways, camera still clicking. Her mom, my sister Rita, who lives in Tulsa now, far removed from this wild-hearted country, says, "Aw, let's just leave it alone. It'll go on, won't it?"

"Not necessarily," my sister Ruth says, very matter-of-fact. She knows: stirred up and frightened as it is, that rattler might stay under the rock for hours. Days, even. When would we ever know for sure it was gone? This is rural, mountainous, deep-in-the-bojacks Oklahoma. You're not going to just call up the friendly folks at *Animal Planet* and have them come remove the diamondback from your property. The fact is, we have to kill it.

Trouble is, nobody's got a gun. Paul and I still don't have one. Ruth and Les didn't bring one. Rita and John only get garter snakes in Tulsa. They're not gun people. Our daddy owns three shotguns, a rifle, a muzzle-loader for black powder season,

the magnum pistol he wears in a holster for shooting cottonmouths from his four-wheeler when he's crossing the creek. But for my father, and for most of the men I know around here, a gun is a tool; it serves a specific purpose: to get food for your family, to protect your livestock from coyotes and rattlers. If there's no purpose for the gun, it stays put in the gun rack or behind the basement door. Daddy would never dream of going to the woods without a gun, but he'd also never think to bring one to Thanksgiving dinner.

So. No gun. Kids and dog in the yard. One useless and ineffective frog gig. A riled and lethal and very huge western diamondback holed up under a rock a few dozen yards from the front door. What would *you* do?

This being rural southeastern Oklahoma, what we do is, we call a neighbor. Daddy comes toward me now, the gig laid back against his shoulder. "You reckon Richard and them are down at Dixie's?"

"Sure," I say. "It's Thanksgiving."

"Call down and see if you can borrow a gun."

I quit taking pictures with my phone long enough to use it to call down the mountain to our near neighbor Dixie to ask if we can borrow her son-in-law Richard's gun. "Preferably a shotgun," I tell her, echoing my daddy's instructions in one ear. "Paul will drive down and get it," I say, echoing my husband's words in the other. "Or a twenty-two, a pistol," I say, listening to my dad again. "Just anything. We got a rattler in the yard."

Dixie relays the message to Richard;

she comes back on the phone. "No problem," she says, "but y'all don't need to drive down here. Richard says he'll bring his shotgun up there."

Within minutes his tan work truck comes bouncing up the mountain on our pitted gravel road, and I can see a couple of passengers in the cab with him. Well, of course. A rattler in the yard is big news. Richard climbs out of the cab, reaches in and pulls his twelve gauge from the gun rack, heads toward us, trailed by a dark-haired young man and an eight-year-old boy, his stepson-in-law and grandson. Because that's how it is here: the necessity and excitement of snake killing gets handed down man to boy.

Richard steps onto the large sandstone slab in front of the crevice, and my sister and I corral the kids out of the way, positioning ourselves to try to see the snake at the moment of killing, which we can't, of course: the space underneath the boulder is too low, cavernous, shadowy almost to black. Once he has the snake located, Richard doesn't even slow to take aim but hoists the shotgun to his shoulder and fires in one smooth motion, *Ker-poww!* a great blast, followed by a furious, tortured hissing *rattle-rattle-rattle-rattle* as the snake thrashes in the dark, dying, and we all creep forward to see.

The high sizzling buzz, so heart-stopping and terrifying when it comes from a roused rattler ready to strike, seems sad now, feeble, vibrating more and more weakly beneath the ledge. My young nieces utter soft sounds of dismay. The men stand back a smart distance from the black crevice, unperturbed. They know how dangerous a dying rattler can be. When the buzz has slowed to almost nothing, Richard uses the frog gig to drag the body out, jabbing it behind the head and hoisting it up lengthwise for all to see. A murmur of amazement ripples through us. The rattles are silent now, the thrashing stilled to an occasional small tremor, a slow useless lifting of its tail. Richard lays the snake out on the sandstone slab; we gather in a circle, marveling at it size, how clean the shot is—a neat, bloody wound across the back of the head, keen enough to kill it but not destroy the carcass. The men's voices are calm, their excitement expressed now in dry, understated Okie drawl: *Big snake. Uh-huh. Right at six foot, I'd say.*

"Can't we just kill it?" Faith keeps saying. "Put it out of its misery? There's a shovel right over there." She's a tenderhearted girl, devoted to all living creatures, especially cats and guinea pigs; she feels the snake's suffering. The men eye the stretched-out body. "Aw, it's dead," Richard says. A snake will keep moving long after its head has been blown off, we all know that, but this one's head is intact, and there's something mighty alive looking in its eyes. And the fact is, even a dead rattler can strike. We've all heard stories of severed snakes' heads striking and injecting venom because the nerves in the jaws are still alive. So we keep our distance, gradually moving in closer as we become surer the snake is not a threat.

The dying takes a long time. Our conversation stalls on how long it's taking, how many rattles the snake's got and how many have likely broken off over the years. One thing we don't talk about is who will keep that prize snakeskin. Richard shot the rattler. Even if it is on our property, the understanding is that the snake goes to him. I ask to keep the rattles, though, and that, too, seems fitting, or in any case, no one questions what I might want those smelly old rattles for. The men speculate about how long in feet and inches the snake will measure when its muscles finally relax, how thick through the middle it is. "'Bout as big around as a pop can," Richard says. *Thick as my upper arm*, I'm thinking.

When the snake is doorstop dead, I stretch out on the sandstone beside it with my arm laid next to the thickest part to verify the comparison while my husband takes pictures. Faith, too, kneels beside the dead rattler, petting it slowly, the way you might stroke a favored pet. At first I think she wants to know, safely, what a rattlesnake feels like under her hand, but then it occurs to me that what she's really doing is trying to soothe the already dead snake, to say, in some way, she's sorry. Maybe I think this because that's what I feel.

On through the afternoon and into the evening, as Richard loads the dead snake into the back of his pickup to drive it down the mountain and we all troop back inside the house for leftovers and a

> We've all heard stories of severed snakes' heads striking and injecting venom because the nerves in the jaws are still alive.

second helping of pumpkin pie, through the slow letdown after all the excitement, the goodbye hugs, the drawn-out end-of-the-holiday family farewells, I feel a kind of increasingly sick-to-my-stomach regret. I hate that the snake had to die.

But this is our home, our yard. Tough enough to step out the door on warm days never knowing if that which can kill you lies in wait on the path to the pond. We couldn't simply walk away from a six-foot diamondback holed up beside that path. Richard told us that his father-in-law, Fred Ezekiel, who built our house, had to clean out a rattlesnake den from the rocky bluff behind the house when he laid the foundation. They're trying to repopulate, maybe, Richard says. Trying to move back in. It's one thing to live on a rattlesnake superhighway, and quite a dangerous other thing to dwell in a house where rattlesnakes gather for their winter rhumba among the very rocks and crevices beside you.

The men never considered anything but that the snake had to be killed. Our mother wouldn't come outside to see it even after it was dead. Later, when we showed her the pictures, she shuddered and dreamed bad snake dreams for a week. The girls, our nieces, a young generation, a city generation, found the snake beautiful. They have never lived on this land. They've been watching PBS nature shows all their lives. Their sympathies were definitely with the snake. And their mom, too, my sister Rita, had to go on into the house before the snake died because she didn't want to see its suffering.

But my sister Ruth, who lives here, stayed right through to the end. She knows what my dad knows. What anyone born and bred to this rough landscape knows: you can't allow that which can kill you to dwell in your living and walking and working space. This is a land without mercy. You might hesitate to kill a rattlesnake, Ruth says, but that rattlesnake would not for an instant hesitate to kill you.

I still have the dried rattles from that diamondback. Richard's stepson-in-law Steven brought them to me the next day after they'd skinned and laid out the snake. He told us it measured five feet ten and a half inches, missing that six-foot guess by not much. Then Paul and I drove into McAlester to buy a gun.

His views on gun ownership had shifted—not out of fear for us, he said, but because of what could have happened to the children: to little eight-year-old C.C., her toddler twin brothers, our young-lady nieces and their small yippy dog. We went to the pawn and ammo shop Richard recommended. The place was packed with men and boys in red hunting caps—it was still deer season—and a few grizzled old characters in full camouflage. We wandered the aisles looking at rifles and shotguns hanging in rows with tags we couldn't read, except for the prices. Hoping for advice, we waited at the counter, listening to the clerks and customers converse in a language we did not understand—the language of weaponry. After a while my husband and I looked at each other, shrugged our shoulders, and left.

The next Sunday, in Red Oak, I told Daddy we were looking to buy a gun, finally, but we didn't know how to do it. "I'll come with you," he said. "We'll go to Walmart." Then he thought a minute. "No, here, tell you what." He went downstairs to the basement and came back carrying his dad's old twenty-gauge shotgun and handed it to me. So that's part of my inheritance now—my papaw's old rabbit gun. It's stored in the bedroom closet, unloaded, stock down, the shells in a zippered pouch on the top shelf. Paul and I keep saying we're going to take it out and fire it one of these days so we'll know what to do with it when we need it.

The dried rattles I keep on my bookshelf, along with a desiccated scorpion, lying on top of a small Oklahoma-shaped piece of sandstone I found in the road. Not a trophy but a talisman. A reminder. "Watch out for the snakes," my husband and I tell each other on warm days. Inside the house, we watch where we step. We never put a hand or a foot where we can't see what we're getting ready to touch. ◈

ESSAY ON URBAN HOMESTEADING

The dumb hours blunt the after
    noon with bottleneck

with clover & weeds
    almost meadowed

& black widows & the mint.
    There are so many ways

to be tired. All summer list
    & ungather, place strategic

plywood over yielding
    planks. The beginning

a swelter now settled :
    now not new :

We have our pick of bars
    & a new bullet

ratio : a little less day-to-day
     interruption : a little less

metal : barrel : slate : syringe.
     Less watch-how-the-dark

-performs-our-ghosts.
     We settle in,

accommodate the history
     of what is left

to us, blue marl & viaduct,
     cold storage units

turned into lofts; sirens
     & blackouts;

a rampage of ten-year-old boys
     throwing rocks.

Camino Real

Lawrence Osborne

He got off the bus from Placita at the end of the afternoon, just as the mine sirens were echoing across the hills, and he walked from the terminal into town with his bag shouldered and his boots frayed apart. The cantinas were long abandoned, and the factory that had sustained them had closed the year before. The gas station still did business with long-distance truckers and above the salt-white desert rose the first three letters of the word *Pemex* in neon. What had once been a square of irrigated grass had turned to dust, and its edges were burned brown like old paper.

Angel already looked far older than twenty-eight. Two years wandering the deserts, drifting from job to job, had turned his skin a darkened copper and made his eyes both harder and more wounded. A year he had worked on the border at a gas station, sleeping near the freeway in a trailer moored at the bottom of a sand hill. He had waited for something to come along that straight American road. Nothing had improved his lot and one day he came to blows with the owner and walked south, back into the desert from where he had come. Someone at the station had told him that carpenters were needed in the mining towns.

He walked past the square to the beginning of Cardenas and turned right into the last living street. There was a hardware store, a cantina called Lagrima, and a Western Union bathed in white light. At the far end of the street he could see the salt-white again and the beginning of another road leading to the mines. The sirens echoed down the valley and reached the taquerias, where old men sat outside with domed plastic cups of *agua de jamaica* stuffed with ice and penetrated by transparent straws.

He went into a hotel at the end of this street and procured a room, was taken up by the maid. The room was on the top floor with a view of the street and the fairy lights of the electrical company, which still maintained a line here. Fifteen by fifteen and a crucifix. He lay on the bed and took off his hat and lit up a Cubano. He crossed his boots and blew the smoke across them, then did his peso calculations. He had enough for dinner and the bus to La Mira the following day, with some extra for lunch if he didn't get too many beers tonight. It was enough for twenty-four hours. He smoked half the Cubano, then decided to save the rest. He shaved, had a depressing and oily bath, and went back down into the street to eat five tacos. Now, the lights—all seven of them—were on and the dusk light behind the canyons had become a fine steel blue. He ate with surly slowness and then strolled into Lagrima, where the music was turned up and a few retired miners sat under posters of Jennifer Lopez. He went up to the metal bar and put his left-hand fingers onto the plates of the Eletrucodador.

"It's one free shot per shock," the barman said.

"I know how it works."

"Sixty volts, a shot of mescal. Eighty, a tequila. One hundred for a Sauza."

"Tequila."

The miners looked up as he took the shock, received his free shot, and demanded another.

"Too many will damage your ear hairs," the barman said.

"It's fine. Shake me up."

It hurt a little more the second time and he bolted down the tequila in one go. He went up to a hundred for the Sauza. After four shots he wiped his mouth and walked out not a peso the lighter. A stiffer wind now bowled down the street and half the lights had been shut off. It was about eight o'clock. He walked toward the neon of the gas station, which shone ever more brightly, and crossed over the rectangle of desert grass that separated it from the edge of the town. Long-distance rigs stood here, their grills covered with plastic dolls, Virgins of Guadelupe, and lengths of bronze tinsel, and the drivers stood at the perimeter of the light, smoking, with cans of Tecate. He walked past them until he could smell the open desert with its faint urine-like whiff of salt. Far off, a few dim lights speckled the horizon, but they were not trucks. He walked along the road a little while, past the spidery ocotillos trembling in the wind. The stiff red flowers were out. Chollas at ground level were also blooming, the white spines shining by the light of the gas station and the yellow blossoms shivering.

Back in the room he checked his phone but there were no calls. He half-closed the shutters with the rusted latches and stood by the window, looking down at the swinging doors of the cantina, through which fat little men were rolling like billiard balls. The dirt in front of it was peppered with bottle tops. There was a fight of some kind going on inside the cantina and soon bloodied men would be falling about with colorful phrases, swinging their arms and spitting their recent meals among the husks. He drew the curtains shut and then went to lie down, throwing his straw hat across the room like a frisbee. The sirens from the mine died down and there was the sound of trucks moving across the desert. Their horns occasionally echoed across the emptiness.

He didn't take off his clothes. He smoked for some time, the Cubano proving its worth as it burned down slowly and richly, and then he lay awake with the lights off, listening to the nocturnal events. It was his habit. The laughter of women came from far off, perhaps from the gas station. So that was their whorehouse. He always wondered about those things. The smoke swirled up to the light cord and he thought about his mother, long dead and forgotten. He felt her within him, a force waiting to extract her vengeance.

He was awakened at first light by the clatter of trash cans wheeling down the street. He was always ready to jump at a trivial sign. He went downstairs gingerly in his peeling boots, his mouth dry and aching. The lobby had an electric coffeemaker on standby and he drank down half the glass pot and ate a stale donut from a plastic container.

A man was sitting there, leaning against the wall, an ancient and flamboyant figure in tooled boots beautifully polished. He was in a crumpled pale gray sharkskin suit, '60s variety, with a windowpane shirt and a dark gold neckerchief. He was about halfway through his seventies but with no residual youthfulness, no smooth patches in his sun-worsened skin, but the white beard and chops trimmed and dapper. He was drinking a cup of black coffee, alone with the hotel cuckoo clock, and now he had Angel for company.

"Buenos días," the man said, raising his brimmed hat. "Señor Patrick Mendes. Have a coffee with me." For once it was cooler outside. They went and sat on the steps and watched the wind socks coming into visibility as the night receded. The older man looked Angel over and he seemed to do it carefully.

"On the road?" he asked.

"Yeah, just traveling and looking for work."

"For work? You must be mad. This is a dead place. You aren't going to find any work here. No one finds work here unless they're a miner."

"I ain't a miner."

"You don't look like a miner. You look like a houseboy on the run. What's your line of business?"

"This and that."

"This and that? Swell. Well, that'll get you far up here. This and that."

Mendes had a rough, charming laugh.

"What about you?" Angel said.

"I'm on the road to sell some proper- ties up north. It's bad days for real estate in these parts. The cartels are ruining everything."

"They must be."

"Sure they are. They're fucking us good. They're hanging people from the bridges in Chihuahua. *La chingada*."

"Yeah, they are."

There was a fight of some kind going on inside the cantina and soon bloodied men would be falling about with colorful phrases.

"Everyone's selling. I'm off-loading most of my portfolio up north. No one wants to live with the threat of death at every moment of every day."

"No, sir."

"The towns are emptying out. Did you find any this and that?"

"So far, nothing."

"That's how it is, boy. It's a desert in all senses now. You'll be getting nowhere fast. Are you waiting for the morning bus?"

"Guess I am. Nothing doing in this dump."

"I have a car. I'll drive you."

"You do?"

"Yes, I do. You think in my line of work I'd be riding around on a stink- ing bus?"

"I guess not."

"Where are you headed?"

Angel shrugged.

"I see. Let's get some huevos rancheros first. I always eat hard and fast in the morning."

They went to a place two blocks down from the hotel. The windows looked over a gully filled with wildflowers and the back of an abandoned slaughterhouse. Mendes ordered for both of them. He could see Angel was broke and mangy. They ate eggs and salsa and churros caked in white sugar and *café de olla* in metal pots with the cinnamon sticks sticking through the lids. It was the best breakfast Angel had consumed in a fair while. His clarity returned and his muscles began to hum. The suspicion that came so easily to him began to relax and he felt something of his old swagger return, the youthfulness that had only recently seeped out of him.

"So," he said now, "you've driving south?"

"Yes, I'm driving home. I am disgusted with my portfolio and I cannot wait to be back."

"Are you going to see any properties on the way?"

"As a matter of fact I am. Just one."

Angel cut the fried tortilla under his eggs with the edge of his fork. He was feeling a little pushy and insolent.

> **Mendes knelt in the shallows and thrust his unkempt head into the water. The women giggled and shook their butts.**

"Mind me asking where?"

"What's it to you, my boy? You think I could give you a job?"

"Wasn't thinking that, señor."

"It's all right." Mendes lit a shaggy cigarette and didn't offer one to his new friend. "I can see how a man thinks like that when he's on the rocks. He casts about, that's what he does. I don't take it the wrong way, kid."

"I would be up for a job," Angel said nonchalantly. "I can do most things."

"We'll talk about it in the car. Have another *café de olla*."

The sun rose as they walked to a surprisingly clean Pontiac on the same street as the gas station. A fine, gritty dust blew off the arroyos.

Angel threw his bag in the back and sat next to Mendes in the front. The desert burst into golden light as they moved out, passing the old tanneries and the two motels, which had once, long ago, flourished in morbid splendor. The road was straight now, earnest and unbending and to the point, and they sailed along it mostly in solitude, passed only by long rigs bound for the north. At the distant foot of the mountains to the right there were pylons, white shacks, and to the left the empty plain of dark gray sand and cholla cactus.

"I'd say," Mendes went on cheerfully, "that from the looks of you you were a drifter. But you're not, are you?"

"I'm just moving around."

"Ah yes. Sometimes one has to move around. It's the law of life. Times are bad and you have to move around."

"That's about it."

"When I was your age I moved around. Yes, sir. Then I discovered this highway. You could buy and sell properties along this highway as easy as buying and selling tacos. It was a silver mine. I called it the 'camino real.' We all called it the camino real—that was the term for it. Those were the days, now that I look back on them. A fortune in easy commissions. *La chingada*. It's all done for now."

Here and there, on either side of the road, stood what looked like ruined and forsaken ranches. No greenery could be seen, no grazing land, no crops, no animals, no tractors or other vehicles. Only the old water towers rusting in the heat and the bleached fences decaying year by year, or was it month by month? One could never tell at this latitude. The forgiving lushness of the Tropic was still far off. Mendes told a few tall stories of the old days, by which he might have meant merely the previous decade.

The land was changing. At midday they came to a half-dried river, an astonishing sight, with low jacarandas in full bloom around it. Here, white horses were tethered in the pebbled shallows, their backs colored mauve by the trees. The stream ran pure and transparent across a bed that descended in shallow terraces. Women knelt there washing shirts, their dresses tied around their hips. Mendes stopped and rolled out of the car good-humoredly.

"What asses!" he cried to the women, who were not at all annoyed. They turned their heads with no concern and took this brutal compliment in their stride. "Can I drink?" he laughed, running down to the water's edge. "It's so fucking hot in this country. Angel, come down."

But Angel stood on the bridge spanning the river, looking down at the docile, tenderly hued horses. The sweat dimmed his eyes and he had to wipe them. The heat and the light were no longer separable.

Mendes knelt in the shallows and thrust his unkempt head into the water. The women giggled and shook their butts. *Cabaza hueca*, one of them teased him. It was clear that they had seen him before, that he was part of this shrill, blinding landscape. But what role he occupied in it was not clear. Buffoon, interloper, genie?

He seemed to know the river intimately, wading into it up to his shins and basking in the jacaranda shade. He looked back up at Angel standing on the bridge and squinted, thinking, *So the drifter doesn't care for a fresh river.* Angel was puzzling over the stout stranger whose trousers were rolled above his knees like a grandfather's. There was something obscure about him, something permanently plunged in shade.

They drove on into featureless hills. Aerial masts and pylons stood in a simple clarity, the low shells of abandoned houses. They went through pueblos baking in the hopeless heat; past Pemex stations alive with Christmas tinsel and bars shaded by painted trees where the men sat outside in *jijipita* hats with plates of radishes and bottles of Noche Buena. Mendes drove a little faster now, his hands light on the red leather wheel. He smoked with a slow deliberateness and looked frequently in the rearview mirror to inspect the road behind them. The sweat was loose and free on his dark temples. He talked about the property he was on his way to visit. Perhaps Angel could visit it with him. They would soon be there. It was, so to speak, "on the way."

"A lovely house on the plain, not far from the road. We had to evict the family. They didn't pay the rent."

"Did they leave?"

"We are about to see, hombre. We are about to see. To tell you the truth, I don't want to go into that house. It was a guy from Morelia, a bad news kind of guy. I never wanted to give it to him. But sometimes you don't listen to the gut instinct. You get into hot water."

"Who is he?"

"Some guy. He did time a while back. Probably a drug runner once upon a time. You know the type. A drifter."

Like me, Angel thought.

"But I don't want to run into that *pendejo*. I have been thinking. Maybe you would like to earn a little cash."

Angel perked up. His inclination toward suspicion returned, but at the same time he felt a fresh vibrancy emanating from the very simple word "cash." Against his misgivings, he spoke slowly and calmly.

"Sure I would."

"I thought so. What if you'd go into that house for me and look around? It should be empty. They are supposed to have left a few weeks ago."

"But one never knows, eh?"

Mendes turned cynically and gave him a wink.

"Money is never for nothing, hombre. I said I didn't want to do it. It'll be nothing, though. It'll just be an empty house."

"What if it's not empty, then?"

"Well, you would have to deal with it."

"Hombre?"

"They might have left some animals in there. A dog or a cat."

"So that's why you don't want to go in?"

"Exactly. I hate animals. I'd pay you to clean them up."

"Let them out?"

"Kill them, I mean. What's the point of letting them out? What the fuck are we going to do with them?"

"I don't know."

"Yeah, you don't know. We're not going to do nothing with them. Pests have to be put down. It's part of the job."

"You've done it before?'

"Sure I have. How do you think the properties get cleaned up?"

"Come on, boy. For $500 you won't kill a pussycat?" Angel felt his head go light.

"Shit, man, I don't know. Kill a cat?" Angel had never killed anything other than poisoning rats around the gas station, but he suddenly wondered if the omniscient Mendes knew even this small fact about him. Did he smell of exterminated rats? But a cat, in any case, was a different matter.

Mendes laughed out loud.

"Come on, boy. For $500 you won't kill a pussycat?"

Angel felt his head go light.

"Five hundred?"

"That's what I said. Five hundred. Five hundred not enough?"

The tone was so sarcastic that Angel had to contradict it at once; he agreed quickly to whatever it was that Mendes wanted.

"All right, it's fine. What do you want me to do?"

"Go through the house and make sure it's fit for repossession. I want you to go through it carefully, though. Animals get into cupboards and behind sofas. You'll have to look through it inch by inch. Can you do that?"

"Sure I can."

"Good. We have a deal?"

They shook hands and Mendes rolled down the window. They had come to a flat, scorching plain with dust-whitened trees standing along the tracks, the building walls painted white and dotted with bullfighting posters.

Angel thought. A cat would be a dismal task, and a dog would be worse. But then Mendes had said that there would probably be nothing. It was a spin of the roulette wheel, and Mendes was paying him to accept the spin. A bet was a bet and a bet could pay handsomely, but one had to roll or bail out. Bailing out got you nothing—and if he had to suppress a pet it was worth five hundred. It was worth a lot less than that. He would have done it for a hundred. Somewhere between fifty and a hundred, he would have balked, but Mendes didn't know that. Even he wasn't used to Angel's level of poverty. For all Angel knew, however, five hundred was the going rate for pest clearance.

"There's just one condition," Mendes said. "And listen to me good. When I say I want the house cleaned, I mean I want it cleaned. I want everything living inside that house cleaned out. Flies, cats, mice—everything. Is that clear? I don't care what it is. Every living thing."

> "When I say I want the house cleaned, I mean I want it cleaned. I want everything living inside that house cleaned out."

"Mice?"

"Whatever the fuck it is, I don't care. I don't want no mice in there—no ticks, no horses, nothing. That's the deal. You liquidate whatever is in there for your five hundred. If you leave one thing alive you'll have broken the contract."

"We don't have a contract."

"La chingada. Of course we have a contract. It's written in our heads. Or do you want to stop at a lawyer's?"

"All right, we have a contract."

"That we do. And if you break it, I'll come for you. You can depend on that. I don't give my money away freely."

They broke open two Modelos from Mendes's cooler on the backseat and drank to their agreement. The car seemed to speed up and soon the walls of crazed pipestem cactus, the fields of walnut trees, and the abandoned motels sped by faster, with less consequence. Angel felt like sleeping, but Mendes turned on the radio and the mariachi kept them awake.

By five they were at a wide, shallow river spanned by a metal bridge and on the far side of it were what looked like railway cars parked in gardens of wild cactus and converted into slum homes. Sure enough, they drove over tracks. Beyond them was an older surfaced road that swerved upward toward sharp-tipped volcanic mountains whose lower slopes were dusted with the pale green of irrigated fruit trees. They tore up it nonchalantly, the radio blaring, and they saw the shadows lengthening from the base of the trees when they were among them.

As the mountain road rose and the earth grew more bare, they came to the house that Mendes intended to visit. It was a ranch-style villa set within high walls crenelated with broken bottle glass. A driveway led to an adobe gateway with fancy iron scrollwork. Mendes stopped the car on the side of the arterial road, however, and suggested that Angel walk up to the gate so as not to make too much noise. He should, if at all possible, slip into the house quietly. Mendes gave him the code to the outer gate and the key to the house itself.

"I use my bare hands, then?" Angel snorted as he got out of the car.

The sun hit him directly and he felt his knees weaken.

"I can give you a small axe I have in the back if that'll help."

"An axe?"

"Yes, a small one for chopping wood. It'll serve, no?"

Mendes got it out for him, and they stood for a moment in the baking sun, blinking at each other. Somewhere between them was a desperate, hangman's humor that could not be articulated, a mutual reproach that had no substance because they were still, after all, strangers. *Better that way*, both were thinking.

"I'll wait in the car," the real estate agent said.

Angel walked to the gate and punched in the code; the gates swung open and he strolled through them to a low, Spanish-style villa with tiled roofs. There were faded, pale brown lawns arid with neglect and a few pieces of garden gnomery, a small toy windmill and an empty pool. He picked his way along the shell path, eyeing the untrimmed edges of the lawns and the windows of the villa, where lilac curtains were drawn, and when he was at the door he paused and listened and heard the sound of an aircraft passing, but far out of sight. He pressed his ear to the door.

The key worked smoothly. Inside, the hallway was surfaced with monochrome stone and there was a chandelier with smoked-glass shades. He turned it on. All the windows were closed and the living room was stifling, immersed in darkness. The sofas and armchairs were covered with sheets, the coffee table wrapped in plastic. On the mantelpiece stood a plaster Jesus of the flowing Aryan variety, its eyes turned toward the very place where Angel was standing. The coffee table was piled with magazines neatly stacked. He went into the middle of the room, clutching the increasingly meaningless axe. It occurred to him that Mendes had spooked him for fun and that this was just a routine matter with a very slight risk of an unpleasant surprise, a risk that the cautious agent had not wanted to take himself. The axe, therefore, was symbolic. He laid it down on the nearest armchair and considered his curious situation.

It was hot inside the house and it was clear that no one had been there in some time. He ventured into the kitchen, which still smelled of long-gone gingerbread, and into the dining room, where mass-produced acrylic paintings of waterfalls hung on the walls. The table was glossy and no dust had accumulated upon its surface. From there a narrow corridor led to a series of bedrooms. The doors were closed but not locked and he opened them one by one, peering inside. The curtains were all closed here as well and the windows fastened. Cushions lay on the little beds. At the end of the corridor, visible through an open door, was a kind of nursery with large windows through which the sun blazed. He walked toward it and as he did so he heard a muffled sound, like that of something rubbing against a soft wall. From it came a sweet, different smell that set it apart from the musty deadness of the rest of the house. He came to the threshold and pushed the door open farther, then looked down at a large bag lying in the middle of the floor between two baby pens.

The bag was made of a dark green material like that of a military duffel bag, and it had drawstrings that were tied tight but leaving a narrow aperture. Below this opening there lay a saucer of water. As he entered the room, whatever was in the bag stirred more frantically, sensing his presence. A subdued moaning made Angel want to speak to it reassuringly, and he stooped at once and held out a hand, silent and afraid. The bag shuffled and it was clear in some way that there was a human inside it. He was about to talk to this person but something held him back and he straightened himself and glanced with a sudden panic through the large windows whose blinds were raised. He could see a dusty backyard filled with large ornamental saguaro. The metal barrier around it had rusted slightly and a child's climbing frame stood forlornly on a floor of dark sand. On the side of the green bag there was a single patch of blood, circular and moist, and around it there lay a few grainy pellets of what looked like dried dog food.

He retreated to the door and he thought, with a slow anguish, about the axe lying on the chair in the living room. It would be easy to pick it up, turn it again in his palm, and get used to its weight. He would need to swing it only once and it would all be over—it would be no harder than crushing a melon. But that split second of cool violence would change the story of his life forever. He could not be sure, however, that he would have a conscience about it. It was equally possible that he would not. He tried to calculate, then, but as the heat pressed in on his temples and his hands began to weaken, the will to do it quickly dissolved and he became superstitious again. He was sure that the ghost would follow him all his life.

Quietly, he closed the door and retraced his steps back to the living room, nervous as he listened to the room behind him while his mind tried to reach forward into the space of an impossible future.

In the living room he parted the curtains and peered down the drive toward the gate, through which he could see the road and the front fenders of the car. He went back to the chair and picked up the axe, but it dithered in his grip. "Get your five hundred bucks," he thought to himself. "You won't even see its face. It's just an animal in a sack." He turned and went back to the corridor, his eyes beginning to dim, and the handle of the axe shifted in the sweat that came off his hand.

> The bag shuffled and it was clear in some way that there was a human inside it.

Halfway down the corridor, however, he stopped again and tried to think more clearly. He had been tricked, but surely the trick could be turned the other way? Turning the axe slowly in his hands, he reconsidered, and gradually he realized that he was not going to cross the Rubicon. It was a vast chasm to cross, but its vastness was not even perceptible; it was more like the desert itself, formless and immersing, uncrossable. To kill was to enter a solitude as great as that.

"That bastard," he said aloud. "Five hundred for that?"

Turning on his heel, he went back to the living room and threw the axe into the same chair. There were a multitude of risks, but they could be calculated in seconds. He walked out into the declining sun, slammed the door shut behind him, and strode boldly back down to the gate.

The car was still parked in the same place and Mendes sat on the hood calmly smoking a cigarillo.

"Well," he said, looking up.

"You bastard, you knew there was a dog in there."

Angel got into the car as if furious and Mendes lethargically got in as well, grinning from ear to ear.

"You took the challenge," he said as he put the key into the ignition. "All I asked you to do was clean the house. Nothing wrong with that."

"Get me as far away from here as you can."

"Anything you say, my friend, anything you say. As long as the house is cleared we can leave."

"It's cleared."

They drove south for an hour. As night swept in they saw dark green mountains shaped like stalactites in the distance, the end of the desert. Lights rose up out of the dusk, towns spread along the highway like fossilized rubbish, corrals of horses slit by arc lamps and districts of bars where those five hundred dollars would go a long way. Mendes pulled over just outside of town and opened the trunk. There was a suitcase with money and he pulled out five hundred. Angel got out also, and it occurred to him that he might as well be on his way. Yet he had to keep his cool, to make sure that his companion believed completely in his depravity. He wanted to disappear into this commodious hellhole with its lollipop bar signs and ample motels, and he wanted to never see Mendes's little metallic eyes ever again. He could almost taste the freedom and modest solvency that lay just ahead of him. It was like edging along the rim of a giant crater toward a safe path downward, the rocks slipping under his feet.

"If I find you didn't clear up, Angel, the others will come and find you."

"Shit," Mendes said suddenly as he handed over the money. "What about the axe? We forgot the axe."

"What about it? I left it there on purpose."

"You left it?"

"Yes. It's evidence—it's better left there."

Mendes considered this and reluctantly began to nod.

"Yeah, I guess you're right. Still, I wonder if I should go back and get it."

"I wouldn't bother, hombre. It'll give you bad dreams."

Mendes looked at him with a cold eye.

"Bad dreams? I get them anyway."

He hesitated about going back, and finally he said, "To hell with it" and sauntered back to the driver's seat.

"Where you going now?" he called over the roof of the car to Angel.

"Into this here pueblo. I figure I earned some relaxation after what you made me do."

"I guess you did. So we're parting ways."

"I reckon we are."

Mendes waved and said a curt "Adios."

When he was seated and the car was humming he spoke through the opened passenger window.

"If I find you didn't clear up, Angel, the others will come and find you."

"Let them come. Everything is in order."

Angel kept his tone cool, and his eyes did not panic.

"Sure it is. Have fun with your five hundred, *cabrón*. I am driving on to Mazatlán all night!"

He left Angel standing by the road. After the taillights of the Pontiac diminished, Angel walked over between the tamarisk trees and dipped down a track that led into the town. It was a short walk.

He went to a hotel and got a cheap room on the third floor. He took off his boots and shirt and washed himself down with a flannel soaked in hot water. He counted out the money again and then a second time just to fill himself with the satisfaction of it. Then he packed it into his travel bag, wrapped in a plastic bag, and went down into the street to get a bottle of Sauza at a bar and a plate of radishes and flautas with guacamole. He was feeling anxious and exultant, with a slightly malicious pride.

Yet as he sat in the cantina eating his flautas, he was aware of the men glancing at him sideways, picking him apart. He felt he must look like a man with past temptation on his hands, but with a bright mark of coward-ice too. One who could not make the darker leaps. He wondered what had made him hold his hand. It was not fear. It was the certainty that his life would change either way but that there was a difference in the two roads that were suddenly open to him.

His hand began to shake and he drank half the bottle of Sauza as he ate, and then finished it at his leisure. The children threading their way between tables with bunches of radishes also seemed to know what was in his eye, and beyond it. A drifting fatalism only half aware of itself. It was just a question of roads, those loose ends that cross landscapes belonging to others. At the crossroads, one waited and trembled. But one could not go back along the same road.

Having eaten, he went in search of a poker game in one of the bars. He played until eleven, losing steadily, pulling out his twenty-dollar bills and drinking at an equivalent pace, and then he went to a fairground and walked among the machines, eating bags of *nuez fina* and shooting toy rifles at teddy bears. Before long he was at another gambling table and losing still more. He laid down heavier bets and soon he had lost four hundred dollars. By one in the morning he was drunk and agitated and unaware of where he was. The good old boys played him along; they could see that poker was not his game.

When he was out of cash he walked back to the hotel, staggering around packs of dogs and garbage dumps singing to himself and carrying the night's last bottle of mescal. It was good that he had paid for the hotel in advance. He had enough for tomorrow's bus to nowhere. He climbed up to the roof of the hotel, where there was a hammock, and crashed into it with the bottle in his lap. It must have been only a few hours that he half slept, observing, or so he thought, brilliantly lit pellet-shaped objects high in the night sky, tiny zeppelins lit by a second moon that no one knew about. He stretched himself out and relaxed, waiting for first light, listening to the sound of the rattling cicada-heavy trees and the tree frogs deep inside the fields. He was certain, or as certain as he could be, that by morning he would be dead and his limbs scattered among hungry crabs.

The following morning, though, he didn't die at all. The gracklings woke him, and the sound of children in a garden next door. There was a brightness in his mind, a hardness of purpose, refreshed by sleep. He found that his body was all in one piece and moreover he still had some of his money left; he decided, then, to stay in the town and play what was left to him.

The town came alive only at the end of the afternoon, as the insects subsided and the painful glare seeped out of the streets. The back lots of the houses were filled with manzanilla oaks from which tires were hung on ropes. Little girls swung inside them, like fish on hooks. When he was in the street he walked under shimmering red coral trees, with the hum of mariachi coming from the gardens. At times he was alone in the street, and his neck crawled with anxiety at the thought that he was being watched.

The men stood in the cantinas, rocking on their heels and chewing pickled carrots. They turned to watch him go by. One of them, half gringo by the look of him, a mix of *gabo* and Mexicano, called out into the street, as if addressing only his moving shadow:

"Que onda, gabacho? Tabacha la gabacha?"

Their laughter followed him, a dog snapping at his heels.

He went without dinner, not even a beer, and joined a card game near a small fairground. It was much the same crowd as the night before, and they teased him as he drew up his chair and accepted a free Modelo.

The game went on for hours to the sound of a jukebox. Slowly he began to win back what he had lost and when he had gotten to seven hundred he quit and bought the table a round of Sauza shots and walked back into the heat of the street. He turned the first corner, not knowing where he was going, and walked and walked until he came to the first of the arroyos, glittering under a half-moon. There he stopped and counted his cash, feeling a vivid satisfaction that fate could turn this way and that. It was still early and he thought he had seen a garage by the road where he could score a secondhand car for a couple of hundred. He walked there by the back streets, coming through a large lot decorated with pennants where old cars awaited buyers.

He paid the two hundred and drove out of the lot in a rusted Saber. It was filled with trash and the seats ran with oil, and a mile out of town he stopped by the roadside and cleared it out. This was the same road by which he and Mendes had come, the only road that ran past that town, and he had already forgotten where it came from and where it went to. He thought it went from northeast to southwest, but he had never seen it on a map; it was just straight and inflexible as it cut across the desert, going from one unknown town to the next. He remembered the Pemex stations infrequently positioned along its length, the dust storms and the whitewashed posts set into the hard shoulder, and the women selling gorditas in the shade of blue trees. It went on forever and ever and at the end of it was another room in a hotel where they would find him eventually, but just like a card game he would never know when and nor would they. It was, after all, the same camino real that had made Mendes rich and that might, one dark night, make him rich as well. It was paved with silver as well as dust and as he drove on toward La Mira he wondered even if his luck might change again. 🔹

Patricia Spears Jones

SELF-PORTRAIT AS MIDNIGHT STORM

Tossing the steel mesh trash cans is so much fun
Not as much as juggling broken umbrellas
Or rocking the yellow taxies or the last of the Lincoln Town Cars
Ferrying passengers drenched and stimulated

The start of a new day and the pitch is black with stimulation
SHIRR SHIRR SHIRR SHIRR   my sheets of rain
SHIRR SHIRR SHIRR

Oh look at the angry boys drunk and holy as they try to mimic storm
The really large guy's huge fist hits a bus shelter's carousel

It pebbles to the sidewalk, hundreds of green nuggets
His holy hand unblemished by blood. Foolish boys

Foolish boys, your anger is no storm and your howling
Bears little glamour—the wolves in your throats have long since left you

And here in the rain, your pain is small, durable and yet
The pebbles scatter about reminders of uglier private deeds.

As for my winds, my rain, my tossing back the moon's soft gleam
Means little to windows stood still storm after storm—centurions

Of design. They raise my ire and lash lash lash I throw against
Glass; the sash a square reflection of domestic armature.

As for the painted wood doors—hey are so easily broken.

FICTION

I, Buffalo

Vauhini Vara

The event in question took place at the end of the summer. I don't recall which day. That summer the days failed to distinguish themselves from one another, and given that failure, I don't see why I should do the distinguishing for them. I can tell you that this anonymous day began warmly. I know this because I began the day on the bus and recall perching on the edge of the seat so that my thighs wouldn't stick to the plastic. I had woken early and, unable to sleep, decided to go to the park.

The only other people on the bus were a young black woman and her son, who sat across from me. The mother wore a fur coat, and the boy sat on her lap facing me with the hem of his mother's coat tight in his fist. He might have been four years old.

"Hot day for a coat like that," I said to the mother.

"Pardon?" the mother said defensively, as if I had cast an accusation.

"Hot day," I said. "I'm going to Golden Gate Park."

The mother ignored me. The boy fidgeted and squirmed on her lap and, finally, his mother said tiredly, "Baby, you want a grenade?"

The boy looked up at her with delight and nodded.

"What do you say?" she said.

"Momma. Give me a grenade."

"Nuh-uh. What do you say?"

"Please, Momma. Give me a grenade."

The mother seemed satisfied with this. She said, "All right," and reached into her purse.

As I watched her fumble, I realized I was sweating. The heat was part of it, but I was also starting to feel anxious. I had my hand on the bell cord, ready to pull at any time, as if it were some sort of alarm, but when the mother drew her hand from the purse and opened it to the boy, her thick-lined palm was empty.

"Here you go, baby," said the mother.

The boy took the imaginary grenade, pulled on an imaginary pin, and the next thing I knew, he had his eyes fixed on me and his arm pulled back. A gasp flew from my lips, and one of my own arms threw itself up in defense. I put it this way because they, the gasp and my arm, seemed to act of their own accord. I never would have done such a thing myself.

The boy froze, then turned to look at his mother, who shook her head at me.

"Child's just playing. Dang."

"I'm sorry. I've got a hangover."

I've always had a habit of sharing too much with strangers. In my youth, my mother coached me against this, and for a long time I held back. But over the past eight months, my opportunities for con-versation had been limited. No more morning banter with the man and the dog. No more phone calls with clients. I couldn't help it.

> I haven't lied since I took an oath, long ago, to behave in a manner consistent with the truth.

"I don't drink," the mother said through pious pursed lips. "Haven't in five years." She indicated, with her chin, the boy.

"That's good," I said. "Nothing good comes of it." I added, "You hear stories like that—a woman has a child, and it saves her life." I wanted badly for the mother to think well of me. "I like your coat," I said, when she didn't respond.

But she didn't respond to that, either—only pushed a big horse's breath of air through her nostrils, then turned her gaze toward the front of the bus and sat silently.

Nothing good does come of it. I wasn't lying about that, nor am I lying about anything else that happened that day. I haven't lied since I took an oath, long ago, to behave in a manner consistent with the truth. At the time I found the language strange—that I behave not necessarily in a truthful manner but only in a manner consistent with the truth—but after a while I got used to it.

That was a long time ago.

Still, I know some facts consistent with the truth.

I am a woman. I am thirty-six years old.

At the time of the event, my apartment had been recently vacated by the others who had formerly inhabited it with me—a forty-four-year-old man from Oregon and a sixteen-year-old dog of unknown breed. The man was a hopeful and bighearted man who demanded much goodness of others and was therefore often disappointed. I trusted him completely.

He had taken the dog, too.

They left behind them a great and holy emptiness. It resembled the alarming emptiness that cathedrals and mosques hold for those of us who believe in nothing beyond what is proven to exist. We feel ourselves surrounded only by unfilled space. That's where I lived at the time of the event.

> Any addict who says she's not ashamed is lying to you or to herself. I believe it makes matters worse if you don't fit a particular profile.

I awoke that afternoon to the smell of spoiled fish and a fierce headache, and I could remember nothing of what had transpired between the bus and my awakening. Not a single detail. The morning on the bus seemed as far away as another continent.

This was not, I'll admit, an altogether alien feeling. I'll be direct. I've blacked out many times in my life. I was a teenager when it began. I'm ashamed of this. Any addict who says she's not ashamed is lying to you or to herself. I believe it makes matters worse if you don't fit a particular profile. You spend your days all buttoned up in your white shirt and pressed pants and iron-flattened hair like a perfect productive citizen. It's not a lie—it's not as if colleagues say, "Are you an addict?" and you say, "No way!" Still. *Fraudulent*—that's probably the term.

The smell of spoiled fish brought a couple of details back. At some point earlier in the day, I recalled, I had opened a take-out box of sushi and a bottle of wine. I had finished the wine. I had vomited.

That's all I had.

My apartment has two floors, which makes it sound larger than it is. I woke in my bed in the bedroom, which is upstairs, with the door open to the hallway. It seemed that the smell came from the hallway. I ventured out there and found that my hunch was correct: out in the hallway, the smell was truly noxious, as if the entire, brackish marine world had washed up into my apartment. I felt a prick of recollection: something had gone wrong. I hadn't reached the toilet in time; I hadn't reached a garbage can; I hadn't found my way to the kitchen sink.

But where had I done it, then?

Downstairs, the smell was fainter—enough that my sense of urgency diminished. In the kitchen, the sun shone warmly onto the countertop. The sky that day was fogless and clear and blue. I checked the living room, ducking to inspect the fireplace for good measure, but saw nothing. I felt clearheaded and alert as I went through these motions, but as soon as I became aware of this, my anxiety welled up again. I'd been through enough evenings like this. I knew the hangover was only dormant. It would surely come alive at some point later in the night. *Good God*, I thought. How had I slept so long?

That's when my sister called.

They were on their way up from Los Angeles for the weekend.

"Who?" I accused.

She and Sam and Mara, she said. Right now they were outside of Sacramento.

"You're staying here?"

"You're asking?"

"This is an ambush. Whose idea was this?"

"Where do you want us to stay? The Hyatt?"

"Did they put you up to it?"

"Oh my God. Are you seriously that paranoid? Hold on. She's being paranoid. Hold on. Mara's got an audition. She's all excited. Sam says we'll be there in a couple hours."

"Cool," I deadpanned.

"You act like you don't want us to come. Mara wants to know why you don't want us to come."

"Tell Mara it's because I know you have ulterior motives."

"She doesn't know what that means, ulterior motives. Hold on. Nothing, Mara. She says she does want us to come. Hold on. Mara wants to know what's for dinner."

"Dinner?" I said. "Pizza?"

"Takeout?"

"No. I don't know why you'd assume that."

"I'm not assuming anything. We get takeout all the time."

"It's not takeout," I said.

Because I know how to make pizza. In fact, I'd already had the idea earlier that week at the grocery store when I came across the cheap premade dough sitting next to the hummus like a bagged breast. I had tried to pick out good tomatoes for that purpose. To make good pizza sauce, you have to pick tomatoes that smell a certain way, according to an Italian friend of mine—yeasty, my friend said, almost like beer. So I had held a tomato to my face and sniffed. The tomato smelled only like itself—tomatoey. I had picked up another one and smelled, then another, then another. My mind had latched onto this one word, *yeasty*, and wouldn't allow me to move on. *Yeasty*, said my mind, *yeasty*, and finally I just picked the best-looking tomatoes, the reddest and closest to bursting, and continued to the meat department.

By the time I hung up with my sister, I'll admit, I'd forgotten all about the smell. I started making the pizza. I chopped the tomatoes. I rolled out the dough. I had a great satisfying sense of being a civilized person in a civilized world. Only when it was all ready to go did I pour myself a drink. A glass of wine. I can handle, you understand, a glass of wine.

At the sound of the doorbell, panic rose in my throat. I lit a vanilla-scented candle and set it on the kitchen table. The candle had already burned down nearly to the bottom. When I opened the door, and Mara came bounding inside and took a running leap into my arms, I can't explain the feeling I had. I want to call it euphoric. But I know how that makes me sound. As if this might have been the onset of some kind of episode.

"Auntie Sheila!" she said into my shoulder.

"Mars Bar!" I said. I'll tell you—I had nearly forgotten how much I love my niece. My Mars Bar. When was the last time we'd seen each other? I never saw her these days. Mara was wearing what looked like pajamas—a dinosaur-patterned jumper with built-in footies. Sam and Priya stood shoulder to shoulder in the doorway. They were the same height and had grown to look alike over the ten years of their marriage—the same mildly skeptical smile, the same slight stoop of their shoulders. "Let's play!" I said.

"It's almost bedtime," Priya said.

"She has to wake up early for the audition," Sam added.

Mara is a child actress. She auditions for all sorts of roles. I knew they sometimes traveled. But San Francisco? What kind of a film got made in San Francisco? Who had ever heard of that? Once Woody Allen made a movie in the Haight. A colleague of mine saw him at Zam Zam. So maybe this wasn't only a pretense for checking in on me. Maybe our parents hadn't put Priya up to this after all. I started to let my guard down. Then Sam sniffed at the air, and I felt a sharp synaptic twitch as I remembered the vomit. I shifted Mara's weight onto my hip.

"Come in, come in," I said to them all. "Give me your coat," I said to my sister. "I like your coat."

Et cetera.

I was trying to distract them from the smell.

"Give me your coat, give me your bags," I said. "Give me all of it—I'll put it up in the room. How was the drive?"

They didn't give me any of it. "Don't be so formal," Sam said. "We'll take it up, no problem."

But the smell, I told myself. *But you don't want to act weird,* I answered myself. "Whatever," I said.

> When I got off the bus, I stopped and bought a little bottle of bourbon. The smallest, cutest bottle.

While they went upstairs to put their bags down, Mara wandered around the living room, picking up various objects—a snow globe on the television, a framed photo of me and my ex that I couldn't bring myself to take down—and setting them down again. She wore enormously thick eyeglasses, and her hair was done up in a pair of uneven pigtails. Glasses aside, she looked strikingly similar to how Priya had looked as a child, despite Mara's bland-faced whitey of a father.

I suddenly remembered another part of what had happened between morning and evening.

"Hey, kiddo," I said, "you want to see a buffalo?"

"I've seen one," she said.

"Are you sure?" I said. "A real one?"

"They have them at the zoo," she said.

"This is different," I said. "These ones are in the park."

Because that's what I had been going to do that morning. I was on this kick. I had been treating myself to the sights of San Francisco that I had been too busy to visit during my working life. When I got off the bus, I stopped and bought a little bottle of bourbon. The smallest, cutest bottle. A child could hold it in one fist. The bourbon glowed from within like liquid sun. It took all my willpower to put the bourbon back in its paper bag and to hold that bag tight till I got to where I was going. Good God, it was hot. When I got to the paddock, I was drenched in sweat. There were supposed to be nine of them—three adults, six children, all female, because the park had moved the males when they figured out the obscene amount of humping all the males and females were doing—but I saw only one. She had the top-heavy build of a boxer—this barreled chest, these thick shoulders, this impenetrable wall of a forehead, all balanced on top of four matchstick legs. For her to stand on those legs and get from one place to another should have been impossible. It defied all good sense. Yet that's what she did. She walked with great grace, as if nothing mattered but to walk. Her shoulders pumped with strength. Her legs, truth be told, tottered a little. When she came to a patch of yellow grass where some wildflowers had sprouted, she stopped and lowered her head as if for benediction. She was massive and shaggy and humpbacked and ancient. Her grace made me feel like the smallest of creatures. She ate the flowers.

> Who was I to allege that I existed? For what reason should I exist? Where was the proof?

I pressed my face to the grid of the wire fence, cool against my skin, and I called out to her. "Hey, girl," I said. "Hey."

She ignored me. Truly, it was as if I wasn't there. And maybe I wasn't, I started to feel. There was not another human being in sight. Only me and the great animal. Who was I to allege that I existed? For what reason should I exist? Where was the proof?

And it's true that it was hot that day. And it's true that I was sipping from my bottle. But the strangest thing happened. Having eaten, the buffalo raised her head again, and I felt a great topspin of joy at this. She continued her walk in my direction. She was so close I could see her eyebrows, and this, too, seemed miraculous. An instant later, she tumbled to the ground on her side as if felled. Her body sent up a puff of brown dirt. In that moment, I had a really strange experience. I felt as if I had fallen to the ground myself. I could taste the dust in the air. Every muscle in my body relaxed. I was not a thinking being. I was free. This lasted for only an instant. Then the buffalo rolled onto her feet and stood, and I was myself again. I stood there gripping the fence waiting for the feeling to return, but it didn't.

Mara came across as very comfortable in her own skin, the way child actors often do.

"You want to know something interesting?" she said.

"What?"

"The Donners ate each other. You know them? The Donner Party?"

I was taken aback. I hadn't remembered her being this gruesome. By the time I thought of what to say—"Not personally," I wanted to say, to be a little funny—Mara had moved on. She was wandering around the room, every once in a while asking a question: "Who's this?" Or, pointing the remote control at the TV, "How does this work?" She moved really fast. I couldn't keep up.

"Sheila?" she said after some time.

"Yeah?"

"What's that smell?" she said.

"What smell?" I said. "Must be your upper lip."

Over dinner, they explained that Mara's audition was for a film about the Oregon Trail. Mara had been doing her research to get into character—getting Priya to take her to the local library and read to her from musty hardcovers. That was how she had discovered the story of the Donners, who had eaten each other.

"Gross," Priya said.

"I wouldn't eat you," I said to Mara, "unless I was really hungry."

"Come on!" Priya said.

I chewed on a pizza crust, took a swig of beer, and grabbed another slice. I had fled Mara's question about the smell by giving my flippant answer, then running to the kitchen to put the pizzas in the oven. Now all seemed nice again. *We'll go see the buffalo tomorrow*, I thought. *Maybe tomorrow the others will be out.* I would say to Mara, "Did you know that the American bison is the largest mammal in North America? Technically, they're bison. At one point there were sixty million of them in the United States alone. That was before the United States existed. Then people showed up and hunted them so bad that there were only a couple hundred of them left. They were about to go completely extinct. So some people decided to save the bison. They got together and put a bunch of them in Golden Gate Park, and maybe some other places, too, and all these bison had a bunch of babies, and now they're not even close to going extinct." All of this was true. I had been surprised by this information, which I'd found on a big, faded tablet in the park.

"Do you know what 'extinct' means?" Priya asked Mara. "It's when every single animal of one kind of animal dies."

"Yeah, like the Donner Party," Mara said.

"Oh, God," Priya moaned. "Sam."

"She does this great cannibalism routine," Sam said. He took a giant bite of his pizza and chewed with his mouth open. Spit and cheese sprayed from between his teeth. "Nom-nom-nom," he said, and when he finished, he patted his stomach. I laughed. He had grown one of those soft, domestic paunches. My own, lost man had one of those. A place to cup your hand at night. A place consistent with the truth if ever there was such a place. My God, I had lost it. "Method acting," he said—this other man, Priya's man, said this.

"Don't make fun of me!" Mara clattered her fork against her plate. It seemed she would cry, but she started laughing shyly.

"Don't mess around, you guys," Priya cried. "Sheila, Sheila, this gruesome streak of hers, it's actually sort of freaking me out."

At first, I felt a surge of pride that my little sister would still confide in me, after all that had happened. Then I wondered if my sister was implying something else. The truth was this: I had been a dark and gruesome child. I would persuade my poor baby sister to watch as I stretched a live worm with my fingertips until the tiny creature snapped in two or allowed a mosquito to rest on my thigh and fill itself up with my blood before thwacking my palm onto the sucker and smearing the resultant brown gunk across Priya's face. But our parents had ignored this, in light of my excellence at school and in piano lessons, and had focused on berating Priya for her learning difficulties and clumsy-fingered musical efforts.

Now, I recognized what was happening: Priya must have been waiting to find me in a moment of weakness. Now, here was that moment, and here was Priya's chess move: "this gruesome streak"—the implication being that there was a direct line, one that our parents had willfully ignored, between my own childhood gruesomeness and my recent fall from grace.

Oh, that.

Fine.

I might as well tell you about it: the so-called fall from so-called grace.

My scandal involved a high-profile, married client. He had been in San Francisco on business for a day and a night, and we had agreed to meet for a drink at the martini bar atop his hotel. We were supposed to discuss a case involving asbestos in a housing complex in the Western Addition, but after a few drinks, we discovered that we had both spent part of our twenties in Shanghai, and all of a sudden, we were trading obscenities in Mandarin. I turned to look out at the sunset. This was a historic hotel, the kind of place at which girls were said to have sat in their sailors' laps before sending them off into the cold Pacific mist, and, thinking of this, I slid my hand across the table until my fingertips rested atop his own.

I don't know what to say.

I was in a sort of fix with respect to my man.

We had been together for ten years. But recently he had proposed to me, and after this, I had found myself hating him. I hated him for wanting to commit himself to me forever. He was the only person who knew me to my core. Yet he would have himself committed to me forever. Was he some kind of idiot?

I had accepted, of course.

But now this.

The truth was this: I had been a dark and gruesome child.

Before long, my client and I were back in his hotel room, and I was sharing with him several lines of cocaine, and I flirted with him by admitting that for other clients—who I at least had the good sense not to name, though all that came out in the end—I charged a lot of money for my drugs.

Then we were jumping on the bed. We were touching the ceiling with our fingertips. We were having so much fun. I was sucking on his thigh. This was a foreplay trick that my man with the dog liked. My client was making these sounds. My client sounded different from my man. He also looked different. He had this massive orb-like stomach and a pink coloring to my man's slim brown self.

I was considering this when I realized that my client was sobbing. The sight embarrassed me, especially because I had mistaken his boyish little gasps for noises of anticipatory pleasure.

"Could you just hold me?" he whispered.

The fun seemed over much too quickly.

But I shimmied up the bed's twisted sheets and allowed him to lay his bearded head on my chest and whisper about how little he loved his wife, whom he respected for her intellect but with whom he had no romantic chemistry. His tears and snot salted the valley between my breasts. But the kids were still young. They were all he had. He pulled his phone from his pocket. Would I like to see some pictures? On Facebook? Maddie at the beach. Rico on his birthday. It was for them that he made his living taking advantage of the vulnerability of undocumented immigrants, because, we might as well both face the facts, lawyer and client, this was what we were doing. "I plead guilty!" he said. "Ha-ha!"

At this, my horror was complete. I finally stood and brought a hand towel from the bathroom and dabbed forcefully at his tears and snot.

"This didn't happen," I said. "I swear to God."

My indiscretion was discovered within days: due to a slip of the finger, the client accidentally sent a drably suggestive e-mail meant for me (he wanted me to know that he couldn't stop thinking about my mouth) to the office manager in my firm, who was also named Sheila. Soon after that, the client confessed all—I have no idea why he did such a thing, but he did. I was fired. Of course, I had to tell my man. You know the rest, about his departure with the dog, and the emptiness.

> "The smell?" I said, still standing at the sink. I said, like it was nothing, "I threw up somewhere."

It was the cocaine that turned them all against me. I guess it was his first time. People could say about the other behavior: *Well, it happens to the best of us.* But the best of us don't operate side businesses selling drugs to law clients. The best of us—maybe you're among them—feel that if attorneys, who take an oath to behave in a manner consistent with the truth, go around selling drugs, then everything is permissible. Well, what if it is? Can there be a fall, I ask you, if there is no grace?

I went to the sink to refill the pitcher of water. "That's how kids are," I said. And I feinted: "In fact, just this morning on the bus, a little kid tried to throw a fake grenade at me." After freezing like a little statue, his arm pulled back, the boy had dropped his hand to his thigh. While his mother had spoken, he'd filled his cheeks with air and slowly expelled it, meanwhile drumming his fingers on his leg.

"It's shocking," Priya said, "how many irresponsible adults there are in this world."

None of us spoke. We bent our heads over our pizzas, we munched our crusts from end to end, we pinched between our fingers the bits of sausage and pepper that had fallen to our plates and ate those, too.

Sam sighed and went to the fridge for a second beer.

Priya burped. "Oh God," she said. "I'm tipsy."

"Are you kidding?" I said. "You're not drunk."

I hated those women who would have two drinks and claim to be drunk. *Ooh, my delicate constitution.* I couldn't believe my little sister had turned into one of them. And she used to be the one our parents worried about. *Keep an eye on her*, they told me. *She's not studying.* And now you looked her up online, and she had this great social media presence. She wrote about being a stage mom, or whatever you call it. She got invited to write these guest posts on these blogs. Meanwhile, an online search for my name turned up reams of lurid detail. I held out hope that other, more prominent Sheila Reddys would soon overtake me. Most of them seemed unlikely candidates: a self-published poet in Virginia, a doctor in Detroit, and three engineers—two in San Jose, one in the Seattle area. But some seemed promising. I had my eye on the freelance journalist who had recently published an essay in *Marie Claire* and the marketing vice president at Proctor & Gamble who, according to LinkedIn, had been slowly moving up the managerial chain. I prayed for the rise of those Sheilas.

Now, Mara spoke again. "Sheila, serious—what's that smell?"

Priya and Sam turned to look at me, and I stood to clear the table, making a noisy pile of the plates and then going to the sink to slide the scraps into the garbage disposal. I could feel pinpricks under my arms, and I wondered if I was visibly sweating. "What?" I said, but even as I spoke, I knew I sounded stupid. I had to confess. "The smell?" I said, still standing at the sink. I said, like it was nothing, "I threw up somewhere."

"Oh, Sheil," Priya said. I didn't know which was worse—my sister's passive aggression minutes ago, or her pity now.

"I don't know where it is," I said, feeling smaller than the smallest person ever to have existed. "It's weird," I said.

There was silence. Then Sam said, "That's okay!" He grinned. "That's okay, Sheil! It happens to everyone." Priya opened her mouth as if to protest—it does not happen to everyone—but Sam had already scraped back his chair and rolled up his sleeves. "We'll help you," he said.

I wandered around the kitchen. Priya was drawn to the laundry room. Mara went upstairs by herself.

"Found it!" she called out to us. We went scrambling up the stairs to where she stood peering down into the laundry chute. That dark limbo space of the house.

"Mara, move it!" Priya cried out. This was dirty business. Grown-ups only. Mara stepped back in alarm at the sharpness of her mother's tone, and the rest of us crowded around the laundry chute.

The vomit had dried middrip along one side of the chute into a purplish brown crust of yellowtail, tuna, and fish eggs, decorated with rice globules and seaweed bits.

"Whoa," Sam said.

And suddenly—just like that—I remembered.

I had found myself, after visiting the buffalo, in the BART station downtown. How had I gotten there? That I don't remember. It had been rush hour. This had felt strange, I remembered, to be there among you working people—you weary, bowed-backed working people, your fingers working your phones as if they were rosary beads: you who I once had been. You were not identical. I don't mean to suggest that you were. You were in fact quite the opposite—each of you so very different from one another, your private concerns yours alone. One woman perched in the hollow of a phone booth with an accounting textbook open in her palm. She pressed the other hand to her forehead and mouthed the words as she read. People passed by and didn't notice her, nor did she notice them. You were like trees to one another, or pylons in an obstacle course. You had once been trees and pylons to me, too.

But now, I was undergoing a change. I felt ghostlike that morning, as if I had left the world of the living and was now paying an invisible visit. I stood in one of the long and orderly lines and when the train screeched and shuddered into place, I closed my eyes against its wind and opened them only when the air stilled and I heard groans and sighs of frustration among my line mates. The door where we'd lined up was stuck shut—USE ANOTHER DOOR, said a sign—and now we all scrambled to the next car, and when I entered that car along with everyone, instead of staying put, I pushed open the door to the first one—the shut one—so that I could be in there alone.

There was a handful of others in the car, and we exchanged looks of complicity. And over the course of the ride I came to think of them all as my friends and was sorry when I left. I raised a hand in parting. Some of them raised hands back. And by the time I returned home, I'm pleased to admit: I was happy. Yes. Happy. I'd stopped to pick up some sushi and wine. Then I set the radio to play through all the speakers in my house, and I went to lie down on my bed. There was a French song on the radio. I don't speak French, but it was a nice song. The lyrics went something like

"Eska poo poo yay yay yay! Vuh shashay la moonay pay!" And I stripped and dropped my clothes to the floor, and I went through the closet, putting on outfit after outfit. I stood before the mirrored closet door and shimmied and sang. "Eska poo poo yay yay yay! Vuh shashay la moonay pay!" I stood in my pile of clothes, and I trembled and sweated and felt joyful. I lifted my breasts and felt the cool air on their undersides. And then I felt nauseated.

"Of course Mara was the one to find it," Sam said. "Your sense of smell hits its peak when you turn eight and declines when you hit your twenties." How Sam loved to make perfect sense out of everything strange and mysterious in the world. He looked at Mara, who, in the wake of my sister's rebuke, stood quietly and lip-tremblingly to the side. He put a hand on her shoulder and said, "The first step is to clean what we can reach from up here." He held the laundry chute open and peered inside. "Sheila," he said, "do you have a sponge?"

> I lifted my breasts and felt the cool air on their undersides. And then I felt nauseated.

I went down to the kitchen and got the dish sponge from next to the sink, then returned and handed it to Sam.

"Sam, let her do it herself," Priya said. "For fuck's sake. Mara, stay back."

"Oh, let me try," Sam said, and he gave Priya a look that was compassionate and trite. *Your sister is in trouble—we have to put aside our disgust and try to help.* Scrubbing with the dish sponge, he loosened and cleaned the crust around the top edges of the chute, and the fish smell tangled with the lavender scent of the detergent. But the vomit had dripped deep into the chute. Sam couldn't reach far enough to get all of it.

"I'll try," Priya said, avoiding my eyes. She took the sponge from Sam and stuck her arm into the chute, twisting at the waist to reach as far as she could. Her shirt lifted as she stretched, and I could see the light down of hair at the small of her back. Sam touched the small of Priya's back. *How bourgeois*, I thought, *for a husband to still be attracted to his wife.* "I can't get it," Priya said.

"My turn," I said. But I couldn't reach either.

The problem was that the space was too small for us; we were stymied at the shoulder. Priya had the idea to go downstairs to the laundry room and try to reach the vomit from below, and she took Sam with her to investigate while I stayed upstairs. Soon I heard my sister's voice bellowing up through the chute: all they could see were some drops of puke atop my towels in the laundry basket. "It's too far," Priya called. "It's all up there."

From the top of the chute I could see her poke a broomstick around. It made a hollow rattle. Mara crept closer, her eyes aglint. Was she thinking what I was thinking? I bent to her and waited for her to say it.

She did. "I could try," she whispered.

"You want to?" I whispered.

"I can?" she whispered. She touched her mouth.

"Shush," I whispered, "they'll hear. Let's get you in there." I handed the dish sponge to her. "Go at it, sweet pea."

> I suddenly felt worn out and dirty. I felt vomit on my palms; I smelled it in the air. It turned my throat sweet.

What I did was, I hoisted her up by the waist and let her shimmy into the chute. Then I was holding her by the thighs, then by the ankles. Only then—when I had her by the ankles, all of her weight in my hands—did I realize how heavy she was. A full-grown child. I felt it in my forearms. I felt it in my back. "Gross," Mara said in a voice that seemed echoey and overlarge.

"Mara?" Priya sang out from the laundry room—two trembling notes, rising low to high. She could probably see Mara from down there. I don't know why she said it as if it was a question. Mara didn't respond. She only grunted like a mechanic.

"Sheil?" Priya shrilled. Her voice rose. "Mara, you in there? Sheil?"

Then came Priya surging up the stairs with Sam on her heels. You want hysterical? Here was hysterical. "For God's sake, pull her up, Sheila!" she cried.

I hoisted Mara out by her ankles and deposited her on the carpet. Priya swooped in and picked Mara up in her arms.

"Mom, I'm fine," Mara said and squirmed out of Priya's grip. "Gosh," she said.

Standing, she smoothed her hair and scanned the faces of the adults. The smell of lavender swelled in the hallway, and for a moment, it was all we could smell.

"Done," Mara said. She sniffed and smiled. "Actually, I love vomit," she said.

"Good girl," I told her.

Back downstairs, we washed our hands in turn. We didn't speak. We didn't make eye contact. We sat on the couch. I suddenly felt worn out and dirty. I felt vomit on my palms; I smelled it in the air. It turned my throat sweet.

The Donners ate each other, I thought.

"Priya, I want to make you a martini," I said.

"I'm wasted," Priya said.

"You're sleeping here!" I said. "Who cares?"

"I'll have one," Sam said.

"Sam," Priya said.

I felt impatient. I went to the kitchen. I made the martinis and brought them back on a tray. Sam took one. Priya hesitated. Then she took one and I took one. I felt great as soon as the gin touched my lip. It was like swimming in a long, deep pool and finally getting to the end of the lane. You come up for air and feel great before you've even taken a breath, because you're anticipating all the breathing you're about to do. That's how I felt.

"Sam, you have mine," Priya said softly. "I actually don't want it."

"Aw, babe, I don't think I can," he protested. "Don't drink it, then."

She glared at him. I knew what she was doing. What she was doing was straight out of some textbook. Some idiot's guide. But I felt great and would not be made to feel less great. "I'll have it," I said, and I took the glass right out of her hand, and I had it. Right there, on the spot, I had it, and then I finished my own, and I felt, for the first time in months, a kind of triumph.

I sat back into the couch and watched Mara. She was building a fort. She had pulled the cushion from the easy chair and taken it to the wide space near the fireplace, where she dropped it. Now she went to the dining room table and got a heavy, tall-backed chair, which she carried, struggling, to the living room. Then she went back and got another, then another. All these she arranged into a tight enclosure. Finally she came and squeezed onto the couch between me and my sister and regarded her creation.

"Nice fort, kiddo," I said, reaching down to take a swipe at Mara's ear.

"Hey. It's a cave."

This struck me as a great thing for a child to say, smart and original. "It's a cave." I wondered what other thoughts were whirling around in my niece's head. I thought about all that I was led to believe in my childhood: olives are bad for you; if you don't brush your teeth at night, they will rot and fall out; blowing one's nose in a towel will leave a dark stain that can never be removed; children have two stomachs, one of which is reserved for dessert;

and so on. But Mara could not be deceived! This was not a fort! "It's a cave," Mara had said. "I love vomit," she'd said. I was struck hard by the force of my love for this child. Every other love of my life seemed small compared to this love. I grabbed Mara by her arm and pulled her to me. "You're perfect," I said.

"My arm," Mara said. "Stop."

"Sam," Priya said. She seemed tired and sad.

I let go. "Don't ever grow up," I said.

"Okay," Mara said, and she scampered across the room and ducked into the cave.

"Remember how we used to do that?" I asked my sister. "We used to make a fort and pretend to be wild animals living in there?"

"I wanted to be the lioness," Priya told Sam. She was doing this thing where she wouldn't talk to me.

"No. You liked being the boar. I did your hair."

"This one time," Priya told Sam, "she did my hair in a braid and then she took the gum out of her mouth and wrapped it around the bottom of the braid instead of using a hair tie, and our mom had to cut it out."

"Oh, come on," I said. "It wasn't tragic," I told Sam.

Mara came crawling out from her cave. She surveyed the room, plucked a knitted blanket off the armchair, and put it over the front opening of the cave to make a door. Then she disappeared again.

"She has an artist's mind," I said. "I was thinking tomorrow we could take her to Golden Gate Park."

"Can't," Priya said to Sam. "The audition."

"After the audition?" I asked.

"Maybe?" Sam said to Priya.

Priya squirmed. "There's something under here." We all stood, and Priya lifted the couch cushion. There, among the lint and the hair, was a brown apple core. Frankly, I couldn't remember the last time I had eaten an apple. Yet there it was.

"Oh, God, Sheila," Priya cried out. Her face contracted, and I was afraid she would start sobbing.

"Don't be a baby," I said. "It's just an apple core."

Priya put her hand to her mouth. She was really crying. She really was. I hadn't seen her cry, I realized, since we were small. I looked to Sam, who put his hands on her shoulders. "Shh," he told her. "She's okay," he told her.

I actually thought for a moment they were talking about me. I felt touched. I felt, for a moment, that all was not lost.

"She could have fallen," she said. "Jesus Christ."

Sam glanced up at me, then down at his hands. "Let's get some fresh air," he said. "I'll have a cigarette," he said.

Priya looked at the cave, at me, at him. Her gaze made a triangle. She tucked a loose strand of hair behind her ear and wrapped her arms around herself as if she was cold. "Okay," she said in a small voice.

I swear to you, the sound of her voice. It reached into me. It passed through some kind of barrier and got inside. I wanted to say something to her. But I didn't know what to say. What do you say? *I love you?* How insufficient. I couldn't. I couldn't even look at her. I don't even know what she looked like in that moment. But I felt so close to her. I don't know if she felt it. I guess she didn't. They stood. They put on their shoes. They went out the door. They shut it. All was quiet.

> I actually thought for a moment they were talking about me. I felt touched. I felt, for a moment, that all was not lost.

I stood. I sat. I stood again, stumbled, and fell to the floor. *Water*, I thought, and I went crawling to the kitchen. This was a good way to get from one place to another. I'd forgotten how good. I hadn't crawled in a long time. When I got to the sink I stood, steadied myself, and poured myself a glass of water. I drank. The water tasted healthful and mineral, as if I were sipping from the palm of God himself. The palm of truth. Your palm. I drank. I poured another glass. I drank and drank. I felt desperate. I remembered that I had shed my clothes earlier in the day and stood in the pile of shed clothes and sung. Now I mourned that moment and all the others that had died. I placed my glass on the counter and knelt on the floor, and once I was there, it seemed impossible that I could stand again. So I didn't. I got on my hands and knees. I padded across the kitchen and into the living room. My shoulders pumped. I felt nothing but the knowledge that I was to go to the cave. And when I arrived there and pulled back the blanket and peered inside, I found what I had known, on some level, I would find. There emanated from inside the cave—in the person of the child inside, may you bless her and keep her ever safe—the hot radiance of truth.

The cave was warm and dark and smelled of corn chips. The child lay curled on her side, her arms tucked at her chest, her cheek pressed to the floor. Her mouth hung open as she breathed, and a thin thread of drool dangled from the corner. Her bowed mouth was of the reddest red. I moved carefully into the cave, not touching the walls, and remained on my hands and knees before the sleeping child.

But I shouldn't say *I*.

I wasn't there.

The buffalo gazed upon the child and felt a deep sense of peace. The child's eyelids fluttered, and her mouth made little movements, and the buffalo held her breath and stayed still. Then the buffalo let herself fall down at the child's side and rolled so their bodies were close. She wanted to be closer still. She pressed her chest to the wings of the child's back, and she cupped in her paw the round of the child's belly, and she pushed her forehead to the child's soft neck, and she wept. For she had been alone for so long. And now this child with her warmth and goodness and her smell of childhood. Oh, God. Did she hold the child too close? Did she make some sounds that a child might find frightening? From outside the cave came the distant sound of a door opening and closing. The sound of a person calling the child's name.

What can I tell you?

An instant later, all would be lost—the walls of the cave torn asunder so that all the goodness and warmth dissipated; the child's mother flying in, pulling the child out from the buffalo's grasp. Then I lay alone. What more can I tell you? Good God, I would tell you if I were the buffalo, let it be. Enough with all these words. Enough with the endless questions and endless answers. It's cold out here in the kingdom of man. But it seemed, for a moment, that this one child's heat might warm a creature amid the dying of her species.

Mark Irwin

A FLY

zings through the century of a window all day
till dusk, then finds a light bulb to orbit. Yesterday
in the hospital I marveled at the newborns, pink
sacks of time, their faces scrunched with the future's
weight. Walking outside now, beyond the baled
alfalfa, I gaze up where a comet dashes like a mouse
across the kitchen floor of heaven, and there, just below
the Belt of Orion, the photo-ionized gas of the Trapezium
Cluster glows part red blood cell, part luminous wing.
As we get older each look in the mirror gets farther. "Come
back," they say. On the third floor of the ward I sat with Lonnie,
head shaved like a monk's, talking about that pond
in Pennsylvania where we once as lovers swam. Now
I stare and would like to part the glass of this sky's window.

PRIMER

When I learned to write it was spring. For trees I drew
short vertical lines with a circle resting on each. For birds
I drew small X's in each circle. That autumn I learned
to read words—*trees, birds*—while letters blew like leaves
across the earth. Now I write pages of words but underneath
I still hear trees, birds, and sometimes I'll circle a word
or X out another, or other times the page will kite
beyond my hands like a swallow and I'll remember
to press harder into each furrow because time is brief
and words make us easy, and sometimes if someone dies
I'll climb a tree, make a circle round it with my arms,
forgetting about words, then scream long into the roots of things.

PERCEBES

Jeff Koehler

Stalking the elusive Gooseneck Barnacle

There are certain sea creatures so star-tling in appearance, so seemingly inedible, that one wonders how anyone thought to scoop them from the rocks to eat. I doubt it was inspired by curiosity so much as desperation. What a surprise it must have been when those early foragers found such bizarre critters to be not only nontoxic but also delicious.

Walk through the seafood section of any covered food market in Spain, and it's clear that the Spanish kitchen ignores little from the sea or its shore, no matter how unappealing in appearance or how tiny the morsel of meat it might contain. Whatever can be caught, netted, or dug up, prized from the rocks or discovered cowering under them, finds its way to the market and, soon after, into the cooking pot. *Bígaro* (dime-sized sea "snails"), slimy sea cucumbers, and spiny sea urchins containing no more than an intense teaspoonful of brilliant orange roe are all displayed on chipped ice. So are murex shells—once fished for their purple dye (used in the robes of emperors, kings, and popes) and now boiled and served chilled with lemon wedges—and scuttling *nécoras*, small chocolate-brown crabs no bigger than one's palm, with a fine fringe of dark, damp hair.

But of all of Spain's seafood delicacies, the strangest is surely the finger-sized Galician gooseneck barnacle (*Pollícipes pollícipes*). Its leathery, tube-shaped black body is tipped on one end with a series of hard, overlapping nails, flat and shiny iridescent white, that come together in a curving point like a hoof; the other end adheres firmly to rock. Not many decades ago they were eaten with a whiff of poverty about them. Today they are not only the most expensive seafood in the market but also an epicurean symbol of taste and wealth. And while I see fewer people splurging on them in restaurants or buying them in the market, the price for top-quality Galician *percebes* has remained high during these last few years of deep economic hardship in Spain.

Gooseneck barnacles are not unique to Spain's coast. I have spent time among young men collecting them in the Western Sahara, where the desert meets the Atlantic in a shelving of sandstone cliffs; they thrive in the warmer water there, but tend to be skinnier, with less meat. They are also found in Canada and France, but stallholders in every Spanish market will tell you with authority and without hesitation that the best grow in Galicia, namely along the treacherous Costa da Morte ("Coast of Death") at the far northwest of the country. The area around the village of Corme, on Cabo Roncudo, is the preeminent spot.

This is one of Spain's wildest, most untamed places, a ragged coastline that inspires both awe and fear and arouses the highly religious and the highly superstitious. It is called "Fisterra" in Galician—"Finisterre" in Spanish—from the Latin *Finis-terrae*, "land's end." The Apostle Santiago (Saint James) appeared here in a stone boat guided by an angel, and ancient pilgrims along the Camino de Santiago would burn their clothes when they arrived, as a sign of purification that they had reached the end of the world. Standing on the westernmost point of the Iberian Peninsula, the pilgrims looked out at a forbidding watery expanse that swallows the sun as well as ships and sailors. Wrecks off this coast are legion: twenty vessels in a flotilla went down on November 28, 1596, taking 1,706 people with them. In September 1870, the HMS *Captain*, a masted turret ship of the British Royal Navy some 320 feet long, completed only that previous April, capsized, drowning 482. And how many smaller fishing boats with two or three men aboard—a couple of brothers, say, and a young nephew, his hands raw, his hand-me-down parka cinched at the waist with a leather belt—have disappeared beneath its frigid waves?

Some of the white crosses that dot the Costa da Morte's shoreline mark these lost fishermen. Others remember those who were gathering *percebes*.

I had been living in Spain for a decade before I began eating *percebes*, having been kept largely at bay by their astronomical price and their mystery (just how do you eat them?). Then, a couple of years ago, as I began working on a cookbook about traditional (which is to say, rural) Spanish food, my wife, two young daughters, and I spent the summer in Galicia. We stayed at first in Muros, quite far north on the west coast, in an attic space with views out over the fishing port and a small terrace on each side like clipped wings where we could sit, sheltered from the wind, and watch the boats return. Seagulls patiently wheeled above the trawlers, and the first fish were laid out on ice in the town market within an hour.

We frequently drove north along the Costa da Morte, looking for a secluded beach, a crescent of sand cradled into a nook of coast, or a market, or a restaurant for an inexpensive seafood lunch. We poked around ancestral fishing villages that live by the sea: huddled places of narrow lanes, a granite church, and a narrow bar where a dish of preserved cockles is set out with a glass of Albariño white wine. The road winds slowly along the unsheltered headlands among plunging cliffs and solitary lighthouses and, in places, beneath multicolored, mineral-rich escarpments moistened by streams and small waterfalls. The sea churns with swells, riptides, and savage currents, and the unrelenting winds have buckled and deformed the scattered trees to resemble the wizened hags from the region's pre-Christian folk tales. One day we spotted a pair of *percebeiros*—*percebe* foragers—far down at the water's edge and stopped to watch.

Standing on the bluff, we could see two men wearing wet suits moving agilely along the treacherous and craggy shore, jumping from rock to rock, disappearing between boulders and into grottos. *Percebes* grow where the surf pounds against the rocks—the harder, the better. They use the oxygen from the foamy turbulence and catch suspended plankton with feathery lashes that extend out from under their "nails." Amid the surge and spray of battering waves rolling in off the Atlantic, braving cold water and the dreaded *séptima ola* (seventh wave), the *percebeiros* scampered and crawled among the slippery rocks to pry *percebes* loose with a long, wood-handled metal rasp. They placed their spoils into a sturdy mesh bag and moved on quickly, dodging—almost teasingly so—the menacing breakers.

There is no tougher or more dangerous job. You have to be fearless, but not reckless, I heard once, and never turn your back on the sea. Braced against the headwinds whipping up off the water, these two neoprene-clad men were keeping one eye on the cracks and crevices of the rocks that hide *percebes* and another on the surf and its unpredictable, roguish waves. "*El mar es un toro: no te puedes fiar,*" the Barcelona newspaper *La Vanguardia* quoted a seasoned *percebeiro* saying a few years ago. "The sea is a bull: you can't trust it."

From Muros we moved inland, to a seventeenth-century stone farmhouse set inside an ancient oak forest beside the Río Minho and then, at the end of the summer, back to the coast. This time we went farther south down the Rías Baixas, renting an apartment in Cangas de Morrazo, across the deep inlet from Vigo. We spent many days in the tiny fishing town of Bueu, on the north side of our narrow peninsula. After lunch in one of the *pulperías* (restaurants specializing in octopus), we would stroll over to the town's wholesale seafood

> You have to be fearless, but not reckless, I heard once, and never turn your back on the sea.

marketplace. Sardines and small fish were auctioned at 7:30 AM, but shellfish—including *percebes*—were at 3:30 in the afternoon. (Larger fish came at 6:00 PM, and at 7:15 PM, octopus.) A long, piercing siren would sound in the port to announce that the auction was commencing.

Inside the cavernous space, *percebeiros*—young men mostly, but some middle-aged women, too—stood behind plastic trays that held their morning's effort: a few kilos of live barnacles. Each had arranged the shortest and fattest on top. So firm is the *percebes'* grip to the stone that most of them had chunks of broken rock attached where the heavy rasp had broken not the barnacle but the stone.

Buyers rummaged brusquely through the trays, taking fistfuls from the bottom to see how many skinny *percebes* were hidden beneath the fat ones. Some just dumped an entire tray out on the stainless counter. "*No vale para nada,*" I once heard one say dismissively. "These aren't worth a damn." As Galicia's greatest literary chronicler and food writer, Álvaro Cunqueiro, once specified, a *percebe* should be the thickness of a carpenter's thumb.

One day—it was early September by then—the first lot of particularly fat barnacles sold for 96.25 euros a kilo, and the final ones for 20.15 euros, a reflection on the keen appreciation of the highest-quality *percebes*. The lobster might be the queen of seafood, but the *percebe* is king.

Or rather, it is king, *then* queen. Nothing is more bizarre about this crustacean than its sex life. "[The *percebe*] changes sex with age, starting as a male and later transforming into a female," wrote one of Spain's most erudite food writers, Ismael Díaz Yubero, in *Las estrellas de la gastronomía española*. "Its penis is proportionally extremely long—some three times longer than its body—and thanks to its flexibility, can be guided into the females' sexual organs, into which it deposits semen to fertilize some 100,000 eggs."

The hatchlings free-float around the turbulent sea until they attach themselves to rocks, where they will remain their entire lives. They tend to grow in clusters, with a handful sprouting from a rocky base, and take about six months to reach a commercial length of about 1 1/2 inches. While there is little chance of these hardy barnacles disappearing, the already failing industry has worsened since the *Prestigei* oil spill decimated much of the *percebes'* coastline in 2002, making the effort to gather them even more risky but potentially more rewarding. Somewhat cruelly for foragers, prices are highest around Christmastime, when the sea is at its roughest.

The following morning, we went shopping at our local market in Cangas de Morrazo and brought home half a kilo of *percebes*. Any hesitation had evaporated: I finally understood why their price was so justifiably high.

The older woman who sold them to me gave precise cooking instructions. "Serve them hot enough to scald the fingers," she insisted. In our small kitchen, I blanched half of what I'd bought in a large pot of boiling salted water, covered them snugly with a kitchen cloth, and whisked them out to the table in the living room before they could cool.

Eating *percebes* is trickier than cooking them—at least to the uninitiated. I attacked the first one haphazardly and got a shirt-splattering of hot seawater, and then mangled the rest trying to get at the meat inside the tube.

I walked back to the market with my oldest daughter. She was turning eight in a few days and stopped to gawk at a display of cakes in a bakery window. Leaning in close enough to brush her summer-lightened curls against the glass, she pointed to one. It was similar to the cake we had ordered that morning with "Felicitats Alba!" to be written across its chocolate face.

"I forgot to ask," I said at the market, embarrassed but determined, to the woman. "How do you eat the damn things?" She laughed, noting, no doubt, my splattered shirt.

Back in the apartment I cooked the remaining *percebes* and carried out round two.

As instructed, I held a hot barnacle over my plate, carefully broke open the bottom, and gently squeezed out any liquid. Opening the skin slightly, I grasped the white fleshy meat between my front teeth and slowly pulled a thin, rubbery tube of pale muscle from the leathery outer casing. There was very little in my mouth, a mere hollow slip of meat—firm, chewy, more like a young squid than a clam—but it retained the tight brininess of the sea, a

bold punch of the Atlantic with all of its flavors and aromas, yet, incredibly, without the saltiness. Sublime. They were worth the price as well as the wait. I felt lucky to be eating them for the first time along the Galician coast, to be able to have a lasting association with this untamed place.

From time to time these days, I buy *percebes* in Barcelona's La Boqueria market to prepare at home. Their flavors transport me from the placid Mediterranean I see daily to the wilder Atlantic of the Galicia, from my city life to savage shores lashed by a furious sea.

But that's not the only emotion they elicit.

Every once in a while, on a bar stool in the market, drinking a *café con leche* and paging through *El País* before picking up provisions, I catch news of a *perceibero* taken by the sea. In March, I read of a twenty-eight-year-old gathering them "furtively" near the lighthouse in Valdoviño, a stretch of coast, the article said, "particularly beaten by waves and steep where there are abundant *percebes*." He had taken advantage of the low tide to start foraging in the crevices when "*un golpe de mar*" (literally a "blow" or "strike" from the sea) knocked him off balance and swept him into the frigid water.

Why do they do it? For some, there is a long family tradition, and so they continue these acts of fearlessness that for outsiders are *always* acts of recklessness. For others, though, it is desperation, not out of delirious hunger like that of early ancestors who pried them from the rocks, but out of the need to earn money in a place where jobs are scarce and the national unemployment has risen to twenty-seven percent.

As my wife and girls and I sit around a plate of steaming *percebes* in our dining room, I am keenly aware that the efforts of *perceíberos* are insanely hazardous, that a rogue wave threatens them at all times as they forage in the angry surf for our high-priced treat. While deeply grateful that they do it, I wouldn't want my daughters to take up their foolhardy profession and risk their lives scavenging tasty but far-from-essential seaside delicacies for someone else's table. I wouldn't let them do so even for our own table.

Slipping a *percebe* from its tube with my teeth, I know that I should fully acknowledge to my children how this meal was gathered and recognize the dangers involved in getting it to our plates. But I don't. It might be hypocritical, but the only way I can purely enjoy such culinary *caprichos*—whims, extravagances—is to ignore the reality of human risk involved. Instead, I focus purely on the unfiltered flavors of the sea and the earthiness of its shoreline that fill my mouth—and forget everything else. 🖋

Cooked Gooseneck Barnacles

(serves two to four)

Until ready to cook, place the live percebes in a bowl and keep them covered with moist paper towels; do not cover the bowl tightly. Rinse, but do not try to pry away the sediment or rocks stuck to the bottoms before cooking, as it will kill them. Be careful not to overcook the *percebes*, as the meat will get too soft and become difficult to extract. Serve them with a bottle of chilled Albariño white wine from along the Galician coast.

> 1 tablespoon salt
> 1 bay leaf
> 8 ounces/225 grams fresh gooseneck barnacles

In a large pot, bring 3 quarts/3 liters water to a rolling boil. Add the salt, bay leaf, and gooseneck barnacles. When the water returns to a boil, remove from the heat. Let sit for one minute.

Transfer the barnacles with a slotted spoon to a large platter. Cover with a clean cotton kitchen cloth to keep them hot and moist. Serve immediately and eat hot.

Rilla Askew is the author of four novels and a book of stories. She's a PEN/Faulkner finalist and received a 2009 Arts and Letters Award from the American Academy of Arts and Letters. Her most recent novel, *Kind of Kin*, was published by Ecco. Askew is married to actor Paul Austin; they divide their time between the Sans Bois Mountains in southeastern Oklahoma and the Catskill Mountains in upstate New York.

Arthur Bradford is the author of *Dogwalker* and *Benny's Brigade*. An O. Henry Award winner, his stories have appeared in *Esquire*, *Zoetrope*, *McSweeney's*, and *Tin House*. He is creator of the documentary series *How's Your News?* (HBO, PBS, and MTV) and most recently he directed the Emmy-nominated documentary *Six Days to Air*, about the making of *South Park*. He lives in Portland, Oregon.

Olena Kalytiak Davis's *The Poem She Didn't Write and Other Poems* is forthcoming from Copper Canyon Press in 2014. Her book *Shattered Sonnets*, originally published by Tin House/Bloomsbury USA, will be reissued in paperback from Copper Canyon as well. She is currently finally reading *Infinite Jest*, only during the day and using three bookmarks.

Natalie Eilbert is originally from New York. Her work has appeared in or is forthcoming from *Colorado Review*, *Spinning Jenny*, *Bat City Review*, *Copper Nickel*, *La Petite Zine*, DIAGRAM, and many other journals. She received her MFA from Columbia University and is a founding editor of the *Atlas Review*.

Alice Fulton received a 2011 Literature Award from the American Academy of Arts and Letters. Her books include *Cascade Experiment: Selected Poems* and *The Nightingales of Troy: Connected Stories*, both of which were published by W.W. Norton. Her work also can be found in *The Penguin Anthology of Twentieth Century American Poetry*; *The Open Door: One Hundred Poems, One Hundred Years of Poetry Magazine*; and *The Best of the Best American Poetry, 25th Anniversary Edition*.

Albert Goldbarth has been publishing collections of poetry for forty years. His books have twice received the National Book Critics Circle Award, and the poems in this issue will appear in *Selfish*, due spring 2015 from Graywolf Press. Believing that even a life as charmed as his should have some stumbling blocks, he chooses to live in Wichita, Kansas.

Kimberly Grey is a Wallace Stegner Fellow in Poetry at Stanford University. Her work has appeared in *A Public Space*, the *Southern Review, Boston Review, TriQuarterly, Columbia: A Journal of Literature and Art, Poetry Daily*, and elsewhere. She lives in the San Francisco Bay Area.

Lauren Groff is the author of the novels *Arcadia* and *The Monsters of Templeton*, as well as the short story collection *Delicate Edible Birds*. Her fiction has won Pushcart and PEN/O. Henry prizes, appeared in journals including the *New Yorker*, the *Atlantic Monthly, One Story*, and *Ploughshares*, and has appeared twice in the Best American Short Stories anthology. She lives in Gainesville, Florida.

Mark Irwin's seventh collection of poetry, *Large White House Speaking*, just appeared from New Issues in spring of 2013, and his *American Urn: New & Selected Poems (1987– 2013)* will be published in the fall of 2014. Recognition for his work includes The Nation / Discovery Award, two Colorado Book Awards, and fellowships from the Fulbright, Lilly, NEA, and Wurlitzer Foundations. He teaches in the Ph.D. Creative Writing & Literature Program at the University of Southern California and he lives in Los Angeles and Colorado.

Patricia Spears Jones is a Brooklyn-based African American poet, playwright, and cultural commentator. She is author of *Painkiller* and *Femme du Monde* and *The Weather That Kills*, three chapbooks and two plays commissioned and produced by Mabou Mines. Her work is anthologized in *Angles of Ascent: Contemporary African American*

Poets and *Best American Poetry*. She is also an editor/contributor to *Thirty Days Hath September* for www.blackearthinstitute. org and *Think: Poems for Aretha Franklin's Inauguration Day*, and a contributing editor to *Bomb*.

Matt Kish is a self-taught artist from Ohio, where he lives with his wife, their two frogs, and far too many books. He has created one illustration for every page of *Moby-Dick*, fully illustrated Joseph Conrad's *Heart of Darkness*, and had his work appear in the *Chicagoan, Propeller* magazine, and *Salt Hill Journal*. He has also illustrated *The Alligators of Abraham*, by Robert Kloss, and the upcoming *The Desert Places*, by Amber Sparks and Robert Kloss.

Jeff Koehler is a writer, traveler, photographer, and cook. His work has appeared in *Saveur, Food & Wine, Gourmet*, NPR.org, the *Washington Post*, the *Los Angeles Times, CS Monitor*, and *Tin House*, and been selected for *Best Food Writing 2010*. He is the author of four cookbooks. *Morocco: A Culinary Journey with Recipes* was published in 2012 and *Spain: Recipes and Traditions* is out in autumn 2013. He has lived in Barcelona since 1996.

Emma Komlos-Hrobsky's writing has appeared in *Hunger Mountain*, the *Story Collider, Bookforum.com*, and *Hot Metal Bridge*. She is an assistant editor at *Tin House* and lives in New York.

Ursula Kroeber Le Guin was born in Berkeley and lives in Portland, not far from the Tin House. As of 2013, she has published twenty-one novels, eleven volumes of short stories, four collections of essays, twelve books for children, six volumes of poetry and four of translation, and has received many honors and awards including Hugo, Nebula, National Book Award, PEN-Malamud. Recent: *Finding My Elegy (New and Selected Poems, 1960–2010)*.

Nathan Alling Long's stories and essays have appeared in a dozen anthologies and over fifty journals, including *Glimmer Train*, *Story Quarterly*, *The Sun*, and *Crab Orchard Review*—as well as on NPR. He has received a Truman Capote Fellowship, a Mellon Foundation grant, and a Virginia Commission of the Arts grant. He teaches at Richard Stockton College and lives in Philadelphia, where he writes, bakes bread, and bicycles through the trails along Wissahickon Creek.

Ben Marcus's most recent book is *The Flame Alphabet*. His stories have appeared in *Granta*, *Harper's*, and the *New Yorker*. His new book, *Leaving the Sea*, a collection of stories, will come out in January 2014.

Aspen Matis has, since she was seventeen and discovered John Muir's *Travels in Alaska*, hiked 7,170 miles on dirt-and-bedrock trail and sand and snow. Aspen is a Riggio Honors student at the New School in Greenwich Village, and her work has appeared in the *New York Times*. She is the author of the forthcoming memoir *Knapsacked: A Life Redirected North*.

Rosalie Moffett is from eastern Washington. She is the winner of a 2012 Discovery/*Boston Review* poetry prize. Her work has appeared in *The Believer*, FIELD, *Hayden's Ferry Review*, *Prairie Schooner*, and the anthology *Gathered: Contemporary Quaker Poets*. She is a Wallace Stegner fellow at Stanford University.

Lawrence Osborne is the author of the novel *The Forgiven*. His short stories have appeared in many publications, and his last for *Tin House*, "Volcano," was included in *Best American Short Stories 2012*. Born in England, he lives in Bangkok.

Donald Ray Pollock grew up in Knockemstiff, Ohio, and worked for thirty-two years in a paper mill in nearby Chillicothe. His collection of stories, *Knockemstiff*, won the 2009 PEN/Robert Bingham Fellowship, and his novel, *The Devil All The Time*, was listed as one of the top ten books of 2011 by *Publisher's Weekly* and the best book of 2012 by *LIRE* magazine in France. "The Worm" is an excerpt from a novel in progress.

Ginger Strand is the author of, most recently, *Killer on the Road: Violence and the American Interstate*. Find her at www.gingerstrand.com.

Allison Titus lives in Richmond, Virginia. Her book, *Sum of every lost ship*, is available from Cleveland State University Press, and new poems appear in *A Public Space*, *Black Warrior Review*, and *Gulf Coast*. She is the recipient of a fellowship from the NEA.

Vauhini Vara is a reporter at the *Wall Street Journal* and a 2010 graduate of the University of Iowa Writers' Workshop. Her stories have been published in *Glimmer Train*, *Black Warrior Review*, and *Epoch*, and she has been a resident at the MacDowell Colony and the Yaddo Corporation.

David Varno received an MFA in fiction from Columbia University and lives in Brooklyn. He grew up on the Mohawk River in the suburban wilds of upstate New York.

Inara Verzemnieks is a graduate of the University of Iowa's Nonfiction Writing Program. She is the recipient of a Rona Jaffe Foundation Writer's Award and a Richard J. Margolis Award. In 2006, she was a finalist for the Pulitzer Prize in feature writing.

FRONT COVER:
Heart of Darkness, Illustrated by Matt Kish, Page 171:
"*In front of the first rank, along the river, three men, plastered with bright red earth from head to foot, strutted to and fro restlessly. When we came abreast again, they faced the river, stamped their feet, nodded their horned heads, swayed their scarlet bodies . . .*"
2012, ink and marker on watercolor paper, 6 ¾ x 11 inches

BACK COVER:
Heart of Darkness, Illustrated by Matt Kish, Page 165:
"*As soon as I got on the bank I saw a trail—a broad trail through the grass. I remember the exultation with which I said to myself, 'He can't walk—he is crawling on all fours—I've got him.'*"
2012, ink and marker on watercolor paper, 6 ¾ x 11 inches
©Matt Kish, www.spudd64.com

Heart of Darkness by Joseph Conrad, Illustrated by Matt Kish will be published in November 2013 by Tin House Books.

SAPPHIRE · JUSTIN TORRES · JACKSON TAYLOR · AYANA MATHIS · CHRIS ADRIAN

THE WRITER'S FOUNDRY MFA

MADE IN BROOKLYN

Fall 2013
www.sjcny.edu/mfa

St. Joseph's College
NEW YORK